P9-BYI-015

BETWEEN
the Water &
THE WOODS

BETWEEN
the Water &
THE WOODS

Simone Snaith

HOLIDAY HOUSE · New York

Library of Congress Cataloging-in-Publication Data

Names: Snaith, Simone, author.
Title: Between the water & the woods / by Simone Snaith.
Other titles: Beneath the water and the woods
Description: First edition. | New York : Holiday House, [2019]
Summary: "Emeline must use her inherited forbidden magic to fend
off the Dark Creatures of legend, the Ithin, and prove to the king and
his council that the supernatural exists, all with the help of whip-wielding
Lash Knight Reese and her dauntless family"— Provided by publisher.
Identifiers: LCCN 2018041582 | ISBN 9780823440207 (hardcover)
Subjects: | CYAC: Magic—Fiction. | Supernatural—Fiction.
Forests and forestry—Fiction. | Family life—Fiction. | Fantasy.
Classification: LCC PZ7.1.S65726 Bet 2019 | DDC [FIc]—dc23
LC record available at https://lccn.loc.gov/2018041582

"The princesses decided that words and numbers are of equal value. In the cloak of knowledge, one is the warp, and the other woof."

—Norton Juster,
The Phantom Tollbooth

one

Emeline watched her brother, Dale, fling his pretend whip at his friends, and then duck and spin away. She smiled, standing in the high grass with her hands on her hips, feeling the sun warm the golden bands on her forearms.

Dale was spry and agile, and she felt proud of him, even though it was just a silly game that boys played, way out here on the edge of the village as close to the moat and the woods as they dared. Her gaze was drawn to the wall of dark, tangled trees beyond the water, and her smile faded.

The sight of the woods awoke an age-old fear.

A primeval dread.

The boys had laid a plank of roof slate across the narrowest bit of moat, where the water was only as wide as the length of two men. This was so the bravest ones could stand upon it, on the very edge of danger, at which point Emeline would scream at them to get back over. So far not one of them had risked actually *crossing* the water. It meandered thick and green beneath the plank, littered with lily pads and the long vines that the boys used as whips.

Emeline loved the water lilies that grew in shades of pink and white atop the water. They were like living jewels—delicate, dewy, fluttery—but now wasn't the time to start mooning over them. She was supposed to be playing the girl to be rescued, although her true role was to keep an eye on the boys. Dale was ten and mostly level-headed, but his rag-tag group of friends from all around the village were of different ages and wits. Aladane, especially—a hefty, good-looking boy with glory in his eyes—had the wildest ideas and needed extra supervision. His father, the head fisherman, was constantly apologizing for the trouble he got into.

"Someone better rescue me soon," Emeline called, sinking down into the grass. Dada would need her home shortly to help with supper. She shoved her black curls away from her eyes and laughed as a tiny blond boy called Minnow caught Aladane square in the face with his "whip," then squeaked and ran away. A shout of laughter sprang up from the group.

"Who let him play?" Aladane bellowed, rubbing his face. "Babies can't play Lash Knights!"

The idea that any of them were anything like real Lash Knights made Emeline grin.

"I don't know, Al, he's better than you," Dale said, laughing. Aladane ran after him, his heavy feet thumping on the ground. Dale dodged and weaved, and the other boys jumped into Aladane's way, waving their vine whips and sticking out their tongues.

"Coward!" Aladane yelled, heaving. "A real man would stand and fight!"

No, a real man learns how to cook supper for his children after their mama dies, Emeline thought, glancing back over her shoulder toward their cottage. *And stands around fretting about what he should put in the stew to make them healthy and strong.* At barely sixteen, she had taken on many of the household duties, but Dada tried hard not to depend on her too much.

"Go and play, Little Plum," he told her, using her old nickname. She had been a plump little girl and was still curvy now. "Be a child as long as you can."

A cry struck Emeline's ears and she jerked her head around. Her heart leapt into her throat.

Dale was standing on the middle of the plank across the moat, waving his arms at Aladane.

"Who's a coward now?" he demanded, grinning ear to ear. The sunlight gleamed off his armbands and his cropped black hair.

Emeline jumped to her feet. "Dale, get *off* of there!" she yelled.

The other boys looked back at her and then at Aladane, who seemed frozen in place, staring at Dale. He took one step forward.

"Don't you dare!" Emeline cried, and ran toward them, nearly tripping over her skirt.

Aladane stepped out onto the bridge and lashed at Dale with his vine whip. Dale struck back, the two of them scooting back and forth across the slate. The other boys started cheering.

"Dale Bird, get back here right now!" Emeline shouted, reaching the end of the bridge.

"It's okay, Em!" Dale said, fighting.

"Dada's going to kill you!" she warned.

"Not if you don't tell him!"

Emeline felt a tug on her skirt; Minnow was at her side. "They won't go all the way over," he told her. But his small face was worried too.

A cloud crossed the sun, casting a shadow over the water and the pretend knights. Aladane suddenly tripped and fell, knocking into Dale—the bigger boy tumbled into the water with a splash—and Dale fell across onto the other side. *The other side of the moat.* Emeline's heart stopped.

"Dale!" she screamed. Her brother jumped up immediately, as if to run straight back across the plank, but the boys were electrified now.

"I dare you to stand there for ten seconds!" one shouted.

"Yeah! Bet you can't do it!"

To her horror, Dale hesitated and stood there in the grass. An uncertain grin spread across his face. Then he looked down at Aladane, spluttering as he clambered up onto the slate plank. Aladane stared back up at him, his eyes shining with awe.

"You're crazy!" he said.

"Dale, get back here *right now*!" Emeline shrieked.

"One, two, three..." the boys began counting. Dale put his hands on his hips and turned around to face the dark trees.

"I dare you to touch a tree!" one boy called.

Emeline gasped, and the others yelled, "No! Don't do it!" This was too much.

Dale looked at them over his shoulder and winked. He took one step forward, and all the boys roared. Emeline ran out onto the plank. Aladane fell back into the water as her steps rocked the little bridge.

"Em, I'm just playing!" Dale said, turning around. His face was flushed. "I wasn't going to do it!"

Emeline reached him and grabbed his arm. And then she glanced up, unable to help herself, at the dense tangle of trunks and branches locked together a few feet away from them. Their sheer steepness alone was intimidating; the gnarled trunks rose twice as high as even the meeting hall. There were black hollows in between where no light fell.

Emeline had never seen anyone as close to the woods as she and her brother were now. A shiver shot down her spine, and her chest tightened.

"It's a stupid game!" she snapped. "Let's go!" She yanked Dale by the arm and turned away.

But then there was a sound. The two of them froze, and the rest of the world went quiet.

A rustling. There was a rustling among the trees behind them. She turned, not breathing.

A branch was trembling. Something was moving.

"Emeline..." Dale whispered. A shadow rose up between the twisted trunks. A shadow that moved languidly, like a snake.

Boys were screaming behind them, but the voices sounded far away. Emeline saw the silhouette of a hooded head. And then, in a finger of sunlight, something like an arm—a crooked, bent arm. It was not a human arm.

Her heart beat against her like a giant fist.

She whirled Dale around and shoved him straight into the moat. Then she dropped to her knees, feeling for something—anything—to grab, her fingers groping into the stream, and

snatched up a lily pad from the water. She turned and threw it wildly into the trees.

It hit something. A terrible hiss filled her ears.

She shot back across the bridge and onto the safety of the grass, grabbing hold of the slate plank's end and dragging it away from the moat. Nothing could come across now.

Aladane and Dale were scrambling out of the water, pale as fish underbellies. All the boys were scattering, running for their homes. Emeline stared back across the water at the woods. They were dark and still again. Silent.

"What did you see?" Aladane exclaimed. "What did you see?!"

"Go home, Aladane," Emeline said hoarsely.

She took Dale's hand and turned away, pulling him along with her. Her teeth were chattering; her hands were shaking. She stumbled and Dale almost fell into her. Then they both broke into a run, racing ahead, leaving Aladane standing there behind them.

"You're a *real* knight, Emeline!" he cried after them. "That was real!"

two

Real Lash Knights had not come past Equane since Emeline was six years old.

She had perched on a wall with Sessa as a royal procession flooded the road outside the village gates. There had been a sea of knights up high on their horses, their black armor glinting in the sun. They carried black shields with black whips coiled at their sides, and their helmets were sloped and pointed like dog muzzles. Sessa had insisted that she could see fangs.

Behind the knights had chugged the steam-powered carriage that everyone knew carried King Olvinde, although no one could see through its curtain-drawn windows. It was painted black and was nearly as large as a cottage, with wheels half as tall as a man and a mound of cases strapped to its roof. Light blue and silver flags had fluttered just above the driver, their silk shining in the sun, but otherwise the black carriage and the black knights had made a dark impression. The villagers had stood solemnly in a crowd, watching them pass.

That had been the king's last journey to his summer home by the ocean. He had never returned all these long years, because of his wasting illness. She would never forget the sight of his steam-carriage, at least; there was nothing like it in Equane, only horses, wooden bicycles, and wagons.

Emeline bit the thread she was sewing with and tied a knot, glancing over at Dale as he sat quietly in Dada's chair with a book in his lap. The light from the two fish-oil lamps in the sitting room revealed the tension in his face.

He had better start turning the pages if he wants Dada to believe he's reading. She hadn't told on him, but he was obviously shaken. Their father was sure to notice soon.

A terrifying image flashed in Emeline's mind and she shook her head. *A snake-like shadow in the trees* . . . She would not think of it. It was gone now and they were safe. She sewed diligently.

Dada was thumping in and out of the sitting room, carrying in tools from the field and mumbling to himself. He was a tall man with straight black hair, black eyes, and a crooked nose he'd gotten from a fall in his youth. He grew vegetables in the field behind their cottage, whittled clay figures, and read every book he could get his callused hands on. Dale had inherited his dark eyes and Emeline his absentminded look; neither of them were as pale as Mama had been, but Emeline had gotten her wildly curly black hair and filled out in her curves, which embarrassed her. The buckle-up fish-leather bodices that were the fashion only emphasized it.

Sessa called her podgy and scruffy. They hadn't been friends for ages, but those words still stung. Emeline often *was* a bit scruffy; she spent her free time outdoors with her brother. It was fitting that Dada had not even asked questions when she and Dale came dragging in, both of them dripping wet and filthy.

Dale watched Dada leave the room again and leaned

forward, catching Emeline's eye. She was startled to see the fear in his face.

"It was the Ithin!" he whispered.

"Be quiet," she whispered back.

He snapped his book closed and got up to look at the crooked shelves along the wall where Dada kept his books. She knew what he was looking for: Dada's *History*, which he'd pored over a hundred times before.

Dale pulled out the heavy tome and sat on the floor with it, flipping through the yellowed old pages. With a sigh, Emeline put down the blouse she was mending and sat next to him. Her sewing always came out crooked anyway.

Dale paused, as usual, at the dog-eared section about the Keldares. Mama had been one. Anyone could be, if they ran off and joined them, becoming an apprentice in one of the arts they practiced. Musicians, poets, skalds, and storytellers, the Keldares traveled the kingdom, entertaining those who would listen. They went their own way and had never sworn to the king, but because of their long peaceful history, and because there were so few of them now, they were mostly left alone. Old folks whispered to each other that slivers of magic were kept alive in the realm's most ancient songs and stories—songs and stories that no one but the Keldares knew now. Magic ran in their blood because of it, they said.

Like many Keldares, Mama had worn golden armbands, and she'd made sure that Emeline and Dale followed the tradition, just as generations of her family had: her people had been Keldares as far back as anyone remembered. The gold in the bands had been panned in the cold waters of the north.

Dale flipped more pages until he found the section he was really looking for: the legends of Dark Creatures.

Dark Creatures. Monsters that had roamed the land since the beginning of time. Unnatural beasts that could only exist if magic were real. Dale's fingers swept over the ancient drawings of craggy hides, shadowed eyes, and wicked fangs.

He knew all of them, and so did she. There was the bat-like Gorbin, dropping from trees to smother you with its wings; the Embel, scuttling among the undergrowth on vicious claws, never seen before it struck; the many-mouthed Silgare, whose hundred-bite was poisonous; and the Anthrane, casting alluring little lights that led you straight to its sting.

Dale stopped at the Ithin, a creature wrapped in a ratty, hooded cloak, stretched out along a tree branch like a snake or a giant cat. He shuddered.

"Why do they wear cloaks?" he asked, his voice tight. Emeline reached over and turned the book around. There was another drawing of an Ithin standing upright, just like a man, but its hooked arms showed through the cloak's opening. She read the text beneath it aloud.

" 'The Ithin live in the forest and fear water, like most Dark Creatures. They eat the hearts of men.' " Dale squirmed next to her. " 'Some say the Ithin cover themselves in hooded cloaks because they are too hideous to behold, but it may also be a form of protection against rain, which poisons them. Few have seen their faces and lived to speak of it, but the descriptions are always the same: an elongated head with enormous round eyes, two large fangs in the upper jaw and two more in the lower, no nose or ears to speak of. Beneath the cloak is perhaps a man's form, but one not restricted by the same physical laws. Their arms are bent in the manner of the praying mantis—' "

Dada thumped back into the room and Emeline jumped, almost flinging the book. Dale burst into a hysterical giggle and fell over on his back.

Their father stared at them, bewildered. Then he noticed the *History*, so Emeline shut it quickly and gave Dale a kick. He only laughed harder.

"What in the kingdom are you two up to?" Dada asked. He was holding his pipe, which meant it was time for him to settle in for a quiet evening. The old clock that had been his father's chimed up on its shelf amid the books.

"We were reading the Comedies," Emeline told him. "Dale is having a silly fit."

Dada sank into his chair and shook his head, tapping his pipe. "I'm surprised he can understand them. Those old stories aren't very funny to me. I suppose humor changes with the times." He lit his pipe and watched as she stood up to slide the *History* back onto the shelf. "Anyway, I thought the Comedies were in the back of the book," he added mildly. Emeline cringed. She should have known he knew the book inside and out.

Dada had traded with a traveler for the *History* book before she was born, and to this day it was his favorite. It had been a library book in the capital, once, and there were several names scrawled inside the first page. First names, but no surnames—a custom of capital folk, Dada said.

Dale sobered up and got to his feet. He went meekly to the divan and sat down.

"Any news today, Dada?" Emeline asked, following him.

Dale had sat down on her sewing and she yanked it out from under him.

Dada blew out a cloud of smoke that smelled of sage and bay leaf. "Just more gossip about the king choosing an heir. They say he can barely walk now, the poor man."

"What happens if he dies before he chooses one?" Dale asked.

"He's got that brother that ran off to the Outer Lands, they say. Lord Irwind. I suppose they'd have to go find him."

The Outer Lands were beyond the borders of the kingdom. People said they were barren, uncivilized, but speaking fairly, nothing was really known of them. Emeline had always wondered what he'd found there, if he was still alive.

"Why did he do that?" Dale wondered.

"I don't know. He was supposedly some kind of genius." Their father shrugged and held out his hands. "I wager he had a reason, although there's always been talk he was cast out. Maybe he had a fight with the king—I've heard Olvinde has more than a streak of stubbornness in him. That's how he keeps the Theurgists at bay, with all their drama about dark magic."

"Ma'am Hendel still believes the Theurgists," Dale ventured.

"All the old folks do," Dada said, puffing. "But the Sapients have convinced four kings now that all magic's a trick of the eye, or a natural phenomenon. Most of the time, I'm inclined to agree." He paused. "You know, son, there used to be *one* council, years and years ago, before it split into the Sapients and Theurgists. Things would be a lot more peaceful if it was that way again."

"But what about the woods, Dada? Why are people so afraid of them?" Dale asked. Emeline gave him a look.

Dada pulled his pipe out of his mouth. "You stay out of the woods," he said flatly. "Even without monsters, there're animals in there that would eat a little boy. Doesn't matter if they're magic or not."

"Yes, sir," Dale said, and pulled his legs up underneath him.

The Ithin can't be natural, Emeline thought, pulling her thread. If they were, then why would they fear water? Didn't everything natural need water to live?

People certainly did. There was even a saying in the village that everyone used: "Bless water." Equane had been built around three natural streams, and the waters ran in green canals beside the packed dirt roads. The people lived off of the crops they grew and the fish in the streams, which had been diverted to create the moat running around the fifty-odd buildings of town. They were brightly painted cottages made of cob, mostly—a sturdy mix of sand and mud—with slate roofs and shutters. Deep red was the most popular color, and when the sun shone on the red walls and the green water of the canals, Emeline thought her village was truly beautiful.

The moat had been created as a barrier against the woods, where wild beasts or bandits could lurk...or the Dark Creatures of legend.

Don't go into the woods, child. Stay on this side of the water.

~ ~

At bedtime, Emeline climbed the ladder up into the loft where her little room was. It was a snug triangle with the slate roof slanting down around it.

Dale slept on the divan in the sitting room below, where his snores sometimes woke her out of dreams. On bad nights, she got up and yelled at him from the top of the ladder until he rolled over. Dada slept in the cottage's one true bedroom, the one he and Mama had shared. There was also a washroom with a pump that drew up water from deep in the ground.

One day, Dale would grow too tall for the divan, and then Emeline would probably have to trade with him, as much as she would hate to lose her room. The loft had one window that let the stars shine in at night, and she had strung dried water lilies all around it. There were more of them floating in a bowl on a shelf.

The lilies' fragile beauty thrilled her. She loved all water plants, so much so that sometimes their nearness tugged on her senses, distracting her. If she gazed at lilies long enough, colorful patterns were conjured up in her mind, dancing like light on a mirror. No one else she knew seemed to regard them much at all.

She thought maybe Mama had felt that kind of love for the wind and the sky. The memories of her mother had begun to fade over the years, but she struggled to keep them close. Mama had died when Emeline was seven, from a bad fever that had been too quick and fierce to treat. Dada had drifted around like a ghost for a whole year afterward. Emeline remembered her pretty face and the way she had always been in motion around the house, humming. She had taken her children outdoors as much as possible, her eyes always watching the clouds.

What does that one look like, Little Plum? Like a fish? And look, that one's a flower!

The sweet memory faded as Emeline stared at the flowers in her room. Without warning, the sight of them brought her back to the woods—to the lily pad she'd thrown at the thing in the trees. The languid thing in the cloak...

With a shiver, Emeline unbuckled her bodice, pulled her dress over her head, and scrambled into her round bed, drawing the covers up to her chin. It was best to forget about it.

three

Emeline was walking to the schoolhouse to collect Dale when Sessa and two of her friends were suddenly upon her, circling on their bicycles.

"Emeline!" Sessa exclaimed. "Is it true? Did you go into the woods?"

Emeline took a step back, startled, and Sessa hopped gracefully off her bicycle. Her auburn hair was done up in a knot, and her dress was expertly embroidered with flowers and fish. The tip of her nose turned up in a very pretty way. The other two girls were dressed similarly, and Emeline noticed unhappily that neither of them were stretching the buckles on their bodices.

"Who told you that?" Emeline demanded. She kept walking, and they followed her, pushing their bicycles.

"We heard from Daney Fish, and he heard from Ma'am Arden, and she said that little Janin told his mama," Sessa told her in a rush.

"And Olinn told his mama, and she told my auntie," one of her friends declared.

Emeline sighed and looked over their heads toward the schoolhouse up ahead. It was a low, round building, the same deep red as the dress she was wearing. She could see a cluster of villagers gathering there, much larger than the usual group who came to collect their children. That was an ominous sight. Maybe the whole of Equane knew.

"I didn't go *in* the woods," Emeline muttered.

"But you saw something in them?" Sessa insisted. "A Dark Creature?"

"I saw something," she said carefully. "But I can't be sure what it was."

"Olinn said you threw water at it! How were you so brave?" one of the girls asked admiringly. Emeline shrugged, embarrassed, and Sessa *harrumphed* as if she resented the compliment.

"That was stupid," she said. "You probably made it angry! You should've just run away."

"What if it comes after us now?" gasped the third girl.

"Don't be silly, we have the moat!" Emeline exclaimed, shouldering past them and hurrying toward the school. She could see the crowd ahead moving inward, and she had a feeling she knew exactly who was in the middle—she could hear Aladane's voice as she reached them.

"There was blood on its claws!" he was saying. "Red blood! I saw it!" People gasped in horror, and she caught several wide-eyed stares as she jostled forward.

"Look, it's Emeline! She was there!" someone said.

She broke into the middle of the crowd in time to hear Dale protesting, "I didn't see any claws..." With some relief, she saw that Teacher Rylin was standing behind him and Aladane, her large hands placed protectively on their shoulders.

"You were too distracted!" Aladane said hastily. "I saw its

claws from the water! Big ones!" He was enjoying himself, his chest puffed out.

"You did not, you little liar!" Emeline cried, deflating him.

"Em, I didn't tell," Dale told her.

She pulled him close to her and gave Teacher Rylin a grateful look; the teacher nodded and folded her arms. She was a tall, solemn woman who had decided in her youth to make it her place to teach all the children to read and do sums. Few of the adults in Equane knew how to read—Dada was a strong exception—so they sent along their children to learn, if they could spare them. Emeline had always liked her.

"Is it true, child?" an old woman asked, peering at Emeline.

"They say you threw water at something! What did you see?" a farmer called out.

"It had a hood, the boy said!"

"I don't *know* what I saw—" Emeline said stubbornly.

"Was it the Ithin?" someone demanded.

"I think it was," Dale murmured.

"A Dark Creature!" boomed a frightened voice. "I knew the Theurgists were right!"

Someone else shouted, "The king must be told! We should have a meeting!"

Emeline stepped back, her arms around Dale as she stared at the crowd. The villagers never got this worked up about something. Usually the only excitement was the latest gossip, or maybe an injury. This was strange. Frightening.

"Dark Creature sightings must be reported! It's the law!"

"Let's call a meeting!"

Aladane's father, Mister Gingern, suddenly pushed his way forward and grabbed his son's shoulder with one meaty hand. He glared defiantly at the crowd, his apron covered in fish guts, and the cries died down.

"All right, call your meeting then!" he yelled at them. "But stop standing around and stirring everybody up! Making a scene over children's stories! Come on, boy."

"But Dada, it's true!" Aladane cried as he was dragged away.

Emeline pushed Dale ahead of her as the villagers stepped back, still chattering and whispering with one another, and the two of them wove their way through the loosening crowd.

"It's absolute madness now," Emeline hissed at Dale.

"I didn't tell, Em. It's not my fault—"

"It *is* your fault! You went across the moat!"

They hurried home to the cottage. Dada was rinsing lettuce leaves in a bucket of water, the rest of dinner laid out on the table: grilled fish, a loaf of bread, and turnips, onions, and carrots from the fields. He looked up at them cheerfully, ready to ask how school was, but his smile hung in the air at the sight of their faces.

"What is it?" he asked.

"There's going to be a meeting," Emeline told him.

The meeting bell rang shortly after they finished eating, a distant but determined clangor from the hall at the center of the village.

Emeline remembered the last time she had heard it. A child had gone missing four years earlier, one of the Kayler brood; that was how long it had been since the villagers had needed a meeting. The poor little girl had never been found. There was talk of Dark Creatures then.

Dada had not spoken a word when she told him what Dale had done. He had just turned pale and gone very still, and her brother had hung his head. They sat there that way for a long time before Dada finally got to his feet. He stepped over to Emeline and laid his hand on the top of her head, a silent thank-you. Then he turned and went back to making dinner without a glance at his son. Emeline knew her brother felt the sting of it. There was no further punishment needed.

Now they followed Dada through the door as the bell rang, filing out into the cool, clear evening air. Dada had dressed up in his black flat cap and a nice gray coat that buckled at the waist. Emeline remembered him wearing them on Mama's birthday when she was little; they had borrowed horses and gone riding while a neighbor minded her and Dale.

She shivered nervously as they joined the other families making their way to the meeting hall, wrapped tight in Mama's hooded red cloak. Nearly ankle-length, Mama had said it was for traveling, but Emeline never traveled and so had taken to wearing it often. Even now, its cloth held Mama's familiar scent of basil, ginger, and clove pinks.

Was it true that the king must be told about this? How? Would they send him a letter?

Once a month, a post wagon came to the village gates with letters from faraway relatives, and packages of glass and metal ordered from the catalogs it carried. This was also how they paid the meager taxes they owed to the king, each household wrapping up a small portion of goods and handing them off to the driver. He often had news from the capital, and sometimes he carried formal notices announcing new laws that had been passed. But as far as she knew, no one in Equane wrote letters to the king himself. The village was so insignificant, she was not even sure the post would deliver it.

A tall boy stood atop the meeting hall's domed roof, pulling the rope that rang the great bell. Emeline covered her ears as the clanging blasted over their heads.

A steady stream of people was crowding in through the double doors of the hall. It was a big building with a raised ceiling that caused voices to echo, which seemed to give them more importance. The cob walls had been painted white and built with rows of windows, to ensure that the villagers couldn't be ambushed while they were all amassed in one place. Ambushed by what, she'd never been sure.

Someone waved at Emeline; it was Endrina, the baker's daughter, her best friend in the village. She waved back as Dada hurried her through the aisles to a seat.

Next to Emeline, Dale gazed around with wide eyes at the buzzing, murmuring people. Most people had dressed up for the meeting, which meant there were more hats, cowls, buckles, and bead-and-flower chaplets than Emeline had seen in ages. She rarely saw so many villagers together, except maybe at the market.

"You think they're going to make me speak?" Dale asked Emeline in a whisper. She shrugged, but she'd been wondering the same thing. The bell finally ceased overhead.

Old Mister Henley had the honor of leading the meetings, but he was likely to pass it down to his grown son, Alvine, soon, considering how old and weak of voice he was now. It took several long moments before the villagers realized he was calling out for them to quiet down. Then they hushed each other and settled in their seats expectantly.

"...Thank you all for coming!" Old Henley wheezed. Emeline craned her neck for a sight of him as the voices died down around her. Bent-backed and white-haired, he was standing precariously on a chair at the front of the hall, wearing an ancient pair of spectacles and holding a flattened brown hat in his veiny hands. The wall behind him was covered in a giant tapestry that had been woven in the early days of Equane: It was a map of the entire kingdom, like the ones in the *History*. Large, elaborate fish-oil lamps graced the wall on either side of it, and the embroidered land and water seemed to shift in their flickering light. The capital was marked with a red star in the center of the northwest, Equane with a tiny blue star down in the southeastern corner.

Old Henley was not a man to waste words. "Unless you've been under a rock today, then I suppose you've heard the news that a Dark Creature may have been sighted by two children," he announced. "Now, there's no cause for alarm since we are still protected by our moat. As I understand it, this took place on the wrong side of the water, where no one should have been anyway."

Emeline saw Dada glance across her at Dale, who cringed.

"But we haven't had a sighting on record since the moat was built, so it bears some looking into." Mister Henley straightened up as much as he could and peered out over the crowd. "Where are the two witnesses?"

All the heads in the hall turned toward Emeline and Dale.

Dada stood and stepped aside to let her and Dale walk out from their row. Emeline straightened up, breathed deep, and squared her shoulders. She took her brother's hand and led the way past the ranks of staring eyes, all the way up to the front of the hall where Mister Henley stood waiting. He climbed down stiffly from his chair and nodded at them.

"Tell us what happened, heart," he told her kindly.

She faced the crowd with her hands in her dress pockets, feeling very awkward, and looked for somewhere to fix her eyes. In the middle of the front row sat Mister Fish, which was unfair of him as one of the tallest men in the village. He was square-jawed and broad-shouldered, with kind, blunt features and curly brown hair, and his two nearly grown sons sat next to him, looking just like younger Mister Fishes. One of them winked at her. She colored, suddenly finding her voice.

"The boys were playing Lash Knights near the moat behind the mill. You know, they pull vines out of the water and use them as whips? Anyway, they put a slate plank across the water, just to show off, and then Dale ran across it." Her voice turned sharp, despite herself. Sounds of shock and disapproval sprang up from the crowd; when she glanced down at her brother, his mouth had collapsed into a pitiful frown. She put her arm around him, softening.

"They stir each other up, him and Ala—some of the others." There was no reason to get Aladane in further trouble. "I ran after him and was pulling him back, but then we heard something in the woods." Silence fell around the room. Her heart beat faster, hot in her chest. "And then I looked...It was hard to see what it was...."

"It was moving," Dale spoke up.

"Like an animal?" Old Henley asked.

"Well, its head was about this high," Emeline said, raising her arm high above her own head.

"Standing like a man?"

"Yes, but not moving like one." She bit her lip. "And...it did look like it wore a hood."

Cries and gasps exploded from the crowd; some even sprang to their feet.

"The Ithin!"

"I knew it! Bless water!"

"Ithin! They eat human hearts!"

"They'll tear it right out of your chest!"

Old Henley got up on his chair again, waving his arms for silence. Emeline gripped Dale's hand and took a step back, straining to look for Dada, but she couldn't find him.

"The Theurgists are right!" someone shouted. Several others took up the call, while many more cried out aghast. Old Henley's mouth was moving, calling for order, but his voice was drowned out; no one was paying him any attention. This was worse than outside the school.

Suddenly, Emeline pictured Mama whistling out to Dada in the fields; her whistle had been sharper and clearer than glass. She put two fingers in her mouth and blew.

The piercing sound broke through the clamor, and not a few people jumped, startled. Then they all went quiet, staring up at her. Dale grinned. He knew that whistle.

"All right, let's have a civil discussion!" Old Henley rasped into the silence. "Everyone, take your seats!" He gave them a moment to settle themselves. "All right now, remember, we don't have solid evidence. All we've got is something spotted by a pair of children. We shouldn't get carried away now...."

"Em, you forgot about the lily pad," Dale piped up. There were sounds of agreement from those who had heard the gossip.

"That's right, I pulled a lily pad out of the moat and threw it into the trees," Emeline admitted. "And then...I heard something hiss." The clamor rose up again instantly.

"They're afraid of water! I knew it!"

"The stories are true!"

"Brave girl, that one!"

Old Henley managed to catch their attention this time, but even as they dropped their voices, they stared at Emeline. Embarrassed, she saw Fish's son—the one who had winked—turning to grin at his brother.

"Protected the little ones! That's a good woman," he said, just loudly enough. She blushed furiously and stared at the floor.

"Well, that is certainly more suspicious," Old Henley admitted to the crowd. He stood there for a moment on his chair, scratching his chin. "I suppose we'd best take suggestions on how to proceed."

More than half of the villagers shot their hands up at once. The old man sighed and waved a hand at Emeline and Dale. "You children better have a seat," he told them. "We'll be here a while."

~≪≫ four ≪≫~

T*he* sky was gray the next morning.

Emeline gazed out the window as she ate a bowl of honeyed porridge next to Dale. Only a dim, dusky kind of light was floating in, and it carried the smell of rain. The clock in the sitting room struck eight, and she heard Dada coming out of the bedroom to put his boots on. He was going with some others to examine the edge of the woods, which was the decision that had finally been made at the end of last night's meeting.

There had been no discussion of Emeline or Dale coming along, but Emeline stood up and joined Dada in the sitting room. She was not going to sit quietly in the cottage while her father all but strode into the forest. The villagers had called her brave, and if that was true, then she was determined to keep it up. Dale wisely stayed put, even though she knew he hated to miss anything.

Emeline slid on her red cloak and went to stand by the door. Dada stood and frowned, studying her.

"You stay on this side of the water," he said finally.

"I will."

Unless you're in trouble, she added silently, following him out.

The sky hung low over their heads as they walked, leaves and straw skittering past their feet in a fitful breeze. Dada scratched his chin and glanced at her.

"Am I being too hard on Dale?" he asked.

"You didn't say a word to him," she said, surprised.

"That's what I mean. Maybe it's easier to bear an outburst like your mama used to have than a cold silence." He sighed. "I just don't know what to say. I worry about him thinking that risking your life is exciting."

"He understands," she said, and slipped her arm through his. "He's sorry."

They passed through the village in a comfortable silence. Before too long, the mill loomed large ahead of them, dark against the sky. A broad-shouldered worker nodded at Dada.

"They're gathering back there," he said, gesturing. "I wouldn't go for the kingdom."

Dada nodded back and led the way around the mill to the long stretch of tall grass where the boys had played their Lash Knight games. There was a small group of villagers there now, clustered at the moat. The trees stood tall and sinister, a gray fog settled around them. Goose bumps prickled Emeline's arms. No one had crossed over yet to the woods.

The tall farmer Mister Fish was there; Old Henley and his son Alvine; Aladane's father, Mister Gingern, wearing his apron; the baker Mister Gale; and Sessa's father, Mister Caldin. There were several other men that Emeline knew only barely, and one woman: Teacher Rylin, who had brought a stack of buckets with her. She stood there with quiet steadiness, inclining her head toward Emeline. The two of them were the only womenfolk.

The men shook hands with Dada; some gave Emeline surprised looks, but a few nodded to her. Thin, soft-eyed Mister Gale smiled briefly. The slate bridge had been laid across the moat again, which flowed along quietly underneath carrying its flowers and weeds. She felt a sudden, unsettling stab of longing at the sight of the lilies, but ignored it. Mister Fish and Alvine Henley held up fish-oil lamps, throwing uneven light over the group.

"Those who plan to cross had better fill a bucket and take it with them," Old Henley said hoarsely.

His own son bent to fill a bucket and then started across the bridge.

Emeline stood by Teacher Rylin and watched the other men follow suit. They filed across the bridge one by one, sloshing the water in their buckets, and slowly approached the woods with lamps held high.

She shivered under her hood.

"They have water with them, child," Teacher Rylin said. "They will be safe."

Emeline nodded. The air still smelled of rain, as well, which would surely keep Dark Creatures at bay. If there were any.

The men separated at the line of twisted trees. They peered in between the branches of the forest wall, cautiously examined bark and leaves, conferred with one another. Emeline watched Dada crouch down to study the tree roots in the grass, holding her breath.

The fog seemed to darken around them. A damp breeze

blew out of the forest toward the village, and her black curls swept back from her face.

"I had a letter from my cousin who lives near the capital recently," Teacher Rylin said, glancing up at the sky. "And she said that some of the Theurgists claim the Dark Creatures exist as a punishment for our loss of belief in magic. But others say that perhaps the Dark Creatures only exist because we do believe." Emeline looked up at her, surprised. "I wonder if both might be true."

A sudden cry shocked them both. It was one of the men. Mister Gingern and Dada leaped backward from the trees, covering their faces; Old Henley yelped and stumbled.

On instinct, Emeline lunged for the water in the moat, ready to splash whatever nightmarish thing appeared. The men were scrambling for the slate bridge.

"Rotten flesh!" Mister Gingern roared. Behind him, Mister Fish pulled the bridge back across the water in one powerful, panicked motion. Old Henley was wheezing, and his son patted him on the back, looking terrified himself.

Something brushed her hand and she jumped up, startled. A white lily was standing up out of the water on a very tall stalk. Confused, she stared at it. It had not been there before.

"The smell! It was horrible!" Mister Gale gasped, nearly as white as the lily.

Dada was covering his mouth, but he dropped his hands when he saw Emeline and wrapped his arms around her. She held still, watching him, but his face was blank.

"Did you see something?" Teacher Rylin asked, her eyes enormous. Men shook their heads. Mister Fish retched for a moment, big man that he was, and turned away.

"The smell just blew out of the trees," Dada said grimly.

"Stronger than anything!" Alvine Henley exclaimed.

"It wasn't dead fish, I'll tell you that," Mister Gingern said. "It was worse. Much worse. It was *wrong*."

A raindrop splashed on Emeline's nose as Dada let her go. Everyone's shoulders relaxed a little as the light rain spilled over them. Emeline looked down at the water lily again, a little dazed. The flower bobbed in the rain, a full foot above the water, taller than everything around it—as if its stalk had grown a foot in an instant, right when she had reached for the water.

I should've grabbed a bucket, she thought, feeling silly. It was a strange and ridiculous impulse, this flinging of water plants.

"Let's get out of the rain," Old Henley told them, looking as if he'd aged a few more years. "Gale, your cottage is the closest. Can we talk there?"

"Of course," Endrina's father said. He picked up two of the scattered buckets and led the way across the grass.

"Are you all right?" Emeline asked Dada as they followed.

"Yes, but you go home and stay with Dale," he told her in a strained voice.

"But Dada, I—"

"Heart. Please. Go to your brother."

Emeline hurried off ahead of them, pulling her red hood over her head against the rain. What had just happened? The woods had spit out a stench so foul that some of the bravest villagers had run like children. And a water lily had grown... when she reached for it. She slowed to a stop at the sight of one of the canals, rain splashing into it a few feet away from her.

Had it grown...?

But that was impossible.

She stepped toward the canal bank, where the hard-packed ground met the rushing green water. There were lilies and water-starworts clinging to the edge just at her feet. She stretched out her hand and hesitated, staring at the soaking petals, and then, slowly, moved her fingers closer.

A bolt of energy surged through her—a lovely, shimmering energy that lit up her arm with heat.

And a flower shot up to meet her hand.

She shrieked and fell backward onto the ground, muddying her cloak. A pink water lily stood wavering above the surface of the water.

Its stalk had *grown* to reach her hand.

She had *made* it grow.

Something from unknown depths inside of her had rushed to the surface, just for an instant. Something extremely unfamiliar.

Emeline leapt to her feet, her heart pounding. She slipped and sprawled on the wet ground again, but she was up in a flash and running, slipping and stumbling all the way back to the cottage.

～～

It was hours later, nearly noon, when Emeline heard a rap at the door.

She had been sitting up in her room, holding her hands over her collected flowers in their bowls of water and trying to make them grow. Nothing was happening. If any logic applied to what had happened earlier, she supposed that made sense—cut flowers didn't grow—but she was frightened and had said nothing to Dale. She listened now as he opened the door, and heard a familiar voice.

"Em, it's Endrina!" Dale called.

Emeline got to her feet and started down the ladder, forcing herself to look composed despite the thin film of sweat on her skin.

Endrina was standing inside the door, shaking the rain off her shawl. She was tall and red-haired with kind features, the same as her father, Mister Gale; like him, she had the look of being all hands and feet, but unlike him, she was beautiful. She greeted Emeline with a hug, but there was tension in her shoulders.

"Give me your shawl," Emeline said, and hung it by the door. The rain had begun to pour down in earnest after she'd gotten home.

"I brought you a sweet roll, Dale," Endrina said, handing it to him in a cloth. He perked up immediately and carried it over to the divan.

"Are they still at your house?" Emeline asked.

"Yes, and more have come over. It's like a meeting, only no one wants to call a real one because there'll be too much hysteria," Endrina said hesitantly. She joined Dale on the divan and Emeline sat down in Dada's chair, watching her.

"Are they writing a letter to the capital?" she asked. Endrina shook her head intently.

"Mister Henley got out the old laws and read them to everyone. It hasn't happened in so long that nobody really knew…" She paused, then gave an anxious smile. "The law says that sightings of a Dark Creature have to be reported in person. By the witnesses."

Emeline blinked and Dale stopped chewing his sweet roll.

"The witnesses?" Emeline repeated.

"They have to go report it to the king," Endrina told her slowly.

"But we're the witnesses," Dale said.

Endrina nodded.

"That's what I'm here to tell you. You two and your dada have to go. They're discussing the details right now."

Emeline's mouth fell open. Dale stared at Endrina and then at his sister, his eyebrows up to his hairline. A second later, he jumped to his feet.

"Em, we're going to the capital?" he exclaimed. "We're going to meet the king?"

Endrina laughed at him, the nervousness spilling out of her in a rush. Emeline didn't move, a tingling mix of fear and excitement spreading through her.

"Are you telling me," Dale was yelling now, "that we might see *real Lash Knights*?"

"But how?" Emeline demanded. "It's so far! We don't even have horses!"

"Mister Fish is loaning you his big wagon and said he'll drive you, and Ma'am Kayley's giving two horses, since hers are the youngest and strongest," Endrina explained.

"This is unbelievable!!" Dale was practically hopping up and down, but Emeline felt more than a little dizzy. First the flowers and now this. She clenched her skirt in her hands.

"Dale, stop it!" she snapped.

"I don't know if I wish I were going too or if I'm glad I'm not," Endrina said bluntly. "It's all very exciting, but I'd be terrified." She went to Emeline's side and put her arms around her shoulders. "I'm already scared, knowing there really *is* something out there in the woods."

"But we'll need—supplies…and money," Emeline said uncertainly. "And a map? Directions?"

"Dada will take care of all of that," Dale told her impatiently. "We're going on an adventure, Emeline! Wait till I tell Aladane!"

five

The next few days were like nothing Emeline had ever known. The hustle and bustle of getting four people ready to leave Equane—and ready to travel to the capital, no less—was overwhelming.

Aladane couldn't seem to leave Dale's side, and the two of them were constantly underfoot as Emeline helped Dada pack. Every few minutes, he said something like, "I can't believe I'm not going...Just think, if I'd run across the bridge like you, I'd be a witness too!" Then Emeline would groan.

Even as she folded clothes, blankets, and dried fish into bundles, she could not quite believe that they were going anywhere. Equane was all she knew. Yes, she had imagined that one day, when she was grown and maybe even married, she would like to travel a little and see some more of the world. But not so soon—so suddenly. Not like this.

With the exception of Mama's death, her whole life had been sleepy, comfortable, and very, very small. She couldn't shake the feeling of being suddenly woken up.

It was best to concentrate on packing, so that was what she did. She had three simple dresses, two fish-leather bodices, and two nightdresses, all of which she rolled up as best she could. She decided she would also take Mama's cloak, and wear boots instead of sandals. The north would be colder than Equane, which never had much of a winter.

Everyone said the strong and sturdy Mister Fish was the best road companion they could have. He was not only sensible and handy at repairs, he was the village's spring-gun champion. At the harvest contest, he hadn't missed a single shot. She felt better to have him along.

But she was afraid. She was. Their trip was required by law, yes, but they weren't taking it just to report what they'd seen: It was the safety of the village that *really* concerned them, and they planned to request protection. It was all people spoke of, whispering together in knots, and she saw the strain of it written in Dada's face. The moat was supposed to protect Equane, but would it? Could the thing in the trees leap, like a cat? Could it climb an oak? What if, somehow, the thing—the *Ithin*—got across? The king must send them men.

Dada had not had much to say about the prospect of uprooting his family and taking them to the capital. But he had begun muttering to himself and walking around and around the cottage, his brow furrowed, and when it came time to pack he stood a long time in front of the bookshelves, scratching his chin. Finally, he pulled out the *History* and a couple of volumes Emeline didn't recognize and put them into a bag. She saw his pouch of clay and whittling knife go in as well.

She was glad they were bringing the *History*. She wanted to read about the Keldares on the road. Was it possible the magic they sang of was real? That *magic* was real? And... more importantly... was what she did with the lilies a kind of magic? Real magic?

What in the kingdom would it mean, if she could actually do magic?

She was afraid to think about it, let alone tell Dada. But in her free moments, she would find quiet spots along the canals and make the lilies twist and grow, one thrilling inch at a time. Each time, it was a sparkling rush of energy, and it was exhilarating. *Where did this come from?*

The petals and leaves twined around her fingers almost lovingly. It didn't work with dry plants, and she couldn't make the water itself do anything, but the water lilies, the weeds, the rushes, the kingcups—any wet plant—would dance right out of the water for her.

The trip would take about two weeks. They were to follow the Braedle Road, named for the early king who had commissioned it. It was a long, winding highway, a lifeline of the realm, and it connected to many smaller roads—including the old dirt path outside the village gates.

Mister Gale brought them several hard loaves of traveling bread, and Ma'am Kayley gave them bales of straw for the horses. Canteen after canteen of water was filled. Mister Henley and the other old folks donated what little money they had, most of which was very worn and left over from long-ago travels, for Dada had none. No one in Equane used it; bartering had worked just fine for decades.

Dada and Old Henley worried about whether the payts they had were still current. Had the king changed the money in recent years? Did anyone know? Old Henley went back to look through the laws.

"Mister Fish should teach me to shoot a spring-gun," Dale declared the night before they were going to leave. He was helping Emeline roll their fish-oil lanterns in blankets to keep the glass from breaking. She snorted. "We'd be safer if three of us could fight!" he insisted.

Aladane, who sat on the divan watching them, sighed with envy.

"Fight who, Dale?" she asked, irritated. "No one's going to attack us. We've got nothing of value to anyone."

"He'd be better off teaching Emeline to shoot," Aladane said, taunting Dale. "*She's* the one who fought the Ithin!"

"Shut up!"

"I can't believe I'm not going with you," Aladane added, for the thousandth time. "Just think, if I had run across the bridge like you—"

"Like a fool, you mean?" Emeline said, and Dale frowned.

"I was going to," Aladane insisted. "I would have!"

Emeline rolled her eyes and carried the lamps out the front door. She was relieved Aladane wasn't going—Dale didn't need to be encouraged.

The sun was setting, casting a reddish glow over the wagon that stood before the cottage. Dada and Mister Fish were tying down the bundles, a handful of villagers watching and calling out advice.

"You got those leather blankets I gave you for rain?" asked an old man.

"Yep," Mister Fish said. The wagon had a leather half-roof on hinges that could be raised up over the passengers, but Emeline supposed the blankets were for the drivers.

"If you end up by the Hawking River, you can add to your vittles," a woman offered. "My grand-dada said there's good fishing there."

"Those river hawks are vicious, though. They should keep away from there."

"Ah, Fish could take out a hawk with no trouble."

Emeline handed Dada the bundled lamps and watched him tuck them in the wagon.

"Don't talk to any strangers, heart," a woman advised her. "Stick close to your folk."

Emeline nodded as Mister Gingern came plodding forward with his hands on his hips. "I'll collect that lazy boy of mine now," he told Dada. "I can't seem to keep him away from yours with all this excitement. It's gone to his fool head."

"He's inside," Emeline said with a smile.

"Young folk always get excited when changes happen," the old man said. "They never realize that change just means trouble."

"Hush, don't frighten the child," someone told him.

Emeline glanced back as she turned to follow Mister Gingern into the house. Sometimes it seemed like the old folk in the village were always afraid, but now their words made her heart beat faster.

"Bless water, she ought to be frightened!" the old man continued. "Everything's going to change now."

Emeline woke with a start as Dada called up the ladder for her.

The sky was still dark through the loft window. Why was he waking her up so early? What was happening?

Then she remembered, and it tore the veil of sleepiness away.

She sat up quickly, wide awake. They were going to the capital. She pulled on a blue dress with a pattern of tiny stars and buckled up her bodice, listening to Dale and Dada moving around below. She washed her face, combed her hair, and stepped into her boots. Then she took a last look at the familiar little room and hurried down the ladder.

Dale stood in the middle of the sitting room, dressed, but with his blanket around his shoulders like a shawl.

"We're actually leaving," he told Emeline wonderingly.

"Come on, let's eat breakfast." She took him by the shoulders and guided him toward the table.

The night sky outside was just beginning to soften when they climbed into the wagon. Ma'am Kayley's big brown horses stood brushed and harnessed, and they snorted and stamped their feet, eager to go.

But do they know where they're going? Emeline wondered as she sat next to Dale on the second bench seat. *Or do they think we're just going to plow a field?*

Mister Fish sat on the front bench with Dada, holding the reins. The two of them wore their farming clothes—coarse trousers and button-down shirts—but Emeline knew that Dada's gray coat and flat cap were packed in the wagon.

Fish's wife stood nearby and waved up at him. She was a hardy, cheerful woman, and Dada had asked her to keep an eye on his field as well as theirs.

"Don't you be too long. The boys'll make a mess of the farms," she said, sounding unconcerned about it.

"You tell them I'll wring their necks," Fish told her.

Old Henley and his son Alvine stood nearby as well, looking sleepy, but wishing them luck. Things were moving very quickly now; Emeline gripped the side of the wagon.

Mister Fish flopped the reins lightly across the horses' backs and they started forward with a lurch. Neighbors followed them as they rolled away from their comfortable cottage, but most of the village was quiet and still.

They were clopping toward the village gates, the tall slabs of old, red-painted slate staring back at them expectantly. Emeline had never gone through them. Her breath hitched.

Alvine Henley came around the wagon and pushed the gates open, just as if he did it every morning. She turned and looked back as they rode through; Endrina had joined the farewell party and was waving. Emeline waved back. Then she turned around to face the dusty road ahead, swallowing hard.

Don't you dare cross the water, Ithin.

six

The Braedle Road stretched across a sea of hills and valleys, connecting the patchwork of nameless paths that led to villages like Equane. The wagon trundled along one of those paths, and Emeline stared out at the land around them, unbroken, for the first time in her life, by cottages or canals.

To the south, behind them, lay the receding gates of Equane and the dark smudge of forest beyond.

To the west were open woodlands, too sparsely treed for Dark Creatures, with the gates of another village just visible in the distance.

North and east were rolling hills, lavender-colored in the morning light. They were patched with clusters of black pine, mist drifting between the copses.

To her, everything was new.

After the wagon had rumbled along for nearly an hour, the shadow of mountains appeared, far away to the north. Emeline realized she was gaping at the ridgeline openmouthed, just like Dale, so she elbowed him in the side and drew herself up.

"Are those real mountains?" he asked, a little hoarse. "Is that the Dinene?"

"No, the Dinene's much farther than that," she told him uncertainly.

"What other mountains are there?"

"There are many," Dada said, speaking over his shoulder. "But those up ahead are part of the Spine. Look."

He handed them one of the maps and Dale took it eagerly. It was a thick piece of cloth, painted with a miniature version of the tapestry in the meeting hall.

The kingdom was shaped like a bean, with an inward curve toward the west near the capital. Just above the capital was a line of mountains marked THE SPINE, and at the far northern border of the kingdom was a much larger and more jagged range: THE DINENE MOUNTAINS.

"The ocean," Dale said, running his fingers along the blue paint at the border of the kingdom. The sea swept around the southwest and up to the curve near the capital. Emeline's eyes ran over the rest of the map-cloth to settle on THE VINDANE REGION, a place she thought she dimly remembered Mama mentioning. It was made up of a handful of villages, precariously close to dense forest.

Beyond the borders to the east and the north, the map was painted gray. Those were the Outer Lands.

"Why does the king have his summer home at the ocean down south instead of right there by the capital?" Dale asked, pointing.

"Because of the great harbor," Dada told them. "Too many steamships coming in and out to be very peaceful."

Fish grunted. "If he wants peace, he shouldn't be king."

"I want to see the great harbor," Dale announced.

"What for?" Fish asked, flicking at the horses.

"Just to see it! To see all that water..."

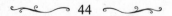

"Not me. What good is water that you can't drink?" Fish said, and Dada chuckled.

"And all the ships," Dale continued, undaunted.

Emeline looked at the gray surrounding the kingdom. There was very little in the *History* about those lands; even Dada knew only a few stories. "Are there any ships from the Outer Lands?"

"They don't know how to build ships in the Outer Lands," Fish said flatly. "They don't know much. Anyone will tell you."

"Well, no," Dada said, "I've read that sailing ships *do* dock from the Outer Lands, and that they're very interesting contraptions." Fish looked surprised by that.

"Really? What happens to the people who are on them?" Dale asked.

"They do their trading and head back," Dada replied.

Emeline had seen pictures of elaborate steamships. She tried to imagine one blowing into the harbor from beyond the known world. What would it be like? It made no sense to say that people of the Outer Lands were ignorant if they could build ships.

"What happens if the crew want to live here?" she asked.

"Well, they have to swear loyalty to the king. If they refuse, they get sent back by the harbor guards. But I'm not sure how all of that works." Dada pointed up ahead. "There's the Braedle Road."

Fish was already turning the horses, and Emeline watched as the broad, flat strip of packed dirt came closer. Before long they were riding on it due north, and the going was much smoother. The great road spread out ahead of them as far as she could see, fading into the mist.

"Does the road go through any forest?" she asked, suddenly worried.

"It used to, Old Henley said," Dada told her. "But now it only skirts the edge of the woods near the Spine."

"See, here." Dale showed her on the map how the line of the road brushed past a section of green near the mountain range. She nodded, relieved.

A shadow in the woods. Moving like a snake.

"Yep, now we just sit back and ride straight for a long ways," Fish said.

The sun was up in full now, warming the top of Emeline's head. She climbed off the seat and settled herself into a space on the wagon floor, leaning against the side. That was one thing about wagon seats: There was nothing to lean one's back against. Dale seemed unbothered by it, slouched over the map as if he had no spine.

They rode along the smooth, quiet road for hours, the scenery unchanging. Emeline grew both sleepy and hungry, her excitement beginning to fade. Fish and Dada had been talking to each other in low voices, but now Fish turned around and said, "Pass me a bit of salted fish, will you, son?"

Dale jerked as if he'd fallen half-asleep. He yawned and then climbed past Emeline into the back of the wagon, looking for the right bundle. "I hope that fog up there doesn't spook the horses," Fish was saying.

Dale suddenly let out a yelp.

Emeline spun around as Fish reined in the horses, jerking

the wagon to a stop. Her jaw dropped. There, among the packed rolls and bundles in the back of the wagon, huddled Aladane Gingern. Dale had clearly just uncovered him. Her jaw dropped.

"Bless water!" Dada exclaimed.

"Aladane!" Emeline cried. The boy tried to seem smaller, squeezing himself deeper between the hay bales.

"You snuck onto the wagon?" Dale asked him. He sounded both astonished and very impressed.

"Aladane Gingern, what in the kingdom are you doing here?" Fish roared. He and Dada jumped down from the front seat and were on him in a second, yanking him out of the wagon.

"I'm sorry! I just wanted to come!" Aladane wailed. His face was red and his brown hair disheveled, sticking straight up.

"Your parents must be going mad looking for you!" Dada said, shaking his head.

"No, no, I left a note! They've gotten it by now," Aladane insisted. Emeline burst out laughing, and Dada gave her a sharp look.

"I'll whip you now and they'll whip you later!" Fish declared, even though they all knew he wouldn't.

"Keep your voice down, Fish," Dada said. "We don't know who else is out along the road."

Emeline realized how far their voices must travel over wide-open land. She glanced around, self-conscious, but the view was unchanged; a cool breeze from the north drifted over them.

"I guess we need to turn around and take him home," Dada said reluctantly.

"What, go all the way back?" Dale exclaimed. "Can't he just come with us?"

"I brought my own food," Aladane said meekly. He looked at Emeline for help, but she shook her head.

"You are absolutely impossible. When were you planning on showing yourself?" she asked.

"When I thought it'd be too late to take me back," he muttered. He looked ashamed, but there was also a glint in his eyes.

"Can't we just take him along? His dada will punish him later," Dale said, appealing to his own father. "We'll lose all that time if we go back!"

"I'm prepared for serious trouble when I get back. I just want to see the world first," Aladane said grandly. Dada snorted at that; Fish grumbled and shook his head.

"You're damn right you'll be in serious trouble," he snapped.

But then he looked at Dada, who sighed and nodded. They would lose a day if they turned around, eating up more food and wearying the horses.

"All right, I don't want to hear one word of complaint from you," Fish told Aladane. "About *anything*."

The boys broke into triumphant grins, and then immediately looked sober. Emeline groaned. Part of her couldn't help but be happy for him, but she had been relieved before that this troublemaker wasn't coming along. He was a bad influence on Dale, after all.

"I won't complain about anything!" Aladane exclaimed.

"Honestly. Like this is all a game," Fish muttered. He and

Dada circled back to the front, looking thoroughly irritated. Dale and Aladane elbowed each other happily until Emeline gave them a disapproving stare. She hoped for Aladane's sake that the trip was worth the trouble he'd be in when they returned.

Fish slapped the horses again, and they were off. They rode for several hours, the boys chattering quietly over the map, and then they caught up with the fog. It settled over them slowly, dimming the light, until the sun faded to a blurry orb Emeline could gaze into without blinking. The horses slowed down, and one of them whinnied, but Fish urged them on gently.

"This is spooky," Aladane said, sounding happy about it.

"Who knows what lurks in the fog of the fields?" Dale chimed in excitedly.

"Well, we know it's not Dark Creatures. Too damp," Emeline said hopefully, peering out beyond the road.

"Dampness doesn't keep away evil men," Fish muttered.

"No, but that aim of yours ought to," Dada told him. He smiled.

"How did you get so good at shooting, Mister Fish?" Aladane asked.

"Practice, son. I was sickly as a boy, so my mama used to make me stay outside all day to sport and toughen up. But my brothers wouldn't let me play with them because I was the youngest." Fish scratched his head under his floppy hat. "I would line up rocks out in the field and knock them down with a dart-shooter. When my dada saw I was good at it, he got me a spring-gun."

Dale's eyes brightened. "Maybe I should start practicing with a dart-shooter."

Emeline reached into the back for a food bundle. She unwrapped it and doled out hard bread to Dale and Dada, then pulled on Mama's cloak against the clinging fog. The horses clip-clopped steadily in the stillness.

⇒ seven ⇐

*E*meline was nose-deep in Keldare stories. In the *History*, they had great strength and daring—they were adventurers as well as troubadours, scalers of the Dinene Mountains, masters of the hunt. But there were also stories of old men whose songs were said to come true, and young girls whose singing could seduce the birds. Was that magic?

One section caught her attention: *It is said some Keldares can interact with elements of nature in a magical sense. This is seen in the story of the Keldare Fire-Bringer who entertained King Braedle. Despite many witnesses, none could determine how he controlled the great flames that danced over the court. Whether such abilities come from a special circumstance of birth or from intimacy with ancient enchantments is a matter of debate....*

Emeline ran her finger under the first line, reading it again. Elements of nature? Like green growth, or water?

The Keldares themselves share stories about a very old, very dark magic, pockets of which still exist in the world. Some believe this bitter magic is the origin of the Dark Creatures....

The page darkened, and she looked up to see a cluster of trees looming ominously over the road. It wasn't the ancient, tangled forest of Equane, but even sparse woods made her uneasy. The sun was setting, casting long red shadows.

At that moment, the wagon suddenly lurched to the left. *Hard.*

Emeline fell forward and grabbed hold of Dada's shirt. The boys yelled, the horses whinnied, and Fish swore.

"Bless water!" he shouted. "What was that?"

Dada jumped out of the lopsided wagon, landing with a thump. "It's a hole! The front wheel's sunk in."

Emeline straightened up and leaned over the side while Fish climbed out and joined Dada. It looked to her like the wheel was half-hidden in the ground.

"A couple spokes cracked," Fish said, crouching down. "I can bind them up in no time and then we can push it out of there. Just let me get my tools."

"Why'd we have to break a wheel here?" Dale muttered nervously. He and Aladane stared up at the trees in the fading light.

"Fish will fix it fast," she said, more confidently than she felt. "Let's eat some supper, Dale. Get our food bundle." He climbed over the seat and into the back.

"I just don't see how this hole came about naturally," Dada was saying as Fish worked on the wheel next to him. "It looks like it was covered up with all this loose dirt."

Suddenly, Fish stood up straight, his arm pointed across the road. It took Emeline a second to realize that his spring-gun was in his hand.

Emerging like shadows from between the trees were two

men, watching them. A chill crept over her. Aladane dropped the sandwich he'd just unwrapped, spilling sliced onions and dandelion greens onto the wagon floor.

"Now, don't get all jumpy," one of the men said. He was as pale as his companion was dark, both of them bone-thin and wearing dirty, ragged tunics. It was hard to see their faces as the sun dropped farther behind the trees.

"We just want to help," the other one said.

"You dug a hole and laid a trap," Dada said evenly. Fish had not moved an inch.

"Now, that isn't kind. We're just poor folk, scrapping it out in the woods," the second man said with a trace of sarcasm.

"If you think this little grove is a wood, then you don't know much," Fish huffed.

"We know you got food and money," the first man snapped back.

"Not one step closer," Fish said quietly.

Emeline held her breath. Dale was pale and serious; Aladane's mouth hung open.

"Look at that sweet thing in the wagon," the first man said with a short laugh. "Give us some food, heart?" Emeline turned to stare at him, not quite sure that he was addressing her. He gave her a leer that confirmed it.

Dada bristled, but Fish put his free hand on his arm. "Don't talk to her!" he growled.

"Look at that gold on her arm," the second man told his companion. They turned slightly toward each other, conspiring. "Keldare gold? Might be worth something."

Emeline gasped and glared at them.

"I'll hold them," Fish told Dada. "You try to push the wagon out."

"'Hold us'? You sure we're alone?" one of the men asked mockingly.

"There's another one!" Dale exclaimed.

Emeline jerked around to see a third man standing on the other side of the road, his spring-gun pointed straight at the wagon. Aladane made a strangled noise.

This man wore a black coat, his hat flat and low over his face. There was a long, tense silence; Emeline could hear a distant bird chirping, and her heart pounding in her ears. Before this moment, she'd never really thought about the fact that spring-guns could kill.

The man finally spoke, and his tone was lazy, almost unconcerned. "Well now, it seems like someone's gonna get shot, doesn't it?"

Then Mister Fish shot him.

Emeline shrieked. Dada yelled, "Down! Get down!"

She threw her arm around the boys and dragged them with her onto the wagon floor. Another shot whistled through the air. There was a shout; someone cursing; the noise of feet pounding. Her muscles clenched, listening, and as the sound of running faded, she realized how loudly the boys were breathing against her.

After a moment, a low, relieved whistle broke the stillness. "He was the only one that had a spring-gun," Fish said, sounding shaken.

Emeline popped her head up, relief flooding her at the sound of his voice. Fish and Dada stood there unhurt, shoulders slumped, facing toward the trees. She didn't see the thieves anywhere.

"How did you *know* the others didn't have one?" Dada asked, incredulous.

Fish shook his head. "Not a lot of places to hide one in those rags they were wearing. One had a knife in his belt, but nothing else. Boots neither."

"Look! Mister Fish killed him!" Aladane yelled.

He and Dale had popped up next to Emeline and scrambled to that side of the wagon to look. The third man was sprawled in the grass, his hat lying nearby. The other two, unarmed, must have run away. They hadn't expected Fish to actually shoot anyone, and neither had she.

"Don't look!" she told the boys, but they ignored her, fascinated.

"He got him in the eye!" her brother called out.

"Fish is a crack shot!" Aladane cried admiringly.

Emeline looked—she couldn't help herself—but she wished she hadn't. The man's legs were splayed out, his long dirty feet bare. Why, she wondered, did people use spring-guns to hurt each other? Why had this man been willing to shoot them? Her stomach curdled. She never wanted to see a spring-gun again.

"You took a huge risk!" Dada was standing with his hands balled into fists, glaring. "What if you'd been wrong and those two had started firing? What would've happened to my children, Fish?"

"Now, calm down, Bird," Fish said, irritated. He tucked his spring-gun back in his belt and turned away. "Don't lecture me, I've got children too. But I wasn't wrong and we're all safe."

"You killed a man! We had nothing to take but food! Would it not have been better to let them have it?"

Fish rounded on him, defiant. "You think they would've left us alone if we had? Don't be naïve, Bird. You heard what he said. If I hadn't shot him, he would've shot one of us, or worse." Emeline and the boys watched apprehensively.

Dada said nothing, but his jaw was clenched. Finally, he turned away and glared instead at the broken wagon wheel. "Let's fix this wheel and leave this place behind," he said.

"What about the dead man?" Dale asked. Fish frowned and looked down at the man he'd shot, his expression softening. He shook his head.

"Well, I'm not hanging around to bury him," he said. "He'll have to stay right where he is."

~⌒~

Night fell, and the five of them ate their suppers in the dark, a lantern swinging from the front of the wagon. Its glow made Emeline think of a giant firefly floating along with them.

Had a man really died today? Crickets sang peacefully all around.

Dada was silent and seemed to be brooding, but Fish was whistling, almost as if he shot thieves every day. Dale and Aladane plagued him with spring-gun questions. Emeline suspected that he was only pretending to be so cavalier.

"If you use poison darts, but you hit someone in the foot, will it still kill them?" Dale wanted to know.

"That depends on how much poison is in it," Fish answered.

"I heard certain kinds'll kill you if they get you in the finger!" Aladane said with his mouth full. Emeline frowned at him. "It's true!"

"Maybe it is, but you don't have to sound so excited about it. I guess we should keep our armbands covered, Dale," she told her brother. He nodded and slid his hand over one of his protectively.

"Maybe we should keep *you* covered," Aladane told her with a grin. "You're the 'sweet thing in the wagon.'" Emeline's fist shot out before she knew it and punched him in the arm. "Ow!"

"Aladane, be quiet!" Dada thundered.

"That wasn't very sweet," Aladane grumbled. Dale laughed at him, his own mouth full.

"Emeline will be just fine, Bird," Fish said quietly. He patted Dada on the back.

"Of course I will," Emeline said, more confidently than she felt.

"I've got my eye on her for one of my boys anyway!" the big farmer declared, turning back to give her a smile. Emeline flushed and grimaced, remembering the wink his son had given her at the meeting.

"Eww," Dale said.

"Over my dead body," Dada told Fish.

"I know, I know." Fish grinned and went back to whistling.

Emeline turned her red face up to the relief of the stars above them, patchy and swirly in the dark clouds. She had not really thought before that *grown* men might stare at her. Where was Sessa now, to tell her she was ugly? She would've welcomed that over the leers of strangers on the road. And she didn't even want to think about marrying one of Fish's sons.

They rode on long into the night, and the brilliant globe of the moon rose above them, casting silvery light onto the road and the dark hills around. The boys climbed into the back of the wagon and lay there whispering for a while before Dale started up his snoring. Emeline yawned and wrapped her cloak around herself tighter.

It was so odd to be out under the stars late at night. No roof, no walls, just the wagon wheels rolling underneath them. It gave her a thrill to think that, from a distance, they were just a tiny moving light in the darkness—like a *real* firefly.

"What do you think old Olvinde will say?" Fish was asking her father. Dada was smoking his pipe, blowing out the smoke into the darkness.

"I don't think he'll tell us if he plans to do anything about it," he replied. "He'll probably just thank us and send us home."

"But what about the village?" Fish lowered his voice and added, "We're not safe if there are creatures in the woods. He's got to send us someone to investigate. Or better, men with arms! Knights, even."

"Only if he believes us," Dada said, puffing on his pipe.

"Well, we have proof, don't we? As much as I hate to believe it myself, the Theurgists are right!"

Emeline watched Dada tap his pipe and shake his head. "Do we really have proof? We have the testimony of two children, and the Sapients are likely to say they imagined it. They don't know that Em's no flighty child."

That's not all they don't know, Emeline thought, nervously staring down at her hands.

Fish turned to look at Dada in the dim lantern glow. "And what about that smell, Bird? We've got testimony too."

"I don't know what they'll make of that."

"Well, I'll convince them," Fish declared. "I won't be laughed at by some feuding council, just for telling the truth."

Dada didn't say anything for a moment. "So you believe in magic then?" he asked him. Emeline held her breath, listening.

"I don't know if I believe in all kinds of magic. I like to stick to things I can see with my own eyes, or things I can dig up out of the ground. But what we smelled in the woods that day...that was like nothing I ever smelled." Fish shuddered. "There is something unnatural in there, and that is a fact. So, if the Theurgists say it's the Ithin, then I'll throw my hat in."

"That's about where I am too," Dada said. "Airlinna used to get quiet whenever I brought up things like this, like she knew some things she didn't want to say." Emeline's ears pricked at the mention of her mother.

"Like what?" Fish asked. "Keldare stories?"

"Maybe. I know she believed the Sapients were too narrow-minded, at least."

"Well, her kind have all sorts of stories the Sapients would throw out. I still remember when she and her mama showed up at the village gates," Fish said with a grin. "All bone-white and black-haired and carrying everything they owned on their backs." Dada laughed suddenly and Emeline's heart warmed at the sound.

"I don't think anyone expected them to settle in so easily. But they wanted to stop traveling. You know, Airlinna never would tell me all the places they'd been to. I think there were some adventures she didn't want to share," Dada said wistfully.

Dale snored suddenly and Dada turned back to see Emeline listening. She reached behind herself and pushed at Dale until he rolled over.

Her father went quiet, smoke drifting past him. She wanted to hear more about when he and Mama first met, but she was afraid to ask. She had *never* asked, because she hated to see the sorrow in his eyes.

She sighed, yawned, and, after a moment, squeezed down in between Dale and the side of the wagon. Then all she could see was the vast black sky floating above. She wondered if Mama's blue eyes—vast and deep in their own way—looked down on her from up there. And what Mama would tell her, if she could, about magic.

✤ eight ✤

I think that's Hollolen," someone was saying. "Or Blyne, they're both right around here." It was Dale's voice. Emeline's eyes opened; she was lying on her side in the back of the wagon.

The sun was so bright that she winced and shaded her eyes.

Mister Fish was stretched out asleep next to her, his hat covering his face, and Dada was driving. She had a hazy memory of the wagon stopping in the night, and Fish brushing down the horses, but nothing else.

"Wait, I brought a spyglass," Aladane said, excited. He climbed over Emeline and she sat up with a start. "Sorry, sorry."

Stiffly, she rinsed out her mouth with water from a canteen and spat it over the side of the wagon, then tried half-heartedly to smooth her curly hair. The boys were both wild-haired and wrinkled, but they didn't seem to mind at all.

Aladane was climbing back onto the seat with Dale, clutching the short tube of a simple spyglass. He held it to his eye and peered at the smoking chimneys of the houses to the west. Emeline joined them, tearing into a piece of rough, dry bread. The cloudless sky was intensely blue.

She could see buildings in the distance, the smoke from their rooftops drifting lazily into the sky. It was a strange sight after riding through so much emptiness, and she craned for a better look. Past them were the beginnings of what looked like woods.

"Why are the cottages smoking?" Aladane asked.

"They do their cooking inside," Dada said from the front seat. "In fireplaces."

"Sounds dangerous." Aladane turned north, still glued to his spyglass.

"Don't I get to look?" Dale asked.

"It's Blyne up ahead for sure! It's big! I see a lot more houses." Aladane passed Dale the spyglass. "It's a real town, Dale, look!"

"Let me see after you," Emeline said, watching her brother. He nodded, squinting, as Aladane flipped through their maps again.

"I've got to remember all these names, so I can talk about them when we get back," he said happily.

"You mean once you're allowed to leave the house again?" Emeline asked, grinning. He sighed.

Dale handed Emeline the spyglass, grinning too. She held it to her eye.

The world leapt forward and warped itself into a bubble shape. She saw the reddish brown bricks of a building first, then shifted the glass half an inch to a small field of grass where geese were waddling. She turned her head and a blur of colors flashed by. There were the bricks of another large building, and two men standing nearby, gesturing in conversation. Behind them was a steam-carriage.

Emeline gasped. It was much smaller than the king's had been, and it was plain and mud-splashed, but it was still a steam-carriage. She stared at the tall wheels and the handled door in the side.

"All right, give it back now," Aladane was saying. She hesitated, sweeping the lens over more buildings, some horses, and a large well.

"The cottages are so close together," she said, pulling her eye from it at last. "The houses, I mean." She gave the spyglass back and took another bite of bread.

"That's what happens when you have so many people in one spot," Dada told her.

"They must have a moat, with the woods so close," she ventured.

"Look, Em, they do. The Hawking River isn't far, either," Dale said, showing her the map. The sight of the curving blue line on the cloth was a relief.

She thought of Equane with a sudden ache in her heart. It was so small, and nestled so close to the forest—*true, deep* forest—where something terrifying lurked. She just hoped the moat would keep it at bay.

But if children could get across...

It was late afternoon when Fish woke up and mumbled about being stiff all over. He dragged himself up and swung his long legs over the bench seat, crowding the boys, then settled onto the front seat next to Dada. Emeline handed him some food.

"We'll have to see if they make a cure for snoring in the capital," he announced, giving Dale a frown. Dada chuckled.

"Now you know what I hear every night," Emeline told him.

"It's not my fault!" Dale insisted.

"Nothing can wake me up. My mama says I sleep like the dead," Aladane said cheerfully.

"If something happens at night, then, we'll just leave you," Dale told him. Aladane scowled.

～～

The sun was setting as the wagon rolled into Blyne. They passed under a large wooden archway, the brick buildings crowding close on either side. The houses here were tall and square, not smoothly rounded like Equanian cottages, and there were bright lanterns shining through the windows. Some had wide porches, and a few had painted signs above their doors. Emeline squinted to read the lettering in the twilight: BUTCHER, SADDLER, FARRIER, TAILOR.

Beyond the farthest buildings were the silhouettes of treetops. They would have reminded Emeline of Equane but for the dark shadow of mountains beyond them.

Loud voices spilled from open doorways and windows. The people here dressed differently from Equanians: The men favored long cloaks and jackets made of a leather that didn't have to be stitched together in strips, like fish-leather did. The streets were busy.

"I bet that's the schoolhouse," Dale said, pointing to a building with a bell.

"And there's the trouble-house," Fish said, jerking his head. Emeline turned to see a building set back off the road, spewing an incredible racket of yelling, arguing, laughter, and music, with the occasional crash of broken glass. The sign over the door read: GALLID'S TAVERN.

"I guess they like their ale here!" Dada said, amused.

The sound of a spring-gun went off, and everyone jumped. Emeline snapped around, worried, but saw nothing; then they heard laughter and the gun went off again.

"This place is exciting!" Aladane said.

"I think you mean 'dangerous,'" Dada muttered.

"There should be an inn," Fish said. "We might be able to stop and wash up."

"Oh yes, let's do that!" Emeline said, and to her surprise, the boys chimed in in agreement. She suspected that they just wanted to see the inside of something.

"They'll charge us for it, but then I guess we'll find out if our money's any good," Dada said. Fish nodded.

"We'll look out for an inn sign," Dale said eagerly. He and Aladane leaned over the sides of the wagon.

The last of the sunlight disappeared into the trees, and the bright glow of windows spotted the darkness around them. It wasn't long before they saw a signpost planted right by the road, a lantern hanging from it. The painted words CARVEN'S INN were plain as day on the board.

Dada turned off the main road, the wagon bumping over the rough path marked by the sign. Emeline could see a tall building ahead of them with many windows in the second story, most of them lit but covered by shades. Figures moved in one or two of them.

"Let's be quick about it," Dada said, studying the place. Emeline couldn't tell whether he disliked it or was being cautious. She felt just as curious now as the boys; she'd never seen an inn before.

They stopped out front, and a boy younger than Dale scrambled out the door as suddenly as if he'd been shoved. He came up to greet them in the dark, squeezing a hat in his hands.

"Hello, do you need a room?" he shrilled. "We've only got one available. There's a stable for horses." It sounded like he was spitting out the words from memory.

"We don't need a room, son," Fish told him. "We'd just like to pay to use the washroom, if that's all right."

The boy stared back at him, his mouth open.

"Go ask your mama if it is," Dada said kindly. The boy spun around and hurried back into the inn; there were a few bangs inside and then he ran back out.

"Half a payt each, except the girl's free. Girls are clean," he announced. Emeline laughed, while Dale and Aladane looked insulted.

"I suppose we'll have to pay for the stowaway," Fish grumbled.

"Oh no, I don't mind not washing," Aladane announced. "I'll just look around."

"If I have to, you have to!" Dale insisted.

Dada turned back to the innkeeper's boy. "All right, we'll come in," he told him. Emeline climbed into the back of the wagon eagerly, digging for a towel and a clean dress—her pale yellow one. The boys followed suit.

"I'll feed the horses while you folk take your turns," Fish said as they climbed out of the wagon. "Somebody ought to keep an eye on things."

Emeline followed her father through the inn door, her legs stiff. The dimly lit lobby was not very warm. A large staircase curved overhead, and the walls were full of framed pictures, but it was hard to make them out in the poor light.

As Dale and Aladane joined them in the doorway, a heavyset matron marched out of a swinging door, wearing a faded dress that buttoned up the front. She surveyed them critically, wiping her hands on a towel as the sounds of clinking dishes and chattering women spilled out of the kitchen behind her.

"Washroom's behind the stairs, to the left," she said with a sniff. "I'll thank you not to bother any guests."

"We'll be as quiet as mice," Dada said politely. He counted out the payt bills from his pocket and laid them on the counter that faced the front door. "Emeline, I'll walk you over and wait at the door. Boys, stay right here and don't talk to anyone."

He put a protective hand on her arm and led her toward the stairs. She realized with surprise that he was more worried about letting her wash alone than about leaving the boys in the lobby, even though she was the oldest.

There were muffled sounds from the rooms above as they ducked under the stairs to a little nook with a narrow door. Someone laughed; someone else was singing in a low voice. She wondered what kind of people were staying the night there, and where they were going.

"Anyone inside?" Dada asked the door. When no one answered, he pulled it open to reveal a large brass basin with a hand pump and a crude bar of soap lying in the bottom. He patted her on the shoulder. "I'll be right out here."

"I know, Dada. I'll be fine."

Once inside, she undid her bodice and pulled off her dress and underclothes, then pumped the handle until cold water came pouring out, making a racket in the brass tub. Footsteps creaked overhead as she splashed herself, shivering; the soap was hard and dry, but she managed to get some lavender-smelling lather.

Suddenly, fast, heavy footfalls thumped across the lobby and up the stairs. She froze. Dada cleared his throat, but said nothing; she dried herself quickly and pulled on her clean clothes, hurrying to open the door.

"Who was that?" she whispered.

"Not sure. Let's go," he said, taking her arm again. They hadn't gotten halfway across the lobby before Dale and Aladane came rushing to meet them, their eyes as wide as platters.

"Did you see them?" Dale hissed.

"One of them was a Lash Knight!" Aladane whisper-shouted. Emeline gasped and turned to look up the stairs, but there was nothing to see.

"A Lash Knight?" Dada looked skeptical.

"He had a cloak on with armor underneath!"

"I could see his whip!" Dale exclaimed. Dada shushed him.

"It's none of our business. Let's go, Aladane, you're next," he said, gesturing. The big boy nodded reluctantly and followed him, still craning his neck toward the stairs.

"There were two of them?" Emeline asked Dale.

"The other man looked like a guard, maybe. They just barged straight in and up the stairs, Em."

"Didn't the inn lady hear them?" she asked, surprised.

"She peeked her head out, but then she just slammed the door shut."

The two of them looked toward the kitchen, realizing it was silent. Everyone on the other side of the door had either disappeared or gone quiet. *Something's wrong here.*

A loud cry upstairs broke the silence—Emeline jumped in her skin. Then a fierce crack tore the air, almost like a lightning strike, and there was a crash. Dada came running back from the washroom just as more cries and thumps sounded.

"What in the kingdom?" he gasped.

A shirtless man suddenly raced down the stairs, ghostly pale and shave-headed. Behind him came a bearded stranger with a strange-looking spring-gun.

"Get down!" Dada roared. Emeline grabbed Dale's arm and dropped to the floor, trying to pull him with her. The two men raced across the lobby, headed straight for the door.

"Stop!" someone bellowed.

But the shirtless man was upon the Birds, his eyes wild, and in one slick movement he yanked Dale from Emeline's grasp. Then he plunged out the door with her brother.

~ nine ~

"Dale!" Emeline shrieked. "He's got Dale!"

The bearded man rushed outside, Dada on his heels. A stranger—a giant in a cloak—caught Dada by the shoulder and pulled him back, running past them both.

Emeline leapt to her feet just as Aladane came hopping out into the lobby, pulling up his pants. She ran after her father, her heart pounding.

It was dark outside, the darkness of a late-summer night. Where was the man who'd taken Dale? She heard Fish call out and run toward them. Panic throbbed inside her head.

Dale! Dale!

The sound of a gun went off, stopping her heart. It was the loudest shot she'd ever heard. Could that really be a spring-gun? She caught up to Dada just as he started running across the road.

"Go back!" he yelled at her. She ignored him.

They plunged between buildings and over uneven ground. Lantern light flashed at them from windows and dogs barked.

"Bird!" Fish roared from behind them. "What's going on?"

"He's got Dale!" Emeline screamed again.

She stumbled and looked up, startled to see trees looming much closer than she expected. Completely out of breath, horrified, she stopped. *Is he taking Dale into the woods?* Fish was catching up to her now, panting.

A harsh voice shouted, "Stop right there!"

She could see Dada freeze ahead of her. She ran to his side.

"Don't move!" the voice cried again.

Dada flung out his arm to hold Emeline back. Breathless, she saw what was just ahead of them—the cloaked man and the bearded man standing taut and alert before the brute that held Dale.

He had one bare, muscled arm tight around her brother, whose kicking legs dangled just above the ground. His other hand held a knife against Dale's throat; the edge of it gleamed for an instant in the darkness. Emeline clung to Dada's arm, staring at the blade.

Behind Dale and his captor, a wide stream ran through tall grass, separating the last houses from the woods. The bearded man stood aiming his spring-gun at them, and the tall man in the cloak had his hand at his side.

"Don't shoot!" Dada pleaded, his voice cracking.

"It's too dark!" Fish added behind them. "You'll miss!"

"Listen to them," Dale's captor snarled, struggling with the boy.

"Dale, be still!" Emeline shrieked.

Then the cloaked man spoke. "Hiding in the dark, Loddril? I suppose it does improve your looks." His voice was so deep and loud it took Emeline by surprise. She squinted at him in the dim, remembering what the boys had said. Was he really a Lash Knight? Could he save Dale?

"You don't know me," the man with the knife snapped back.

"And for that, every day I'm grateful. But I do know what your business is," the cloaked man replied. His tone was disdainful, almost lazy, but underneath it was a dangerous edge.

"You *don't* know! And you'll be getting *nothing* from me about it. If you don't want this child dead, you have to let me go." He took a step backward and Dada gasped.

"And where will you go that I can't find you?"

"You don't know what I can do! I can disappear!"

"Go on, then, show me your magic! Disappear! But I think your concern, maggot, should be how little you know *me*." The emphasis on the last word made the shirtless man flinch.

It was just enough distraction for Dale to wrench himself half-free. His neck jerked back, away from the knife, and Emeline gasped. The blade turned—

A flash of black lightning crossed the distance between them. It struck the knife from the man's fingers, sending it spinning into the dark. He dropped Dale with a shriek.

The whip struck again and slashed the man across the face. He fell to his knees, but Dale was on his feet and running. He came crashing straight into Dada and Emeline, and they threw their arms around him.

"Bless water!" Fish exclaimed.

"You're a failure all around, Loddril," the Lash Knight taunted. His bearded companion was striding toward the man, still aiming his spring-gun. "I'd love to put an end to things, but I have to find out who hired you."

Emeline stared at the tall, broad-shouldered knight in

awe, Dada nearly crushing Dale to death in his arms as Fish reached over and patted them. The Lash Knight turned to look back at them, his face hidden under the hood of his cloak.

"You have unfortunate timing," he said indifferently. "This man was hired to kill someone in that inn—a place I wouldn't recommend to travelers on the best of nights." The four of them stared back at him, speechless. "Wasn't there another boy?" he asked pointedly.

"Aladane!" Fish blurted. He turned around and ran back toward the inn.

"Thank you," Dada told the knight, his breath coming out in a rush. "Thank you for saving my son." Emeline couldn't even speak.

The bearded man was leading the would-be assassin back toward them now, his hands bound behind him. The man's angry white face was bloody, and Dale stared at him as they passed.

"It's someone important, isn't it?" he blurted out. "That he tried to kill?" Dada shushed him.

"That's a sound assumption," the Lash Knight declared. "Innish, does he have anything on him?"

"Another knife and a map. We should check the room," the bearded man answered.

"And collect Rellum. The fool, traveling alone!" the knight said. They left without another glance at Dada, Dale, or Emeline.

"Is Al okay?" Dale asked, a little shaky.

"Let's go make sure," Dada said, sounding strained. Emeline hugged them both again.

When they got back to the inn, they found Aladane surrounded by Fish, the innkeeper, and the kitchen women in the yard. The ladies were chattering excitedly, and several heads were staring out from the windows above. Once he caught sight of them, Aladane ran toward Dale, waving his arms and tripping over his pants' legs.

"Dale!" he screeched. "Did you just get *rescued* by a Lash Knight?!"

~ ~

When the innkeeper heard the story she gave Dale a large cheese tart, which he accepted happily. As the rest of them stood there, still getting their bearings, Emeline noticed an elderly man standing off to the side and speaking with the Lash Knight, clearly pained by what he was hearing. Olive-skinned, he had short-cropped white hair, a lined face, and a sharp nose, which gave him a haughty look. His richly embroidered cloak of blue velvet touched the floor.

He gestured at the assassin Loddril, whom the bearded Innish was guarding. In the lantern light, Loddril was pale enough to glow, and he was wire thin, covered in lean muscle. A long angry welt from the knight's whip cut diagonally across his face, and he grimaced in pain, his mouth full of filed teeth.

Innish was a ruddy-complexioned, hardy-looking man, older than Dada. He had a curly gray beard, with more gray curls spilling from underneath a black cap, and he wore panels of leather armor and trousers with many pockets. Emeline was surprised by how large the leather panels were; they were clearly not fish-leather.

There was a chain around his neck that disappeared into his collar, out of sight. If there was a pendant on it, it was hidden from the world.

"If you don't mind my asking, how did all this happen?" Dada asked him as Loddril spat toward the women staring at him.

"We got word someone had been paid to take out that one," Innish said guardedly. He nodded toward the old man in the embroidered cloak.

Dada followed his gaze, and his dark eyes lit up in surprise.

"He's a Sapient!" he exclaimed. "He's got the cloak!"

Astonished, Emeline turned back to look. In the embroidery on the man's thick cloak, she could just make out the shapes of silver-threaded gears and wheels, symbols of the Sapients. This man was a member of the royal council!

"True," Innish said, sounding surprised that Dada would know such a thing. "He is Rellum Sapient."

As he spoke, the Sapient—still in conversation with the knight—angrily rubbed his face with one hand. Emeline studied him, wondering what he would think of their story about the Ithin, this man who denied the existence of magic.

And what would he think of *her?* She bit her lip, suddenly uneasy, and took half a step behind Dada.

"That scoundrel was going to *kill* a Sapient?" she heard Fish ask, aghast.

"He's an assassin with a reputation," Innish told him. "Sir Reese has heard reports of him before."

Emeline glanced at the tall, muscular Lash Knight. He had pulled the hood of his cloak down when he stepped inside, revealing a black, muzzle-shaped helmet. His armor gleamed darkly in the lantern light, like black fish scale.

As she watched, he pulled the helmet off and shook out a short crop of reddish blond hair. She was startled to see a younger face than his voice and size suggested, a keen intelligence burning in his eyes. He was scowling at something the Sapient was saying.

"We're traveling to the capital to report an Ithin sighting in Equane," Dada was telling Innish. Emeline looked back to see the bearded man's face transform completely.

"You *saw* the Ithin?" he exclaimed, suddenly fearful.

"My children did, and my friend here and I saw some evidence."

"Was anyone hurt?" Innish demanded. Emeline was surprised that he seemed so ready to believe.

Dada shook his head quickly.

"No, no. I only mention it because I suppose we might see you in the capital." He looked over at Dale and Aladane, who were sharing the cheese tart. Dale was yawning enormously between bites, and Emeline realized how tired she was too. She was in no condition now to consider magic and Sapients—none of them were.

"We should get on the road again," Fish spoke up.

"You didn't get to wash," Emeline realized aloud. Fish smiled and patted her arm.

"That's all right, heart. I'll live."

Dada collected the boys, and the five of them wandered to the wagon. Dale and Aladane glanced back at the knight, reluctant to leave, but Emeline wanted nothing more than to lie down under a blanket. The night was cold, and she shivered as she tossed her things into the wagon.

"Did you see that knight's face? He looks as young as my sons," Fish was saying.

Before Dada could reply, a voice called out from the inn. Innish was hailing them from the doorway.

"Yes?" Dada asked, surprised.

"Sir Reese says we shall escort you to the capital!" Innish's voice rang clear in the night air. Emeline stared sleepily, not sure she had heard him right. "If you can wait till the morning, that is! Rellum Sapient is too tired to travel now."

Emeline looked at Dada and Fish in disbelief. They were stunned as well, but not nearly as much as Dale and Aladane—the boys broke into wild grins, gaping at each other. Were they now going to *travel* with a Lash Knight?

"...Certainly! Thank you!" Dada managed to answer. Innish disappeared back inside, leaving them standing by the wagon, still in shock.

"Bless water!" Aladane sat on the ground.

"Bird!" Fish said, staring at Dada. "What d'you reckon? Do you think he wants us as witnesses to all that?"

Dada frowned in thought. "Witnesses? Yes...Maybe... But we saw the same things that he and Innish saw, and I'd guess their testimony is worth more than ours...."

"Well, I don't want to be involved in any of it," Fish said. "But we'll be a lot safer if we travel with those two, if anything else happens."

"I agree," Dada said quietly.

Dale sank down next to Aladane and leaned on him,

overwhelmed. Emeline patted his dark head to reassure herself that he was all right.

"Do we have enough payts for a room?" Dada asked, digging into his pockets.

"I think that woman'll give us a discount, with the children looking so tired and scared," Fish offered.

"I'm not scared," Dale said with a huge yawn.

Before long, they were crowding into one bedroom, chilly and narrow with only two beds. It felt odd to be up so high, on the second floor of the tall brick building. Emeline peered out the large window into the night as Dada spread blankets on the floor: The moon lit up the Braedle Road below, but it was empty and quiet.

"Bird, you and the children take the beds," Fish said, sparing a look of resentment for Aladane. Ignoring the glare, the boy flung himself onto one of the beds with relief.

Emeline climbed into the other one with Dale. The bed was creaky and the mattress was thin, but it was a welcome softness compared to the wagon floor. She put her arm around Dale and he curled against her with a sigh.

"I'm so glad you're safe," she whispered, squeezing him. "Now don't snore."

~ ~

Emeline was last up, still shaking off clinging dream images of vines and underwater flowers—not lilies, but fiery, brilliantly colored flowers that she'd never seen before—while she brushed her hair. Sun shafted in through the room windows.

"I'll go down to the stable," Fish told Dada. "And get the horses ready."

"Do you think the lady will make us breakfast if we look scared?" Aladane asked Emeline.

"I think she's probably tired of us. We've got our own food anyway," she told him, yawning.

"Al, we're being escorted by a Lash Knight," Dale said with a grin. "We can't keep him waiting." Aladane grinned back and the two of them tore out of the room, leaving a couple of towels behind. Dada scooped them up, irritated, and followed.

Emeline dressed and then hurried after them down the large staircase. The lobby was sharp and clear in the morning light: Its brick walls were blackened and stained in patches, and the floor was unswept, scuffed with footprints from the chase the night before. She remembered what the knight had said about not recommending the inn to anyone. *Maybe he's used to fancier places in the capital.*

A young blond woman stood near the front, leaning on the counter and tallying a handful of payts. She wore a ragged dress and her feet were bare, but she was very pretty. She glanced up as Emeline passed and gave her a friendly smile.

"Look at the village girl," she said cheerfully. "Men would pay through the nose for you." Emeline frowned at her, confused, and she laughed. "Didn't you know that?"

Dada came back in through the door, looking impatient. "There you are," he said, grabbing Emeline's hand. "You sure are in a dream this morning." He gave the blond girl a wary look and she blew him a kiss. Harrumphing, he dragged Emeline out the door.

Outside, Fish and the boys sat in the wagon, looking

expectant. Emeline hurried to climb into the back next to Dale, who was staring out at the road ahead of them.

She had to stare too. There was a small, ornate steam-carriage there, puffing clouds out of pipes in the back. It was painted the same blue as the Sapient's cloak, its wheels and doors silver-gilt. A thin young man in simple black livery sat at the front of the carriage in the driver's box, one hand on a large wheel and the other on a handle crank.

With a start, she saw that Loddril—bound hand and foot—was lying across the top of the carriage, strapped in among the luggage cases. She supposed that made sense. He had to be brought to the capital, and he certainly couldn't sit inside with the Sapient he'd tried to murder. But he was in for a long, rough ride up there with the baggage.

Nearby, Sir Reese and Innish sat on horses jet black and larger than Ma'am Kayley's, which snorted at them. The knight no longer wore his cloak, and his armor shone like polished black stone in the sun. He held his helmet under one arm, and his long black whip was coiled on his hip. An engraved symbol on his breastplate reflected the light: It was a perfect circle.

He turned to gaze sharply at Emeline, as if he hadn't really noticed her before. In the sunlight, she saw that he had bright green eyes and striking features to match his build: a straight nose, a strong jaw, defined cheekbones. She met his stare hesitantly, wondering if he was angry that she'd taken the longest to get ready. But she could not read his expression.

He brought up his helmet and shoved it down onto his head. Then he turned his horse around and spurred it forward,

Innish following. Behind them, the carriage driver pulled on the handle crank and the impressive contraption sputtered into motion.

"Look at that. How does it work?" Fish asked as he slapped the reins to make the horses follow.

"It must have some kind of contained fire," Dada said uncertainly. "And some water that it boils into steam."

As they spoke, Emeline noticed a few women standing in doorways or on porches, waving to passing men. She thought of the smiling blond girl in the inn and winced. She was beginning to understand why Dada was concerned about her. Maybe the world outside Equane was more dangerous for women than she thought.

Don't talk to any strangers, heart. Stick close to your folk.

"I hope we get to ride in a steam-carriage at the capital," Aladane said, with his mouth full of breakfast bread.

"Imagine—a Sapient traveling with us," Dada mused. "I suppose Sir Reese must have some idea who wanted him dead."

"Probably the less we know about that, the better," Fish replied darkly.

ten

As soon as they left Blyne, they found themselves at the foothills of the Spine. It was a huge, craggy range, blue-shadowed and steep. The forest that spread over the slopes was covered in mist, while the peaks were patched in a brilliant white that could only be snow.

"I wish we could talk to Sir Reese and Innish," Dale said, trying to see past the steam-carriage to the riders.

"How do you think a boy that age became a Lash Knight, anyway?" Fish asked Dada. "I mean, apart from his size. Shouldn't he still be a squire?"

"It doesn't seem likely that a squire would be involved in the rescue of a Sapient," Dada commented.

"He's got a symbol on his armor," Aladane said. "He has to be a real knight."

"Maybe he's special," Dale said, sounding pleased with the thought. "Maybe he's so good that he beat all the others his age."

Emeline thought of how true Reese's aim had been with the whip. *Maybe so.*

At midday, the Sapient's carriage slowed in front of them. Rellum's small white head popped out of the side window, and Innish trotted up to speak to him. A moment later, the guard nodded and rode over to the wagon.

"A few miles down the road there's a turn-off toward the Hawking River," he told them. "Rellum Sapient wishes to stop at the lodge there."

Emeline's heart quickened at the thought of water plants, cooled by river spray and glistening with damp. Her palms warmed.

But was now really the time for magic? With a Sapient here?

"All right," Fish said. "What for?"

"For lunch," Innish said stiffly. He wheeled his horse around and rode back up to the front.

"Well, my, my!" Fish said, and Dada laughed. "Some of us can just eat while we ride."

"He's an old man," Dada said, smiling. "Traveling must be hard on him."

"Inside that moving cottage?" Fish snorted. "Life must be pretty different in the capital."

"We might as well catch a few fish while we're there. Add to our supplies," Dada said, and the prospect of fresh fish cheered them all up immediately.

Before long, Emeline could hear the faint roar of rushing water. The steam-carriage turned onto a wide, stony road branching off the Braedle and they followed, rattling along in the direction of the mountains. She gripped the wagon's side.

Suddenly, the way opened onto a remarkable view: The woods curved back from a wide belt of rushing, tumbling water, its rapids white as boiling milk. This was the Hawking River, which cut through the Spine and disappeared in the trees to the east. A fresh, clean smell of mud and mist filled the air, and on the riverbank sat a low, half-timbered building.

"Look how fast it is!" Dale exclaimed. The river was loud, crashing and swirling against rocks in frothy eddies. It was at least twice the width of the Braedle Road.

Emeline's eyes were drawn across the water to the dense trees on the other side. They were eerily quiet and still beside the busy river. Watchful, almost.

Were there Dark Creatures behind those trees? Eyeing them from across the water? She looked back at the old wooden lodge and wondered how its builders were brave enough to get lumber from the forest.

Sir Reese and Innish were dismounting in front of the lodge. The carriage slowed to a stop behind them, puffing steam, and Fish stopped the wagon in turn. Emeline gasped as Loddril's head lifted briefly on the carriage roof; she'd forgotten he was there, buried in the luggage.

Aladane and Dale practically vaulted out of the wagon to get to the riverbank, trailing a fishing net behind them.

"Emeline, make sure they don't fall in and drown?" Dada asked, exasperated. "I need to feed the horses."

"I'll try!" She got down quickly and ran after them, glancing at the carriage as Rellum Sapient stepped out. He sized up the lodge with a weary look and wrapped his lush cloak more tightly around himself.

She reached the wild Hawking River and the two wild boys cavorting at its edge. Pulling up her skirts, she plodded through the mud and reeds to join them, river spray catching her deliciously in the face.

There were reeds everywhere. They weren't pretty like her lilies—they were just green stalks—but her fingers tingled with a familiar anticipation.

She looked at the boys—Aladane was helping Dale shake out his fishing net; neither of them was watching. No one was watching, in fact. She couldn't resist.

Holding her breath, she reached an eager hand out toward the reeds. A shot of heat raced down her arm, and one of them sprang toward her.

"Emeline!" Dada shouted. She jumped and put her hands behind her back as he and Fish came through the muddy grass, carrying fishing poles and food bundles. "Don't lean out over the water, heart."

Aladane gave a cry, and they turned to see his meager net disappear off into the rapids. Fish laughed, the sound echoing out over the water.

"I told you the weights weren't heavy enough!" Dale said.

She eyed the long reed that had stretched toward her. She'd made it do that, she knew. How close did she have to be to make it grow? No one was watching her. She took one step back, and then another, and then, surreptitiously, held out her hand.

For a moment, nothing happened. Then the reed pushed itself up slowly, twisting a little as it reached for her. She lowered her hand, slowly, breathlessly, and the reed drooped and came to rest on the ground. Her arm hummed like a just-plucked harp string.

"Em, aren't you hungry?" Dada and Fish were spreading a blanket over the grass and laying their things down. "Have some bread to hold you over."

She wheeled around and hurried back to them, plopping down. Her mind raced: How wet did a plant have to be for her magic to work? If a tree was wet from rain, could she move the branches?

And how long before she had to tell someone?

She accepted the bread that Dada handed her in silence, watching as Fish assembled the fishing poles. Soon both men were casting lines.

A waft of something fatty cooking floated by. She looked back at the river lodge, her stomach growling. Whatever Rellum Sapient was eating had a rich, meaty smell; it was something she'd never tasted.

As she gazed at the lodge, the large black figure of Sir Reese emerged. Helmet-less and glove-less, he strode toward the carriage with something that looked like bread in his hand, tossing it up to Loddril on the roof. The sun was bright on his fair hair and dark armor. In an idle fashion, he started toward the river.

He stopped close to her, frowning at the little fishing group with his arms folded. Fish hooted, swinging a medium-sized grayling out onto the bank; it flipped and flopped on the mud, flashing in the sun a bit like Sir Reese. The knight made a disgusted sound, muttering something under his breath.

"Yes, sir?" Emeline asked shyly, rising to her feet.

"Fish is for a man with no sense of taste," he said.

She blinked in surprise. The idea that someone might dislike fish had never really occurred to her.

"Everyone eats fish in Equane," she told him.

"What a charming place it must be. I'll have to go sometime." He looked out over the river, not even meeting her eyes.

Emeline stared at him. She had never heard anyone sound so biting and yet so blithe at the same time. Perhaps she misunderstood his tone.

"Have you always lived in the capital?" she ventured politely.

"No," he replied coldly. "But I doubt you've heard of where I'm from."

Emeline bristled this time. He *was* insulting her. If all Lash Knights were this rude, then boys had no reason to worship them.

"Must be somewhere they don't teach manners," she blurted without thinking.

Then she stiffened, realizing she had just insulted one of the king's knights. Was that a terrible offense? Was there a penalty? She saw with dismay that he was glaring at her.

"Manners are about as useful as a trapdoor in a boat," he said with some contempt. His gaze turned back to the river. "That's the first thing you learn outside of the *village*."

There was no mistaking the condescension in this remark, and she scowled. He chuckled, surprising her, and she saw that Aladane had fallen backward onto his rump, yanking on Dada's fishing rod.

Sir Reese caught his breath abruptly, his eyes now on Dale. The boy's sleeves were rolled up and his armbands were visible as he wound the crank on the fishing rod. Sir Reese turned back to stare at Emeline, his expression altered.

"Are you Keldares?" he asked. The disdain had vanished from his tone.

"Our mama was," she told him, and pushed up one of her own sleeves. Her armband glittered rose-gold in the sun.

He looked away, frowning, but as he watched her father and brother, his features softened. She was surprised how much it changed his face.

"Are there Keldares where you're from?" she asked.

The knight gave her a sidelong look with his sharp green eyes. "For someone so concerned with manners, you ask a lot of questions." The disdain was back, and Emeline gritted her teeth in disgust.

"I was not aware that two questions were a lot," she said, attempting to match his tone. Then she gathered up her skirts and stomped away to join her family.

Dale turned to show her his catch, then practically jumped out of his skin at the sight of Sir Reese. The others noticed the knight then too, but he turned away from them and began to walk among the rocks.

"Was he talking to you, Em?" Dale demanded, wide-eyed. "What did he say?"

Emeline considered for a moment and decided not to disappoint him. "He hates fish," she said. Dale looked surprised.

"How could anybody hate fish?" Aladane exclaimed.

"I'd like to ask him a few questions about the capital, if he's out here walking around," Dada said, setting his pole down.

"He's not very friendly," Emeline warned him.

"Lash Knights aren't in the business of being friendly!" Fish declared, dragging his catch over to join them. "Let's start a fire and get these cooking."

Emeline helped to gather dry sticks with the boys as Dada walked over toward Reese. They made an odd pair when they stood next to each other; Reese was even taller than Dada and just as broad-shouldered. Dada gestured politely while Reese looked down his nose at him.

"Where do you train to become a Lash Knight?" Dale asked Fish, who was coaxing the first sparks of fire from the kindling.

"There's some sort of academy, but I don't know much about it."

"Were there ever any from Equane?"

Fish laughed at that, looking up at him. "An academy costs money, son! Only a rich man's son could become a Lash Knight. It's not for villagers."

Dale looked crestfallen, but not entirely surprised. Sir Reese was a rich man's son, then. *That's why he's so condescending*, Emeline thought, irritated. *He looks down on farmers like us.* She squeezed Dale's shoulder as fish were laid out across the flames.

"By the time you're grown, maybe things will be different," she told him. He nodded.

"When I grow up, I'm going to leave Equane and make money somewhere," Aladane announced. "You can come with me, Dale, and then we'll save up for the academy." Fish snorted and shook his head.

Dada was walking back toward them now, alone. The knight was heading to the lodge.

"Was he friendly?" Dale asked him at once.

"I wouldn't say that," Dada replied. "He said he came outside because the cook was singing like a dying screech-owl." Dale and Aladane laughed, but Emeline rolled her eyes. Dada turned to Fish. "Did you know they have an underground water system in the capital? He says it's all automated."

"What for? Connecting wells?"

Emeline only half listened as she watched the sullen knight reach the lodge. Out of nowhere, a large dog rushed him, bounding with glee. She tensed, half expecting the knight to yell at or even kick it, but he dropped to one armored knee and started scratching behind its ears. Relieved, she watched as the dog licked him full in the face.

"Sir Reese doesn't believe in the Ithin," Dada said, catching Emeline's attention.

"Oh, no. He thinks we're lying?" Dale asked, dismayed.

"No, he didn't say that." *Surprisingly*, Emeline thought. "I just asked what people in the capital thought about magic and Dark Creatures, with the Sapients and Theurgists going at it," Dada told them. "He said no one knows for sure. Most people just go about their business."

"I can believe that," Fish said, nodding.

Dada poked at the fish on the fire. "He doesn't seem to think much of this Rellum Sapient. But then, I'm not sure he thinks much of anyone."

Fish shook his head, annoyed. "If all the folks in the capital are like that, then I'm glad we won't be staying long."

eleven

They rode for days on end, passing throu waving grasses. Sometimes they saw clusters of glimpsed the gates of towns, but mostly they were

Nights were spent in the wagon under the star would watch Sir Reese and Innish see to Rellum needs, then set up camp for themselves while the slept in his carriage.

Every so often, another steam-carriage would Once, a plain one driven by a boy her age passed th was a very handsome boy in the way that some girls l full lips and a smooth face—and he smiled and nodded Dale waved at him. He didn't interest her, just as no one home ever had, but if someone had asked her what sort o she liked, she wouldn't have been sure what to say.

Was Sir Reese considered handsome, she wondered? Th was something magnetic about him, about his strength a green eyes, but he was all fierceness and arrogance.

One evening, clouds gathered overhead, bringing th smell of rain. A storm was usually welcome weather in th village, since water meant both safety and crop growth, but out in the open, it was unfamiliar. Threatening.

"We better get the cover up," Dada said. "Come on, Dale."

climbed into the back, stepping on Aladane and waking ~ up from a nap. They started cranking the handles that ~ed the leather half-roof.

"Throw me up some of those leather blankets!" Fish called ~m the front. Emeline traded places with Aladane and dug ~ them. The roof of the wagon didn't quite cover the front ~at, so he and Dada were likely to get wet.

"I'd rather be inside for this," Fish grumbled. Dada ~joined him on the front seat, looking worried. They draped ~hemselves in the stiff leather blankets as a distant rumble ~hook the air and a strong breeze swept under the wagon ~over.

Up ahead, Innish rode toward the steam-carriage. He was wearing a heavy cloak and carrying a second one.

"I bet that's for Loddril," Dale said solemnly. Emeline gasped, realizing the assassin would have to weather the storm on top of the carriage. The carriage driver was unfolding a little canopy from behind his seat, but it would only shelter him—and not very well, from the looks of it. Innish tossed the cloak up onto the roof. A bound pair of hands shot up and grabbed hold of it.

"A fitting punishment for that scoundrel," Fish observed. "I can't say I'll be sorry if he drowns."

"Me neither," Dada said. "But then I suppose they won't get any information out of him."

"Do you think Lash Knights will torture him at the capital?" Aladane asked. Innish was riding up to their wagon now, nodding at Fish and Dada.

"They're supposed to have a code of honor. So they wouldn't

torture people," Dale told him, but he sounded uncertain. "It would be wrong."

"A lot of sudden storms in this area!" Innish hailed them. "This could be a bad one. I'll ride back here with you for a while."

"Thank you," Dada told him.

Innish steered his horse to walk beside them as a boom of thunder made Emeline flinch. Dada gestured to her to pass up another leather blanket, which he offered to the guard; Innish took it, nodding his thanks as the first few drops fell.

"The air feels weird," Aladane said. It was chilly but balmy; heavy, but impatient.

"What if it's a tornado?" Dale exclaimed, alarmed. He started flipping pages in the *History* book.

"Those are only in the Outer Lands," Fish told him.

"No, they aren't! There was one in the kingdom when they first built the capital!" Dale said, pointing to a page. "They had to rebuild a lot." There was a drawing of a massive column of wind twisting and slanting through a city.

At that moment, lightning flashed and the horses screamed, startling everyone. Rain tumbled from the sky, slapping the wagon roof with shocking force; the men's leather covers were instantly soaked. This was not the soft, soothing rain that fell in Equane.

Dada turned around and yelled reassuringly, "See, Dale, it's not a tornado! There's hardly any wind!"

He was right. The rain came straight down as if from a giant bucket.

The horses plodded along reluctantly as the torrent continued, drenched and steaming. Thunder rumbled and lightning cracked, illuminating Emeline's view from under the wagon cover: Fish and Dada, the back of the carriage, and a curtain of water. She felt gnawingly guilty for the protection she and the boys had.

"When did they build the capital, Dale?" she asked, since he was still looking at the *History* book. She wanted to distract him from the storm, but she had to shout to be heard.

"It says 970!" he shouted back. "King Eldid!"

"Was that the mad one?" Aladane asked.

Thunder roared and then they heard Innish's voice through the wagon cover. "No, that was Gabane!" he answered. He was riding very close.

"I like his stories the best!" Aladane yelled back.

"He built the underground tunnels!" Dale added.

Fish glared back at them, water dripping from his nose. "Stop hollering back there! Bless water!"

Emeline burst out laughing. "There's plenty of it to bless!"

The wagon rocked to one side suddenly and she stopped laughing, realizing they might break another axle. Innish, a lumpy shape under his rain gear, rode forward to check on Ma'am Kayley's horses.

"Everything all right?" Dada called.

"They're just stumbling!"

Dale put the book away, and everyone fell silent as they plowed on. The rain would ebb for a few moments and then crash down again, like a thousand stones striking the wagon roof. Emeline's head began to throb, almost to the rhythm. It was growing colder, too, and she knew Dada and Fish must be freezing.

After a miserable hour, Sir Reese rode back to meet them, the rain running off his armor in streams. He roared something to Innish, who nodded.

"Shelter ahead!" Innish called to Fish and Dada, and Emeline sighed with relief. She could see nothing now but water and darkness as they followed the carriage off the flooded road. It felt like they were floundering through a shallow canal, and her stomach rolled as the wagon lurched.

Finally, the carriage slowed down in front of them, and Fish reined in the struggling horses.

"Where are we?" Aladane yelled.

"There's a house!" Dada called to them. "Get whatever leather blankets we have left!"

"Maybe we should all just stay in the wagon!" Dale said, and Aladane nodded. They would have to leave the shelter of the wagon to run inside.

"Come on!" Emeline told them. Dada and Fish had already jumped out into the rain and were cursing while unhitching the horses.

"I can't see! What if we can't find where to go?" Aladane wailed. Emeline gripped his shoulder.

"I'll be right behind you! Go on!" She ducked under the blanket with Dale, and Aladane, grumbling, climbed out the front. They heard him shriek—and then they followed.

She landed with a splash in icy, knee-deep water. The rain struck with a force that knocked Dale over, so she jerked him to his feet and dragged him forward, running and splashing through the flood. She was holding her breath, squinting, nearly blind, and then she crashed into Dada's waiting arms and was pulled inside.

They were in a vast, dim room that stank of mildew and rot. A great tree trunk grew up from the floor through the high ceiling, rainwater pouring down its trunk. The walls—what she could see of them in the dark—looked like cracked, heavy stonework, and the floor was covered with dead leaves.

But this high-ceilinged place had been something grand, once. She could see that.

Gasping, she shoved the drenched leather blanket off of her, then unbuckled her bodice and shook out the wet dress underneath. She was soaked, but not completely through—thanks to riding under the half-roof, her underclothes were still dry. Everyone stood spluttering and shaking off layers, dropping them to the dirty floor. The horses whinnied in misery, crowded together in the corner.

"What is this place?" she asked Dada.

"Somewhere abandoned," he told her, crouching wearily and looking more bedraggled than she had ever seen him. His dark hair was plastered to his head, and water ran off him and the shivering Fish in rivers.

"Never seen that much rain in my life," Fish growled.

"We're all going to catch cold and die," Aladane said mournfully. She almost laughed.

"If it weren't for that abominable racket on the roof, I'd have simply stayed in my carriage," an unfamiliar voice announced, thin, crackly, and very indignant.

It was Rellum Sapient. He sat awkwardly on a massive tree root, his long, dripping robe gathered up into his lap. His driver knelt beside him, quivering, his livery soaked through. They were watching Innish scrape a flint against a stick.

Sir Reese was unstrapping his armor. "Now that's what we should've done with Loddril," he said. "Toss him in the carriage and let him listen to that noise."

He caught sight of Emeline as he set his pauldrons on the ground, and stared for a moment. She didn't know if it was because of how drenched she was or because her bodice was undone, but either way, it was embarrassing. She turned away and took off the bodice; her dress was not revealing, anyway, and everything needed to dry.

"I'd rather that than be in here with you," Loddril snarled from somewhere in the dark. Innish chuckled.

"He's just sore because I threw him down like a bucket of dishwater," Sir Reese said.

"There are trees growing right through this place!" Aladane said, hurrying over to the fire Innish had gotten started.

His words brought a pang of fear to Emeline's heart, but it was only a few trees tangled up in the bones of the house, not a forest. Anyway, the rain would protect them from Dark Creatures—surely?

"This is a lonely old manor. Look at this tile underfoot," Innish was saying. "I wonder how long it's been like this."

Dale stopped short at the sight of Sir Reese without his armor; the massive knight was all shoulders and muscles in his wet shirt, which gleamed white in the darkness. He folded his arms and looked down at the boy.

"Is Loddril tied up?" Dale asked him shyly.

"No, I thought I'd let him wander around a bit. Make himself at home," Sir Reese replied. Dale smiled uncertainly and went to join Aladane.

Sir Reese turned his gaze back to Emeline as she stood there in her limp dress in the doorway. She couldn't read his expression in the dark.

"I don't know how you folk live with this kind of weather," Fish declared, startling her. "This would drown all my crops!" He marched over toward the fire, Dada nodding respectfully to Rellum as he followed him. "Thank you for riding along with us back there," Fish added, to Innish.

"Of course. It was Sir Reese's suggestion."

Emeline looked up, surprised.

"Em, come sit by the fire," Dada said. She stepped carefully over to him and sat down on the filthy ground. The fire's meager warmth quickly lifted her spirits.

"What a terrible journey this has been," Rellum said gravely. "I won't unknot until I reach the blessed capital. Remind me never to travel again, Reese."

"Why would I do that, when traveling flushed your assassin? This piece of offal can finally tell us who's been plotting your death." Reese walked closer to the fire but stopped short of joining them, sitting against the wall. The flames threw long shadows across the room, and Emeline spotted the figure of Loddril near the knight, lying in a puddle.

"Plotting my death, yes..." The Sapient sighed heavily. "To think it's come to that." His old face was tired, but his dark eyes were sharp. Emeline noticed that he looked at each of them shrewdly in turn, rubbing his fingers against his cloak. The corners of his mouth had deep frown lines.

"Anyone paying attention knew it was coming to that. Once His Majesty named you a likely heir, it was just a question of when and where," Reese replied. *Likely heir?* Emeline noticed that Dada and Fish looked up with interest. "When I got the tip that this rat was spotted in Blyne, and that you were due to pass through, well, I knew he was there for you." He smiled darkly at Loddril. "Sometimes notoriety works against you."

"And as to who hired him?" Rellum asked.

Emeline looked at Rellum, trying to imagine him as the next king. She knew the king had no children, but she had never imagined that the royal heir might be an old man.

"Well, as to who hired him...I have no proof of anything," the Sapient said, "but Helid Theurgist...He has certainly engulfed himself in this madness. He will *not* see one of us crowned."

"Well, if you're right, he might see himself hanged instead," Reese told him.

" 'If'? Did you know that he's been giving presentations on the history of magic?" Rellum demanded.

"I did not. Is that what serves as a declaration of war these days?" Reese asked. Innish shot him a disapproving look.

"You may have saved my life, Knight, but I won't submit to your sarcasm," the Sapient said coldly. "You know as well as I that folklore features all kinds of magical nonsense. And that's just what magic is, no matter how you dress it up—nonsense. Even what seems like harmless folklore can lead to foolish ideas."

Emeline looked at Dada, thinking of all the stories in the *History* book that he'd read to her and Dale. He was frowning, but he said nothing.

Rellum shook a finger at Reese, warming to the subject. "Consider that popular physician—that Doctor Nallor and his cure-all tonics! There's no science-based medicine in his draughts, but he compares them to the magical elixirs in ancient stories, and the people readily believe him. Young man, the slush he sells *kills* by keeping men and women from real medicine, medicine that would help them."

"True," Reese agreed.

Rellum's tone softened then, catching Emeline's expression. "I enjoy a good story as much as anyone, of course. But there is enough fear and superstition in the kingdom as it is, without dwelling on the unenlightened past. And I suspect Helid is worse than deluded...worse than eccentric. He wants the people to believe in dreck so they'll be soft-headed enough to follow him—to listen to anything he says. He wants the throne."

"Enough to resort to violence?" Reese asked.

"Indeed, he has a dangerous temper," Rellum continued, in a lower tone. "There have been many arguments between us where I was afraid he might strike me."

"Rellum Sapient," Innish spoke up politely. "Did everyone know your travel route?"

Rellum shook his head. "Not my route, no. Only that I was visiting my daughter in Basten. My assistants knew, of course, and Erd, who is trustworthy." He gestured to his driver. Emeline looked at the young man and realized with a start that he was staring at her, smiling. She looked away quickly, feeling suddenly exposed in her sopping dress.

"It wouldn't be difficult to bribe one of the assistants," Reese said. Innish nodded and Rellum frowned, rubbing at his cloak again.

They settled into silence, listening to the crackling fire. The rain was still beating on the broken roof overhead.

"How did you know about the tornado in 970?" Innish asked Dale suddenly.

"From the *History* book we have," Dale said.

Innish gave Dada a curious look and scratched his beard. "I didn't think farming villages paid much attention to the kingdom's history," he admitted.

Dada frowned again, and Emeline could tell he was insulted, but Fish spoke up before he could reply.

"Bird here has always been a big reader. I couldn't see the point in sending my sons to school, but my wife insisted," he said, poking at the fire. Dada avoided Innish's gaze.

"Dale and I like to read," Emeline said defensively. She glanced at Erd again without meaning to and he winked at her, still smiling.

To her surprise, Rellum pointed a finger at her. "But perhaps you read too many old stories. That is surely what convinced you that you saw a Dark Creature," he scolded. He cast a disapproving glance at Dada and Fish, adding, "Your father should've taught you that the Ithin aren't real."

The Equanian men stiffened, and Emeline felt stung. Her cheeks flamed.

"We saw it for real," Dale protested.

"With all due respect," Dada said sharply, "a group of rational men, including myself, went out to the woods to investigate, and something strange had definitely been there. It left behind the foulest stench."

There were two rational women as well, Emeline added silently.

Innish gave Dada an intent look. "What kind of stench?"

"Like rotting flesh, but...worse, somehow," Fish muttered. "It wasn't right."

Rellum scoffed and shook his head, and Emeline watched him, frustrated.

"Dada did always tell us that Dark Creatures might not be real," she told him as politely as she could. "But then we saw something. And everything changed."

"Our old folk have always told tales, but we're practical people," Fish declared.

"Yes, well, the Theurgists will gobble up your story," Rellum told them with disgust. "They never require any proof, of course. No factual evidence! They just so desperately *want* to believe in magic."

"Why?" Aladane spoke up. "Because it's exciting?"

"It's a craze for power, child. If magic exists, then so does magical power to hold over one's enemies." Rellum stabbed the air with his finger again, as if to curse someone.

Emeline squeezed her hands together. Maybe other people wanted magic because they wanted power—she could believe that. But what *she* had wasn't dangerous. It wasn't about power. It was peaceful and natural—she felt that to her very bones.

What would Rellum think if she showed him real magic? Should she, to show him he was wrong? Sweat gathered under her arms, even though she was cold.

No. The old man would be furious, and he was a powerful person, dangerous to provoke. He would just think it was a trick anyway, wouldn't he? And if he did believe it...If he did believe it, maybe he would think it was evil. That she was evil. That she was *crazed for power* too.

Better to keep it to herself.

"Not everyone loves magic for its power," Reese said quietly.

Rellum groaned. "Oh, I see you're still hovering on the edge, young man. You'll learn. In this world, you cannot trust anything that your eyes can't see or your hands can't feel." Fish had said something like that, too, but now he looked confused as he stared at the fire.

"I guess His Highness believes you, if he chose you as a likely heir," Dada told Rellum carefully.

"Yes. We've made so much progress," Rellum said, relieved.

"And then someone tried to kill you," Reese pointed out.

"Well, that's where it stops being any of our business," Fish said. "We'll just tell the king what we saw—to abide by the law—and then take our leave." He cleared his throat as if to end the conversation, poking at the fire.

Except there's so much more to tell than you think, Emeline thought, staring into the flames.

She couldn't keep hiding her secret from Dada, could she? If a Theurgist could plot a Sapient's death for *saying* magic wasn't real, then what might the Sapients do to her if she *proved* magic was real?

People were trying to kill each other already. Rellum Sapient was the king's heir and he had almost been murdered. Her? She was no one.

She would have to tell Dada everything. In the morning,

she decided—as soon as she could. He would know whether or not she should tell the king.

"Do we have to leave the capital right away?" Aladane was protesting.

"You hush," Fish said.

Innish looked at Dada and said thoughtfully, "You may want to visit the capital's academies, Mister Bird. Or at least a library." Dada's eyes lit up at that and Emeline smiled.

Thunder shook the old walls and everyone flinched, looking up at the roof. Rain was puddling around the tree root where Rellum sat, and he stood up with a sigh. "This is intolerable."

"Are we going to have to sleep here?" Emeline asked.

"It seems likely that it'll storm all night," Innish said. "We'd do better to wait it out."

"What, without dinner?" Aladane asked.

"Not unless you want to go out to the wagon," Fish told him. The boys looked as if they were almost considering it.

"All our things will be wet tomorrow," Dada said unhappily. He stretched out his long legs near the fire. "I hope that cover saves the books and maps from ruin."

"And our clothes!" Fish grumbled.

Everyone settled in awkwardly, trying to make the best of it on the damp, filthy ground. Emeline curled up on her side, resting her head on her elbow. They were in for a long, uncomfortable night.

"I'm not going to sleep. There could be snakes," Dale told Aladane. His friend muttered back something in agreement.

"If you're planning on being a Lash Knight, Dale, you can't be afraid of snakes," Fish said carelessly.

At that, Reese suddenly laughed—a deep, warm sound that filled the room. It didn't sound like a mocking laugh; she was surprised at how nice a laugh it was. Dale turned beet red and glared at Fish, but Emeline couldn't help laughing, too. She sat up slightly and looked over at Reese, hoping to see his face in the dark.

"Erd, will you collect some rainwater to drink?" Rellum asked his driver wearily. He handed him a flask from within his robes.

The young man got to his feet and carried the flask over to one of the leaks in the ceiling. Emeline watched him, wondering why he kept smiling at her. Did he think she was pretty? She didn't know him and she didn't want to be smiled at again. Sometimes it was hard to be the only girl in the group.

Look at the village girl. Men would pay through the nose for you. Didn't you know that?

She curled up into a tight ball next to Dada and told herself to sleep.

twelve

Emeline opened her eyes to a strange, dark silence. She heard Dale snore, but still the air seemed empty, weirdly calm. The fire had died down to almost nothing, and her muscles ached from clenching against the cold.

Slowly, she realized why it was so quiet—the rain had stopped. There was nothing to be heard but the dripping of leaks and the sleeping noises of the men around her. Relieved, she yawned and resettled herself, wondering how close it was to morning. She could just make out the shape of her brother curled up next to her, and Aladane....

Where was Aladane?

She sat up, wincing at the pain in her side. Aladane had been next to Dale, but she didn't see him anywhere now. Sleepily, she glanced around at the others and counted the shapes, even Reese and Loddril near the wall, but there was no mistake—

Aladane was missing. Where was he? Had he gone out to the wagon?

A faint sound reached her ears from somewhere deep in the old manor. Unsettled, Emeline sat very still and listened. It was a scratching, rustling sound.

It didn't sound like the horses. It was probably a small animal, but...She should find Aladane.

She got to her feet and stretched, trying to ease the pain in her side. None of the others stirred as she picked her way across the room. They would all be stiff and grouchy come morning, and there was only a wet wagon waiting for them.

She heard the scratching again. It was coming from the left, where the room opened up into a wide, worn corridor. She tiptoed that way, brushing against rain-dampened vines along the wall.

The old hall sagged, long and silent. Moonlight spilled through a yawning window nearly as large as a door, half-full of broken colored glass. The cold, wet air from outside made her shiver.

"Aladane?" she whispered.

The scratching sounded again from a doorway, an open one choked from top to bottom with leaves and branches. It looked like an entrance to the woods.

She stopped, alarmed. A cold drop of rain splashed onto her head and she flinched, turning to go back. Then something rustled in the branches.

Emeline caught her breath, staring in horror as the brushwood parted. The moonlight flashed on a long, wicked claw sliding through the leaves. Another claw appeared, moving jerkily, reaching outward. She stumbled backward.

It was like a nightmare. She couldn't run. She couldn't scream. She was a block of ice.

A hooded head shot out of the branches. Gleaming jaws— huge dead eyes. Sparks flew from its mouth—white hot!

She threw her arms over her face, green magic surging

through her like a wave—powerful, sudden, uncontrollable. Something brilliant flashed.

There was a violent hiss, and she looked, unable to help herself. Vines from the wall had covered the Ithin's eyes. With a gasp, she threw up her arms once more, and the vines flew at her command, wrapping around that terrible head. It hissed again—a harsh, grinding sound—and its frothing jaws snapped.

Someone grabbed her shoulder and yanked her back. A whip-crack broke the air, slashing across the Ithin's snapping face. It disappeared in a flash, swallowed up by branches.

A strong arm hooked Emeline by the waist and dragged her away.

"Get outside!" Reese's voice roared over her head. It was his arm holding her tight; her feet weren't even touching the ground. She heard shouts from the others, the scrambling of footsteps, the horses screaming.

"Emeline!" Dada yelled.

More footsteps, running, and then a rush of cold air. There was Aladane, shocked, standing by the wagon. The others tumbled outside onto the grass around her.

Reese let go of her and she sank to the ground. Dada grabbed hold of her as the horses screamed again in the manor.

"Are you all right? What happened?" he demanded, peering into her face. She couldn't speak. Her heart was hammering painfully on her ribs.

"What's in there?" Fish asked Reese. He had an arm around Dale, who was only half-awake.

"Get clear of here now!" the knight shouted, but he turned around himself and ran back into the manor. Innish was on his heels, his spring-gun drawn.

"Into the wagon!" Dada ordered, pushing them along. "I think he's getting the horses!"

Emeline saw Rellum standing in the grass, looking bewildered. Erd took hold of his arm and pulled him toward the steam-carriage.

She snapped to her senses as Dada shoved her into the wagon. "It's the Ithin!" she gasped. "In the cottage!"

"What?" Dale exclaimed. Dada spun around and gaped after Reese.

"Get in, get in," Fish said frantically. He vaulted into the wagon and reached down to grab Dada by the collar. "Come on, Bird!"

"We can't go anywhere without the horses!" Aladane whimpered.

"We've got to at least hide!" Fish said as Dada clambered in under the wagon roof.

Everything was dark and still now, the manor's rotten doors hanging open. Emeline couldn't breathe. What was happening? There was nothing to hear.

After a moment, the horses trotted out in single file, breath puffing from their nostrils. Innish followed quickly, slapping their haunches.

"Where's Reese?" Emeline asked Dada, worried. "He's still inside!"

"What if he needs help?" Dale exclaimed.

"He's got Innish. Be still!" Dada said.

Then a terrifying scream cut the air.

It came from outside, very close, and it was a man's voice. Emeline's blood turned to ice water.

"Loddril!" Innish bellowed. He mounted his horse and rode into the darkness.

Emeline felt herself dragged backward by Dada and squished against the wagon floor.

"*Shh!* Nobody move!" he hissed.

They were all on the floor now, a miserable huddle of racing pulses and frantic breaths. Emeline's whole body ached.

Had Loddril escaped and the Ithin gone after him?

Were Reese and Innish fighting it? Could *anyone* fight it?

Morning will never come. We'll never be safe, she thought numbly. It was raining again, light drops pattering on the leather roof. Rellum's carriage door creaked open and then shut again, quickly; Emeline imagined Erd had rushed inside. *As if a carriage door will keep him safe!*

Then there were voices, human voices—Reese and Innish shouting to each other.

Her heart swelled with relief. Bless water, they were both still alive! Reese was alive!

"What...is...*happening?*" Aladane demanded, muffled.

"He's dead," they heard Reese call out to Innish. There was a tremor in his deep voice that Emeline had never heard before, and she shivered. Unable to keep still any longer, she pushed Dada's arm aside and sat up, but all she could see were Ma'am Kayley's horses standing untied and confused near the front of the wagon.

"Who's dead?" Dale sat up too. He was pale as a ghost.

"Let's get back to the road, quick!" Reese shouted. "Innish, help them hook up the horses!"

～⁓

The first light of dawn was breaking when the carriage, the wagon, and the two men on horseback reached the Braedle Road. To Emeline's relief, it continued to rain calmly. *That should keep Ithin away.*

After a while, Reese waved at Erd to stop the caravan, then he rode up to the wagon, a determined expression on his face. Fish and Dada just looked at him, fearful and exhausted.

"Loddril?" Dada asked, after a moment.

"Whatever that thing was, it killed him," Reese said, his voice steady but grave. "I found him torn to bloody shreds behind the house. Butchered." Emeline shuddered and covered her face. How horrible, even for a man like him. "That fool chose the wrong time to try and escape."

"Was it the Ithin?" Dale called up to him.

Reese hesitated. "It fit the description." He held up his coiled whip, and Emeline saw there was a scrap of cloth stuck to it—a scrap torn from the monster's hood. The cloth had a burn mark on it, as if the Ithin's very blood was deadly. She shrank back instinctively.

"Well, someone tell Rellum, so he can get off his high horse," Fish declared, sounding less frightened than he looked.

But Reese said flatly, "Mister Bird, I need to speak to your daughter."

She sank down into the damp wagon seat as Dada looked from Reese to her, confused. The knight must have seen the vines attack the Ithin.

He knows my secret.

Well. There was nothing to be done about it now. Emeline nodded and got up, shakily climbing out of the wagon; Reese dismounted, looking pointedly at Dada and Fish, and after a second, they let him pull her aside, too weary to protest.

The knight fixed his green gaze on Emeline. His expression took her by surprise: His eyes were full of wonder, even...admiration. But before either of them could speak, Rellum opened his carriage door and stared down the road at them.

"Reese!" he cried out in a wavering voice. "What in the name of Olvinde did we just run away from?"

Reese raised a hand toward Rellum, asking him to wait. His eyes never left Emeline's face.

"You have magic," he said softly. He smiled then, a warm smile that lit up his stern face. And suddenly, he was *undeniably* handsome. "Real magic."

Emeline blushed, her face burning.

"They don't know, do they?" He jerked his head at the others in the wagon. She shook her head. His face grew serious and she felt the loss of his smile. "Listen to me. Tell your family about this, but no one else. No one. Certainly not Rellum Sapient. Do you understand?"

"I think so," she murmured.

"Think of Rellum's situation. He's been named heir to the king. But if magic is real, his position...Well. It's less than assured." He ran a hand through his hair, frowning. "And don't think the Theurgists will be your friends either. Just— trust me. Tell no one."

He mounted his horse, wheeled it around, and rode over to talk to the Sapient. She felt dizzy enough to lie down, and frightened enough to be sick, but she turned to face her concerned family in the wagon.

"Dada. Dale," she said, climbing back in. "I have to tell you something."

"Heart?" Her father's face was creased with worry. "What is it?"

She took a deep breath. "I fought the Ithin off with vines. Without touching them." The rest of it came out in a rush. "Dada, I can move water plants, wet plants. I mean—I can make them grow. I can control them!"

The three of them stared back, not comprehending. "What are you saying, Em?" Dada asked.

"I think it's magic, Dada! Elemental magic!" she told him.

"What?" Aladane exclaimed.

"Since *when*?!" Dale burst out. Fish just stared at her in disbelief.

Emeline watched as Dada scratched his chin. He glanced over at Reese and Rellum, who were arguing now, and gestured to her to join him on the front wagon seat.

"Now, Little Plum," Dada said. "Tell me everything."

⌒⌒⌒⌒

Emeline told him the whole story while the others listened. She started with the water lilies back home and the reeds at the Hawking River; there were several exclamations of *"Bless water"* from behind her. When she got to the night before, Aladane interrupted to admit that he'd gone out to the wagon for food, which explained his disappearance.

Finally, Emeline came to the point of describing the Ithin, and her voice faltered.

"What did it look like?" Aladane prompted.

The image of that horrible face flashed out at her. It was real. It was so real. More than half of its face was just those giant fangs.... And the dead eyes! She realized she was crying, and Dada held her close.

"Shh, shh, heart, you're all right," he said, sounding hoarse. He kissed her on the top of her head as she sniffled into his shirt, embarrassed, exhausted, afraid. "You know, I used to wonder about your mama. Sometimes there were things she did..." He sighed, long and heavy.

"What?" Emeline whispered eagerly. She needed to hear this.

"You know how much she loved the wind and the sky. Well, there was an accident not long before you were born, where the Trindles' boy nearly died. This whole wagon was coming down on top of him," Dada told her slowly. "But Airlinna was there, and along came this huge gust of wind, out of nowhere. It rocked that wagon backward, back onto its wheels. I remember her standing there, with her arm outstretched, white as a sheet. It wasn't windy that day, heart. I knew that she'd made it happen somehow."

She stared at him in awe. He smiled wistfully, but Dale piped up in a hurt voice, "Emeline! I can't believe you can do *magic* and you didn't tell me!"

"I wasn't sure it was magic," she said, putting an arm around him with a pang of guilt. But Reese's smile as he'd said the word came back to her. *He* was sure.

Dada scratched his head, worry lines visible everywhere on his face. He shot Fish a look that said *Now what do we do?*

The big farmer stared at Emeline for a moment, almost as if he were afraid of her. She couldn't blame him. "Well... I'll just feed the horses some grass and let you folk talk for a while," Fish said finally, uncomfortable. "Most of the hay got ruined...."

Then he hopped off quickly. Dada sighed.

"Hey! If it's Keldare magic, then maybe I have some too," Dale said, delighted. "From Mama!"

"Maybe you do," Emeline told him. Maybe it was lying dormant in him, until he reached her age. If only Mama were around to tell them. *Mama, I need you.*

"I want to see you do it. We need to find some water," Aladane announced. "Man, I can't believe you didn't show us at the Hawking River!"

"Dada, does Emeline have to tell the king?" Dale asked, suddenly serious.

Emeline held her breath and looked at their father. The words of the old man in Equane came back to Emeline suddenly: *Bless water, she ought to be frightened. Everything's going to change now.*

This was no longer just a group of villagers reporting a sighting. Now a Lash Knight had seen an Ithin himself—even had his prisoner killed by one. *And* he had witnessed magic! Her magic!

"Well, I suppose Reese will tell Rellum Sapient," Dada said slowly. "I reckon it's his duty." As a group, they turned to look at Reese and Innish, who were still speaking with Rellum outside his carriage. "But I'd give the kingdom for him to hold his tongue."

"I think he will, Dada," Emeline said quietly. "He told me not to speak of it."

"Bless water, I'm glad. We don't want to get involved in anything above us," Dada said, crushing Emeline to him. He looked over all of them. "Don't tell *anyone*. None of you."

A second later, Rellum Sapient shouted at Reese, "It was a wild animal! Of course it was!" He banged a feeble fist against the side of the carriage, and then cringed. "Shame on you, Knight, for letting your imagination get the better of you!"

Reese gave Innish a disgusted look as the guard scratched his beard doubtfully. The knight looked back at the villagers, and locked eyes with Emeline for a moment. Her pulse quickened.

Don't tell, she thought. . . . *And don't look away.*

"I don't care what creature you saw," Rellum announced, breaking the spell. Reese turned his attention back to him. "The fact remains that Loddril is dead and no longer able to tell us who hired him. My life is still in danger!" He slammed the carriage window shut.

"He's right about that," Innish said. Reese scowled and wheeled his great horse around.

"Son of a maggot in a *rat*," he spat. "That idiot just had to get himself killed." He looked again at Emeline for a heartbeat, and then added, louder, "Well, I can't say I'll miss him. We should push on." He rode past the carriage to the front.

Fish rejoined the Equanians, Dada heaving a new sigh of relief.

"He didn't tell him!" Dale whispered happily.

"Tell him what?" Fish asked, sounding tired and overwhelmed.

"Sir Reese said nothing about Emeline," Dada told him. "And let's keep it that way. Remember: No one say anything." The Sapient's carriage shot out steam nearby, ready to depart.

"But why can't we tell?" Aladane asked. "Why can't she just show them and say, 'Magic is real! Everybody stop fighting'?"

"Because it's not that simple, son. People are trying to kill each other," Fish snapped, climbing up into the front seat. "We don't want any part of it."

His words made Emeline want to curl up into a tiny ball and hide in a bale of hay like Aladane had. For the first time since they'd left Equane, she longed for the safety of their quiet village. She had wanted to tell Dada about her magic... but now she wished desperately that she'd been able to hide it longer. At least until they got back home. Or maybe forever.

A deep anxiety gnawed at her insides.

The wagon was rumbling forward now. Dale leaned over and put his arm around her.

"We'll protect you, Em," he said.

"Yeah, we know a Lash Knight, remember?" Aladane said with a smile. "And Dale and I are going to be knights, too."

She smiled, even as she stiffened at the memory of the Ithin's slathering head bursting out at her. Reese's and Dada's voices were looping in her head: *Don't tell anyone. Say nothing.*

"Son of a maggot!" Aladane called out. "I'm starving!"

Emeline laughed, happy for any distraction. Dada and Fish glared back at him.

"Don't you start talking like that now," Dada warned. The boy grinned and began rooting through the wet food bundles with Dale.

thirteen

That evening, they stopped at a busy, muddy town with a dining hall and a public washhouse. Emeline watched Innish speak to Rellum through the carriage window before nodding and hurrying off, probably to order the Sapient's dinner.

The Equanians gathered up their things and followed the signs to the bathhouse, staring at the people.

Both the men and women dressed in simple shirts and trousers, but there were a few women in heavily embroidered, parti-color dresses cut asymmetrically—women of means, shopping with their ladies' maids for dinner. Many people were as dirty as the Equanians, their slouchy work clothes blackened. Almost no one looked like a farmer.

The washhouse had one entrance for women and one for men, so Emeline turned aside as Dada herded the boys in through the men's. Inside the warm, clay-tiled bathhouse, there were rows of basins with water pumps. She did the best she could to bathe without drawing any attention to herself, a knot of fear in her gut.

No one can tell my secret just by looking at me. They can't.

She washed her tangled hair. What would Rellum *do* if he knew? Would he really lose his chance at being king if he was wrong about magic?

Even if he didn't want to hurt her, he might lock her up. He might lock all of them up. Make them disappear. She squeezed the water from her hair, her heartbeat quickening. Reese had told her she couldn't trust the Theurgists, either, but what did that mean?

She stared down into the basin, where the grime from travel spiraled in the lukewarm water.

I can't show anyone, ever. This will always be my secret.

But...she already missed the touch of cool water, of pliable stems, of leaves. A tiny ache throbbed inside her when she thought of hiding something this lovely forever.

But Mama must have managed that for most of her life.

Slowly she wrapped her hair up in a towel, then changed into her striped brown dress, buckling her bodice back on.

"Are bodice dresses coming back in style?" a beautiful dark-skinned girl asked her friend, glancing critically at Emeline. "They're flattering on some girls, but *so* country village." They laughed.

That shouldn't have bothered her, with all she had to worry about, but it did. She glowered as she marched back to the wagon, reaching it just as Reese was returning from his wash. He wore the same white shirt and black trousers, but his hair was brighter now that it was clean. Emeline noticed that both men and women appraised him as they passed, tall figure that he was.

He spotted Emeline and raised his eyebrows at her towel-wrapped hair.

"Is that an Equanian look?" he asked, with some of his old condescension.

A flash of anger made her flush. This was too much after the comment about bodices. She turned away in disgust.

Miserably, she climbed into the wagon, sat down, and yanked the towel from her hair, glaring at Reese as he mounted his horse and whistled at Erd to start up the steam-carriage.

The knight noticed and gazed back at her, watching as she raked a comb through her wet curls. She wished she could read his expression, but she'd never been able to do that, had she? Abruptly, he rode off to the front.

"We saw a man with a sword in the washhouse!" Aladane crowded as he boarded the wagon.

"Everybody has weapons!" Dale added enthusiastically. Dada gave Fish a worried look.

~ ~

That night's ride was calm until the thunderous, crackling boom.

"What is it?" Emeline cried, startled out of a doze. Another boom struck her ears as a star erupted into blindingly bright pinks and purples. The horses were frantic, stepping sideways into each other.

The stars were exploding! Another one shattered into astonishing blues and whites.

"It's beautiful! Em, I can't believe it!" Dale shouted. "Sky magic!"

Emeline thought of Mama as intense colors flashed in the sky, sparkling red and green. She had never seen anything so lovely and terrifying at once.

"I'm not going any farther, Bird!" Fish roared. "I'm going back!"

"It's safe, I assure you!" Innish called, raising his hand as he rode toward them. "These are fireworks! For a birthday celebration, perhaps! It's not magic, it's science!" A yellow firework flashed, lighting up his face. He was not smiling, but there was a strange, intense excitement in his eyes—just a trick of the light, surely, but it alarmed her. He didn't look quite like himself.

"If that's science, I'll take magic," Fish growled, reining in the horses.

Still dazzled, Emeline realized the wagon was passing beneath an enormous, gleaming silver archway that straddled the entire road. Colored rockets were streaking upward from beyond it, just inside the walls of—

Walls! City walls! *It was the capital!*

She had never imagined that their first view of the city would be at night, under a violent sky of convulsing stars. Her breath left her.

They were halted at a gate, but Rellum Sapient's steam-carriage puffed on through. Innish stayed behind and spoke to the armored guard at the entryway. Unlike a Lash Knight, this guard's armor was a deep blue and his helmet was peaked and rounded. Another guard, identical in armor, stood on the other side of the archway, glowering. Innish beckoned to Dada, who climbed out of the wagon to join them.

"It was nice of Sir Reese to wait for us," Emeline muttered, still feeling the sting of his stupid *Equanian look* remark. She flinched as the fireworks roared.

"He's got Lash Knight stuff to do!" Aladane said.

After a moment, Innish rode on through the gates and

Dada came back to the wagon, illuminated by purples and greens.

"Come on, let's go through before I forget the directions," he said as rockets popped overhead.

"By all the fish in the canal," Fish swore, cringing at the sky. He slapped the reins and the horses darted forward, eager to move in any direction.

"I can't believe it's not magic," Emeline breathed. But of course, it couldn't be. Not out in the open in the capital itself.

"Whose birthday are they celebrating?" Dale asked Dada.

"Some rich fellow, I imagine. All right, past this big park, it's two rights, then a left and a right. . . . The main streets are named after kings and the small ones are numbered."

Behind the wagon the guards began closing the heavy iron gates, accompanied by the sounds of grinding metal and rattling chains.

Directly ahead stood an enormous figure, lit by an eerie glow. Emeline was mesmerized by it; as they came closer, she saw it was a great statue of white stone, ringed by lanterns.

"Is that a statue of the king?" Dale asked amid the firework crackles.

"If it is, it's not a recent likeness," Fish said. The ghostly statue was of a heavily muscled youth, striking an athletic pose.

Emeline turned to look back at the fireworks as they rode past the statue. One fractured into three astonishing blooms of red and gold.

"We gotta bring some of those back to Equane," Aladane said, staring back also.

"People would run screaming," Dale told him sensibly.

"I know!"

The wagon crossed over a small bridge under which a dark canal slogged. Lanterns atop tall poles marked the road ahead of them, and rising around them was the glow of lighted windows in dark buildings.

Suddenly they were in the city proper, and the noise of the fireworks was nearly drowned out by the sounds springing up on all sides. There were nighttime voices, calm and steady, but there were so *many*....The great hum was accented by door slams, shouts, scraps of music, the barking of dogs, and—mysteriously—the jingling of many small bells.

"Listen to all that racket," Fish said wearily.

"That's it—take a right here on Ardellin," Dada said. Fish turned them onto a road full of shadows.

"King Ardellin lived the longest," Dale murmured.

They turned right again onto a road numbered 25, and then there were the two left turns. If it weren't for the noise, Emeline would've thought they were riding through some kind of dream—a dream of floating lights and towering dark shapes. The roads grew narrower and narrower, and the buildings leaned closer on either side.

"This is it," Dada said finally, and Fish slowed the horses to a stop. "The royal lodge."

Before them was a large courtyard, bordered by columns and arches. There was a shape in the middle that was perhaps a fountain; at least, Emeline could hear water gurgling. The voices and night noises seemed a little quieter here.

"Wait. There's supposed to be someone to let us in." Dada

climbed out of the wagon and returned a moment later with a sleepy-looking boy in a wrinkled black suit, who yawned and took the horses' reins from Fish.

"You can have the two rooms over there," he said, pointing vaguely. "You're the only guests here. Master Quaith will sort you out in the morning."

Everyone got up quickly and began gathering their things as the boy waited impatiently, shifting his feet. Then he led the horses and wagon away, leaving them standing there in the dark.

"What if we don't ever see them again?" Fish asked, watching the wagon go.

"Then we'll just live here," Aladane declared. "Let's go look at our rooms, Dale!"

He ran off, Dale following. Their excitement roused Emeline's; she walked along with Dada and Fish for a few paces, then gave in and ran after the boys. They were in the capital! What did rooms in the capital look like?

Across the courtyard, the boys disappeared through an arch and she followed. She almost smacked right into Aladane on the other side; the two boys had stopped dead in front of a couple of open doors, intimidated by the darkness inside. Other doors lined the corridor to the left and the right, all closed.

Emeline stepped into a room and heard the faint sound of a clock ticking. She took a few steps and then bumped into what felt like a table. "Where's the lantern?"

"Maybe on the wall. If this is an inn, how come we didn't have to pay?" Dale asked, warily sticking his head in.

"Because we're here to see the king!" Dada said behind him. "Innish called it 'official business' at the gates. I never felt so important," he added, amused, and Fish snorted.

He stepped inside, Dale and Aladane following, while Fish lingered warily in the corridor.

"Don't break anything," he warned them. She could hear them groping around.

"What's this?" Dale asked. There was a sudden cranking, winding sound, and the room flooded with a painful light. Emeline cried out and covered her eyes.

"Bless water!" Dada exclaimed over the others' shouts of astonishment.

Dale stood near a short crank-handle on the wall near the door, which was slowly unwinding itself, ticking softly as it went. Overhead, a collection of glaringly bright bulbs dangled from the high ceiling, suspended from several slow-turning gears. Emeline was reminded of Rellum Sapient's cloak.

"It's electricity!" Dada said with a smile. "I've read about it, but I didn't think we'd have it!"

Fish grunted and squinted up at the ceiling. "That's some kind of generator in the back, keeping it going," he said, sounding reluctantly impressed. "I'd hate to have to repair that mess. Seems like a lot of trouble when you can just light a lantern."

"But you can just turn it on with this!" Dale reminded him, patting the crank-handle.

Emeline looked at the room itself. There were two narrow beds in elaborate, silver-etched iron frames, two iron and silver dressers with mirrored doors, and one narrow table with matching chairs. The walls were darkly paneled in wood with framed paintings of unfamiliar land- and townscapes.

There was also a large ticking clock with a pendulum underneath, a washroom door, and a large diamond-paned window with sheer curtains revealing only darkness beyond.

She put her bundle of things down on one of the silver beds. "It's beautiful here," she breathed.

"These are just guest rooms! Imagine the King's Hall!" Aladane did a bizarre little dance that made Emeline laugh.

Dale threw himself onto the bed while Aladane started opening the dressers. He pulled out several blue blankets and thick furry towels.

"Put that back, Al, and Dale, don't break that bed," Dada said sharply. "I'm sure we'd have to pay for *that*." He sat down next to Emeline and shook his head. "I wish your mama could see this."

"Well, I'm going to sleep in the other room where it's nice and dark," Fish said, yawning. No sooner had he spoken than the lights switched off and the room went black. Aladane yelped and knocked into something.

"The crank unwound all the way," Dale said. There was the sound of the handle turning again and the bulbs switched back on immediately.

"It's a good system. Saves the power," Fish admitted, leaving.

The washroom turned out to have a basin large enough to lie down in, and a large silver knob that twisted to run the water, not a pump handle. Emeline hung her worn dresses on the many wall hooks and sprayed them with a bottle of perfumed water that sat on a shelf. The tub water was hot, and there were loads of sweet-smelling soaps and soft towels, which altogether made her feel like she was melting.

When she curled up in one of the soft beds, however, her thoughts flew back to her fears in the washhouse. She was sure Dada was turning restlessly, worried about tomorrow too. She imagined the Sapients and Theurgists would start shouting and arguing the moment Reese told them about the Ithin—all while she stood there with her burning secret.

Aladane was right, though. Couldn't her magic end this conflict that had become desperate and dangerous? Was it right not to tell anyone at all? Shouldn't they find someone important to tell in private, someone neutral?

Or maybe they had already done that by telling Reese. The idea soothed her a little.

There wasn't much time to figure things out anyway. The king was likely to simply thank them for their testimony and then send them away, especially now that Reese had seen the Ithin himself. He was a much more important witness. She knew they would be lucky if the king even agreed to investigate their woods.

But he has to. He must.

Out of nowhere, Emeline realized that she was eager to see Reese again, and she frowned at herself. An image of his smile and his eyes was interrupted by his stupid comment, *Is that an Equanian look?* She huffed and rolled over. *Are bodice dresses coming back in style?* The washhouse girl's voice came back to her too. *They're so country village.*

She groaned inwardly. It was very possible that they would

all look ridiculously rustic to the king and his council. All things considered, she knew it wasn't the slightest bit important, but she still wished she had the time and money to buy clothes in an appropriate style, whatever that might be. Maybe it would up their odds of being listened to.

But time was what they had least of all. She sighed and tried to will herself to sleep.

fourteen

Emeline stood looking through the sheer curtains at a patch of green grass and a bench painted deep red.

"Morning, Em," Dada said, giving her a thin smile. He did not look rested.

"Dada, it's a garden out there," she said, her elbows on the windowsill. The sun was bright and clear, and she could see grass sectioned off by hedges. The sound of water trickled from a nearby fountain.

"I hope we can restock somewhere," Dada said, counting the few payts he had left. He was wearing his nice gray coat, and his hat was out on the table. "I don't suppose they'll feed us, and there's only a bit of dried fish left."

"Will someone come get us?" she asked, turning around.

"I imagine that Mister Quaith will. Wake your brother up."

Emeline looked at the clock on the wall just as it struck seven. Then she poked the two boys still huddled in the soft bed. Dale groaned and rolled over, but Aladane popped up like a rabbit.

So much for "sleeping like the dead."

"Dale, get up! We're in the capital!" He grabbed his friend by the shoulders and shook him.

Emeline went to the room door and opened it a crack.

The corridor was shaded by arches, but in the courtyard beyond, sunlight sparkled on the water spraying from a beautiful stone fountain. It was a statue of a young girl with outstretched arms pouring water into a basin; she was cracked and green with moss, but still lovely.

Lush vines twisted along the edge of the basin, and Emeline's heart skipped a beat.

I should never show anyone, ever... But the pull was so strong. She almost vibrated with it.

She looked around quickly. The courtyard was quiet, a big, silent square surrounded by empty rooms behind columns and arches. Hadn't the boy who had taken their horses told them that they were the only guests?

Dale and Aladane were bustling around and Dada was in the washroom, so she grabbed her cloak and slipped outside without saying anything. It was cold in the shade, but warm in the sun. The ground was tiled in large brown squares, smooth underfoot.

Emeline walked out to the fountain, birds fluttering around it, twittering. She looked down into the gurgling water and saw that the basin was half-choked with vines and leaves. That familiar, shimmering sensation was already growing inside her.

She reached out over the water and a tendril came up to meet her hand, curling and dripping in the sunshine. It was a sweet rush, a little thrill of magic that surged through her blood. It felt so natural.

Carefully, she drew the vine up into the air, startling the

birds, and twirled it slowly around one of the statue's arms. It looked pretty there, like jewelry. She reached for another one.

"Emeline! I saw that!" Aladane's voice made her jump. The vine fell back into the water with a splash.

The boys stood just beyond the corridor, staring out at her. Aladane's mouth hung open, but Dale was grinning. She was lucky it was only them.

"Maybe I can do it too!" Dale cried. He ran to join her at the fountain. "How do you do it? Show me!"

"Shhhh! Quiet," Emeline snapped. "Someone might walk by."

"How does it work?" he asked again, in a lower voice.

"I just hold my hand out," she said as Aladane joined them. She looked around them just to be sure, then called up a bit of vine through the water.

Dale tried it for a moment, but nothing happened. His shoulders drooped.

"How come you can do it but not me?"

"I don't know," she said, feeling guilty. "Maybe you have to grow into it."

"Maybe only girls can do it," Aladane said, and Dale frowned.

"Do you think Mama could do it and we never knew?" he asked Emeline.

"I think she could do other things," she said seriously.

Aladane looked up at the vine that she had twisted around the statue.

"You should do them all like that. It looks good."

He sounded a little awed, and it made her laugh. She rose up another one and—

"Em!" Dada's strained voice spun her around. He and Fish were watching, stunned, from the corridor. She put her hands behind her back.

Fish whistled. "I have to admit, Bird, that's quite a trick."

Dada nodded, too overcome to speak. Then he crossed to the fountain and put a squeezing hand on Emeline's shoulder.

"That's what you have to say, heart, if anyone else sees it," he told her. "That it's just a trick. Stage magic that you learned at home." His face was so serious that it pained her, and she dropped her eyes to the ground. "But *no one* should see you do it, Emeline. Especially not here. Do you understand? Please tell me you understand."

"Yes," she said quickly, her heart heavy. It was like being asked not to hum, not to smile, not to let her eyes sparkle. She would just have to avert her gaze from any fountain or stream they passed.

Footsteps sounded on the tiles and everyone jumped. A tall, trim man was walking toward them, very dapper in a long black coat and striped blue-and-silver trousers. His graying brown hair was long and tied into a little knot at the back of his head. He stopped and nodded at them, giving no sign of having seen anything unusual.

"I thought you might rise early," he said pleasantly. "My name is Quaith, and I will be taking you to a café near the King's Hall for breakfast. Whenever you're ready, you may follow me."

"Thank you," Dada said, sounding embarrassed. "But

I'm afraid that we may not have enough money left." Fish straightened his shoulders, as if refusing to be ashamed.

Quaith smiled somewhat patronizingly. "Not to worry. It will be taken care of."

Hurrying back inside to get dressed, Emeline wondered if this was how the king treated all lowly subjects who thought they'd seen a Dark Creature, or if it had more to do with their association with Reese and Rellum Sapient. The latter seemed a lot more likely.

Everyone else was ready, of course, so she threw on her blue dress and combed through her hair, checking herself frantically in the washroom mirror. She looked flushed, her hazel eyes shining bright. She hesitated with her bodice for a moment but buckled it on reluctantly; the dress underneath was completely shapeless, so she couldn't imagine that it looked better that way. Frowning, she pulled her red cloak back on to hide her unstylish outfit, pulled the handle crank all the way around to click the lights off, and then ran back outside.

The others were standing in a semicircle around Mister Quaith.

"Where's our wagon and horses?" Fish asked.

"They're in the lodger stable, safe and sound, and will be returned to you after your testimony is heard," Quaith assured him. He spoke very clearly and with an air of importance. "I'm afraid I can't guarantee that you will see His Majesty today, however, as he is very ill, and all appointments depend on his current state. But we will receive further instructions after breakfast." Dada and Fish looked at each other in surprise as Quaith turned and led them out of the courtyard, walking briskly.

As they followed, Aladane whispered eagerly to Dale. "Did you hear that? The longer we wait to see the king, the more time we have in the city! Maybe we can explore!"

Emeline had thought the very same thing. Would they be allowed to, though? Or would they have to stay in their rooms, waiting?

Quaith marched them up to a small vehicle waiting in the road. It was a very small steam-carriage, but it had no roof. The cushioned seats were open to the air and an empty driver's seat perched low in the front.

"All aboard," he said with a smile. Dada stepped into the carriage uncertainly, the boys pushing their way in right after. Emeline sank into a soft padded seat while Fish squeezed his long legs in.

With a loud rattling and several puffs of steam, they started forward. She held on to her seat nervously, but the carriage was very smooth—so smooth, in fact, that it glided along at an alarming pace. The sun shone warmly, but the wind was so chilly that Emeline was glad for her cloak; the end of the summer bit more deeply here than in Equane.

Now they had the chance to really look at the buildings of the city. By daylight, they were beautiful. Made mostly of cracked, weathered stone, their large windows were framed with oversized shutters in a wonderful variety of colors and styles. Some shutters were carved to look like doors, others like animals, especially dogs; a few were even shaped into pairs of bird or butterfly wings, and one pair formed two halves of a golden sun. It was clear that many of them were very old—their bright paint was cracking—but Emeline admired them all.

Most houses had dark tile roofs and chimneys, and most were fronted by small patches of grass, sometimes planted beautifully with flowers. The city as a whole was dotted with trees, but she noted that none of them were clustered together. It was always one tree alone.

The streets on which they drove were quiet, but before long they turned a corner and came out onto a much wider road, where steam-carriages of all sizes puffed by. Here, a great many people walked along the avenues, and if the Blynians or Equanians had seemed varied in color, these people were a rainbow.

There was no shouting or running here, no drunken laughter spilling into the air. The capital folk moved in a stately fashion, their outfits proving that Quaith's blue-and-silver motley was a popular look. There were also one or two other men who wore their hair long and tied up in a knot.

Quite a few people had guns at their belts, but their holsters looked rather elaborate, even from afar. There was also no end of layers and accessories, such as fitted caps, fine rings, beaded purses, and gloves, although it certainly wasn't cold enough to require them.

Some people even wore bells stitched onto a sleeve or a pant leg. They sent a faint jingling up into the air, which explained what Emeline had heard the night before. She also saw with surprise that several people wore spectacles with colored lenses.

"Why does everyone have so much clutter on them?" Fish asked as they all stared openly at the city people.

"Clutter?" Quaith asked, surprised.

"It's for decoration," Emeline said, smiling and admiring the knit caps that she saw some girls wearing.

"Look at those shoes!" Aladane exclaimed, pointing rudely at a man whose shoes curled up into a point in the front. Emeline slapped his hand down.

"A whimsical new fashion," Quaith said airily.

"Don't tell me their feet curl up like that inside," Fish muttered, and Emeline laughed.

Soon the houses had been left behind, and now there were shops, places to eat, and services for hire. Emeline squinted through the windows as they passed, catching glimpses of gowns on racks, books on shelves, furniture on display, and more. It was a whirlwind of things to buy, if you had money. She realized that the people here would probably be astonished to learn that Equanians didn't even *use* money.

"Is this a market?" Dada asked Quaith.

"Oh, no, the market is much more crowded. These are just a few shops."

A tall spire in the sky caught Emeline's attention as their carriage made another turn. It was a massive stone tower that vanished and reappeared among the dark-tiled rooftops and scattered trees.

"That's the tower over the King's Hall," Dada said, following her gaze.

"You are correct," Quaith said. "A most formidable keep."

"What's a keep?" Dale asked.

"Sort of a hideout for when there's trouble," Fish told him.

Aladane looked doubtful. "It's not very well hidden," he said, and Quaith laughed.

The tower loomed closer and closer, until Emeline could see that it was made of truly ancient gray stone. Narrow slits of windows were carved into the walls.

Soon it was directly before them, set far back behind a high stone wall that stretched in either direction. Front and center in the wall was a pair of elaborate silver doors, nearly as tall as the arched gates at the city's entrance.

"Look!" Dale cried as a pair of Lash Knights rode past the carriage; city folk turned to watch them too, in obvious admiration. Emeline caught herself looking for Reese, but neither of the knights was tall enough, nor did they wear his circle symbol. Riding up to the silver doors, the knights cried out for entrance and were admitted; the gates gave a loud mechanical groan as they opened.

"I didn't know they had so much silver here," Dada said, watching the doors close again.

"Where does it all come from?" Dale asked.

"His Majesty's royal colors are blue and silver, so of course he has made great use of the silver mines. Here we are," Quaith announced, stopping the little carriage in front of a low building. A sign out front read MOTHER'S MILK in painted, curly lettering. There were long, tall, square-paned windows in the front that revealed a handful of people sitting inside at tables. "The Mother's Milk will be your kitchen while you are here."

"I'm starving," Dale said as they all climbed out.

"I hope they'll feed us something we can keep down," Fish said, under his breath.

They followed Quaith into the plain, low-ceilinged café. Several aproned young women were hustling about, picking up plates, carrying drinks, and sweeping under tables. The oldest one approached when Quaith waved her over.

"Please give them the royal lodger breakfast. Have the guards arrived?" he asked.

The girl nodded, gesturing to two sturdy men who rose from a nearby table. Their clothing was like Innish's—black caps and panels of leather armor. They nodded to Quaith respectfully.

"Ah, here you are. I'll be at the hall for a short while, and then I'll come collect them," he told the men. Then he left without another word.

The guards studied them silently. One was young and wiry and the other hefty with a beard.

"He left us with guards?" Fish muttered to Dada, who cleared his throat uncomfortably and nodded at the two men.

Emeline noticed that the other diners were watching them. "We should sit down," she said quickly, herding the boys toward a table facing one of the windows. The guards remained standing off to the side. She wished they wouldn't just stare at them.

"Did you see how everyone looked at the Lash Knights when they went by?" Dale asked no one in particular. His voice was a little dreamy. "I wonder where they practice fighting."

One of the aproned girls brought them five plates full of

food. There was toasted bread, slices of meat that were clearly not fish, and chunks of long, pale-colored fruit.

"What's this?" Fish exclaimed, and Emeline cringed. The serving girl gave him a disparaging look.

"It's beef and yellow-fruit. What you think it is?" she demanded, her speech much less proper than Quaith's.

She set down mugs of a steaming black liquid next. Aladane reached for his, taking a big sip—and then he choked and spat it out across the table, splashing Emeline's cloak. She and the serving girl shrieked.

"*Aladane!*" Dada and Fish roared at once. The boy cowered and turned red.

"It's disgusting...!" he murmured defensively. The serving girl glared at him, but she untied her apron in one practiced move and began wiping up the liquid with it.

"Don't you even know what coffee is?" she asked angrily.

"We're not from here," Emeline muttered, shaking out her cloak.

The girl gave a shake of her head. "If you follow me in back, you can rinse that out."

With a frown at Aladane, Emeline got up and followed her. They crossed the room, passing curious faces at other tables, and went all the way back into the kitchen. It was a long hot room full of steam and women's voices, rich with the flavor of the strange meat cooking. The girl gave Emeline a bucket of cold water, and she stood in an out-of-the-way corner and pulled off her cloak to dip it in.

"Cayle, who do you think I saw this morning?" one girl called to another.

"Why don't you just tell me?" came the smart reply.

"Your Sir Reese, that's who! He's back!" the girl said gleefully. Emeline glanced up, surprised.

"*Her* Sir Reese! In her dreams!" a different voice shrilled.

"Oh, but he is gorgeous. And already a knight!"

"Gorgeous, my eye. He's a big lug!" This was followed by a cackle of laughter, and Emeline grinned.

"That's how I like 'em!" Cayle insisted. "You know he's the best in the field, they say. That's why he's knighted already. Fastest and strongest."

"He had to be, to get knighted in the first place. Started out just like us," a stout woman with a red face declared. Emeline stopped wringing the water from her cloak, confused.

"Oh, right!" the first girl said with scorn. "He's *just* like us."

"He was brought up poor, that's all I know."

"That's why he's my favorite," Cayle announced. "A poor boy from Aliddser, grown up a knight!"

Emeline stood up straight and put her hands on her hips. This could not be the same Reese who had spoken so disparagingly of her village. She lingered, wringing out her cloak again.

"Haven't you seen how the other knights torture him? Not good enough to serve with them and all that."

"He's never seen with any fine ladies either. My friend Arti works in the hall and says so."

"You think they don't think he's good enough?"

Emeline's indignation faded as murmurs of agreement and the clucking of tongues followed.

"Or *he* doesn't think he's good enough," the stout woman said with sympathy.

"Well, he can stoop to my level any day. He can put on whatever airs he likes with me!" Cayle said. There were several shouts of laughter at that. Emeline found herself smiling again, then turned quickly and went back out to join the others.

fifteen

Emeline listened absently to the others as they ate their strange breakfast under the watch of the silent guards. The meat was dense, but its flavor was good, and the sweet yellow-fruit was pleasantly soft. Aladane was right about the bitter taste of the coffee, but the warmth of it was soothing, at least.

"If this is meat from a cow, I can't say it's all bad," Dada said, chewing.

"It's not as good as fish, but it's all right," Fish allowed.

Emeline's mind kept turning over the words of the kitchen girls. Could it really be true that Reese was a poor boy who'd worked his way up to knighthood? It was the very thing Fish had scoffed at Dale for. If his disdainful air was a defense that he had formed against the other knights, then that was understandable, but that didn't explain why he maintained it with her and her family. Unless it had become a habit he couldn't shake.

"Have you ever heard of Aliddser?" she asked Dada. He shook his head, drinking from his mug.

"I think I saw that on the map. It's a village in the northeast, past the Spine," Dale said, his mouth full.

A village! Emeline thought with delight. *He is the same as we are!*

"Look, there's Mister Quaith coming back," Aladane said, his eyes glued to the windows even as he ate. "If he asks how the food was, don't tell him I spit out the coffee." Emeline and Dale laughed at him.

"What'll you give me?" Fish asked with a smirk.

Quaith came in and joined them, his expression clouded. Dada and Fish nodded at him politely. "Well, I'm afraid the news is not good," he began. "His Majesty is very interested in your report, especially as Sir Reese wishes to corroborate your account, but he is not at all well today and must postpone his appointments." He sighed, then straightened himself up. "I will have to escort you back to your rooms for now."

"I understand," Dada said slowly. "Thank you."

Emeline looked at Dale and Aladane, and saw that they were ready to burst.

"Mister Quaith?" she said politely. "Would it be all right if we were to walk around the city for a little while?" The boys nodded earnestly.

"No, indeed," Quaith said, surprising her. He frowned and glanced at the guards; she thought he seemed to be considering his next words carefully. "I must be aware of your whereabouts at all times, you see, in case His Majesty summons you."

Was he worried about them?

Emeline looked at Dada and saw that he was ready to agree. She couldn't imagine spending hours sitting in their rooms, nice as they were.

"What if we picked one place and stayed there?" Aladane asked.

"Aladane," Dada warned.

"And the guards came with us?" Dale chimed in.

Dada shot him a stern look, but Quaith finally smiled indulgently. "I understand the capital must be rather exciting to you," he said. "I suppose we could spare the guards an hour with you, as long as it's somewhere nearby. And, er, public."

"Well, that beats sitting around and twiddling our thumbs," Fish declared.

Emeline gave her father a hopeful look, and Dale said, "Dada, we might never be here again!"

Their father sighed and nodded, looking very troubled.

Quaith waved for the guards to approach, asking, "Where would you like to go?"

"Can you take us to see the Lash Knights practice?" Dale blurted out immediately.

Emeline felt a little thrill at the thought of watching Reese going through his paces, skillful, powerful. But then she was angry at herself, her face coloring. What was he to her?

Quaith tilted his head in thought. "Hm. Yes, I believe that can be arranged. They'll have started already this morning. Are you ready to go now?" Aladane and Dale leapt out of their chairs; Aladane's fell over backward with a clatter.

"I would've liked to see the library or the underground water system," Dada told Fish, getting up reluctantly.

"Well, I guess you should've spoken up," Fish replied.

"Maybe they'll have spring-gun shooting at the practice, Mister Fish," Dale said.

Quaith laughed, surprising them all. "Spring-guns! I haven't seen one of those since I was a child." He exchanged a smug look with the guards. "Guns in the capital shoot bullets, my boy, not darts. Mostly bullets made of silver."

Emeline looked at Fish, wondering what *bullets* were. He frowned, clearly ignorant too. Darts seemed deadly enough to her. She thought of the bandit Mister Fish had shot, and went cold at heart.

Outside, Quaith spoke to the guards; they were taller than him, but he somehow managed to look down his nose at them. "You may use my carriage, but *please* drive carefully. Take them to the viewing deck on the field. One hour, no more." He nodded to Dada and Fish and then marched away toward the silver gates.

As soon as he left, Dada reached out to shake hands with the bearded guard, startling him. "Thank you for your help," he said, and the man smiled.

"Never had to watch over villagers before, instead of fancy folk," he said in a rough voice. "Be a nice change."

"I heard you got important news or something like it," the younger guard ventured, but his elder nudged him sharply to be silent.

"We're not entirely sure of that ourselves," Dada said cautiously. "But we certainly don't know our way around here."

"The knights' practice ground's as good a place to start as any," the bearded guard said. He opened the carriage door and, to Emeline's surprise, mimicked Quaith's voice expertly. "All aboard!"

They rode alongside the massive stone wall, away from the silver gates. Emeline craned her neck to look up at the tower, suddenly nervous about watching Reese practice with the other knights. Would they see evidence of what the kitchen girls had said? What would Dale think if he saw the other knights mistreating him?

She could not understand what was so terrible about being from a poor village. *We're all nearly equal in Equane, and everyone has everything they need.* It was something she had always taken for granted.

But maybe it was a rare thing.

They were approaching the walled practice ground. Two tall poles marked the entrance to the field, topped with long black banners fluttering against the sky. The figures of men on horseback could be seen maneuvering across the muddy grass.

The carriage parked and they got out, listening to the thunder of horses running. The boys barely restrained themselves from pushing past the guards; the younger one noticed their excitement and grinned. He steered them to the left, toward a raised platform with rows of bench seats for spectators.

"This is the viewing deck. Up you go, boys! Give 'em some cheers!"

"We'll be down here till Master Quaith comes back," the bearded guard told Dada and Fish. "One hour."

The knights were facing off in pairs on armored horses, cracking their whips through the air and catching the impacts on their black shields. Dale and Aladane rushed up toward some open seats, and the rest of them followed.

Emeline looked at the row of boys and young men who sat along the front of the stands, cheering and waving. Their legs swung down into the field, and they laughed and elbowed each other knowingly. Most of them wore leather armbands and leather patches on their trousers; a few had striped vests and one had long hair tied up like Quaith's, but in a much messier fashion.

They all stopped for a moment to gawk at Emeline and the others mounting the steps to sit above them. The seats were tiered so she could just see over the heads of the row in front. Directly across, the field ended in an arched entryway that cut straight through the King's Wall.

A loud bell rang out over the field, and the knights traded places with each other quickly, shaking the ground with their horses' hooves.

"Look at that!" Dale yelled as one knight lashed the shield out of his opponent's arms. Fish hooted and looked at Dada.

"So, Bird, if spring-guns in the capital can shoot pieces of silver, are we supposed to believe these shields can stand up to them?" he asked, incredulous.

"Probably not at close range! Not the armor, either," Dada agreed.

One knight was forcing his opponent backward with powerful lashes, both of them coming closer to the viewing deck. The boys in the front rows jumped up to see.

"That's Mallin! He always charges like that!" one of them shouted.

"He'll lose in the racing!"

"Not if he's up against Asai!"

Emeline strained to see farther out into the field, looking for Reese's ring symbol among the shiny black breastplates. Perhaps he wasn't there today after all? The bell rang out again, and a handful of young men in brown tunics ran forward from the arched entryway. They were carrying sheaths that held long blades.

"It's the knife lashing!" a boy shouted.

The knights were each given a sheath full of shining, long-bladed knives. They paired off again, and then they waited. At the sound of the bell, one knight in each pair began to throw his knives at the other—firm, skilled throws, one blade at a time.

Emeline sat up straight, alarmed, but the targeted knights were whipping the knives aside in the air. In fact, some of them lashed the blades from their opponents' hands before they were even thrown. Black whips cracked all over the field as the stands cheered.

"Look, there's Reese!" Aladane cried, jumping up.

And there he was. A large knight with a circle on his chest, wheeling and slashing at the flying blades. Emeline's heart leapt. He *was* amazing! He was blindingly fast.

As if irritated by his ability, the opposing knight began to throw two knives at him at once. Emeline gasped.

"Don't worry, Em. Knives can't go through his armor," Dada said, glancing back at her.

"Look how fast he is!" Dale crowed.

Reese was catching all of the blades, lashing them right out of the air. One of the knives went astray, thrown badly, and he struck it with his whip anyway, as if to prove a point. His speed was truly incredible.

"Bless water!" Fish said, riveted. The boys in the front row roared with approval.

"There you go, Reese!"

"Show 'em how it's done!"

All of a sudden, another knight broke away from his partner to fling a knife at Reese too. Emeline cried out and several of the boys turned her way, surprised.

Reese struck the extra blade with his shield even as he lashed his partner's knives away. The third knight threw several more, showering Reese, as other pairs of knights stopped to watch. Emeline saw that they were laughing.

"That Gundan, he's always riding on Reese!" one of the local boys yelled.

"He won't take it for long!"

"Get him, Reese!"

Reese roared, whipping Gundan's entire sheath of knives to the ground. Surprised, Gundan yanked the bridle, and his stallion reared and almost threw him off—he just barely held on. The bell sounded again and Reese spurred his horse toward the nearly thrown knight.

They rode by each other, smacking shoulders as they passed, and then wheeled about to face each other again. Emeline could only imagine the expressions on their faces, hidden by the dog-muzzle helmets. Another knight had to intervene, riding in between them and holding up an arm.

It occurred to her, watching, how much these sons of rich men must hate Reese—a poor young upstart who bested them on the field.

He glanced up in their direction as he rode into the next formation. She suddenly wondered if he'd heard her cry out—she was the only girl on the viewing deck and her voice had probably carried farther than she'd thought.

The young men who had brought out the knives were now carrying something new: guns, guns that Emeline knew were not spring-guns. She clenched her hands together in her lap.

More people were making their way onto the viewing deck. A group of girls a little older than Emeline clattered up the steps, chatting; they all wore the neat round caps she had admired from the carriage, but their clothes were like nothing she'd seen before. Two of them wore long tunics with deliberate tears, revealing a layer of mesh material underneath; another wore a loose, shimmering dress, pinned up at the sides to show her parti-color stockings.

Most surprising of all, one girl wore a beautiful pair of wings shaped out of silver wire.

Must be another "whimsical style"!

The girls caught the eyes of several of the young men in the front row as they took their seats. She could see why— they were as fresh and pretty as a rose garden.

"Oh, we missed the knives!" one girl said. She jingled, revealing bells on her sleeves.

"Where's Gundan? I've been daydreaming about him!" another one said, and they all laughed.

Emeline tucked her plain red cloak around her and turned to look at Dada. "Are the knights just going to shoot each other next?" she asked unhappily. He shrugged, watching just as eagerly now as the boys.

A row formed of ten knights armed with guns, while the others waited, unarmed, in a line nearby. She gripped the edges of her cloak, the cloth beginning to soften with sweat.

The bell sounded again, and an unarmed knight kicked his horse forward. He raced directly across the sights of his armed brothers, and as one they started firing on him. The knight dodged what he could and shielded himself against the rest, while another knight spurred out behind him to enter the gauntlet. The clanging of bullets against shields rang through the air.

Emeline winced as she watched, but the rest whistled and cheered, even the other girls. The sound of the bullet-guns was sharp and violent, worse than spring-guns.

Then it was Reese's turn, and Emeline held her breath. He charged through the melee of bullets, flashing his shield so fast that it was a blur. Before he reached the end, his whip shot out and lashed a gun from someone's hand. Everyone on the platform burst into cheers, some of them leaping to their feet.

She alone sat very still and heaved a sigh of relief.

The shooting was over now, and the boys in the front row began to talk about racing. She shifted in her seat, watching Reese detach himself from the others and ride very slowly toward the viewing deck.

Dale immediately stood up and waved. Emeline expected Reese to simply nod at him—if anything—but he rode all the way up to their seats. An excited whispering broke out among the girls.

"Good job, Sir Reese!" the local boys sang out.

"Bravo!"

Dale and Aladane rushed to the railing and leaned over; on impulse, she got up and followed. The locals moved over reluctantly to give them space.

"We asked Mister Quaith to bring us," Dale called down to Reese.

"So I assumed." His deep voice carried easily through the helmet, but he took it off and shook out his hair, which was damp with sweat. Emeline heard distinct giggling from the girls behind them and she laughed.

Reese eyed her. "Am I entertaining you?" he asked suspiciously.

"Aren't you supposed to? That's why there's a viewing deck," she replied.

He broke into a wide grin and looked away. She was surprised to feel her heart flutter, and even more surprised to see the locals staring at them with a mixture of astonishment and envy.

"Quaith didn't leave you here alone, did he?" Reese asked, frowning slightly.

"No, we have guards," Dale told him.

Is he worried for us, too? She clenched the railing. *Does he think we need protection?* Her chest tightened, half with fear, half with something else.

"You were great!" Aladane exclaimed. "Are you going to race now?"

"No, I'm not fond of racing. Running in circles is tedious." Emeline couldn't help smiling at the boredom in his voice. "Are you lot going to sit here all day?"

"We wanted to go sightseeing, but Mister Quaith has to know where we are," Dale told him.

"Can *you* take us sightseeing?" Aladane asked abruptly. "I bet Mister Quaith wouldn't mind that!"

Reese looked startled, and Emeline cringed.

"Aladane!" she said sharply. "Don't be stupid. Come on, let's go back."

She reached for Dale's hand, but he was looking at Reese, waiting for an answer.

The knight's horse moved restlessly under him and he settled it. Then he looked directly at Emeline. She stared back at him with her chin up.

"I suppose I could. I don't have anything else to do today," he drawled, finally.

Dale and Aladane cheered as if he had done something spectacular out on the field. The local boys looked at one another in disbelief.

"Let's go tell Dada!" Dale turned and squeezed past Emeline; Aladane followed, nearly knocking her over. She peered down at Reese one last time. He was watching her, his brow furrowed in thought. Then he turned and led his horse away.

As Emeline followed the others down from the platform, she saw that the girls were eyeing her up and down, whispering. She knew they were wondering why Reese had spoken to them and who they could be. One flashed her a curious smile; one gave her an encouraging wink.

Strange: All of them had straight hair. In fact, all of the girls she had seen had straight hair. She had seen a few curly-haired men, like Innish, but no women. How was it possible that girls in the capital all had straight hair?

The guards met them beneath the platform with mystified expressions. Emeline waited for them to ask about Reese—they'd seen everything from the ground—but they held their tongues.

"I feel safer if it's Reese showing us around," Dada said

quietly to Fish, who nodded. The ground shook beneath them as the knights ran relays on horseback.

"Doesn't racing just prove who has the fastest horse?" Emeline asked Dada over the battering of hooves.

"Racing makes them better horsemen," Dada told her. "They have to turn the chargers and keep them in line."

"I never used a horse for much more than plowing," Fish said. "Wouldn't know how to get one to do all that!"

Reese reappeared after a long while. He was wearing a black leather vest over a white shirt, and black pants with black boots. His whip was still coiled at his hip, but his hair had been toweled dry. His lack of layers, bells, and accessories made Emeline smile.

"It's kind of you to take us around," Dada said as he reached them.

There's more to this than kindness. He's scared for us. Somehow she could see it.

Reese nodded stiffly. "I've informed Quaith." He looked at the two guards, who stood respectfully silent. He considered for a moment, and then said, "As it happens, I've rescued this calamitous crew twice before. You can return to your duties."

The guards ducked their heads and strode back toward Quaith's carriage. Reese looked down at Dale, who was practically hopping in place. "What do you want to see?"

"Now hold on, he got to choose the first time," Fish said. "Bird wants to see the underground water system."

Reese stared and then gave an incredulous snort. "The plumbing?" he said with disgust. Dada and Fish looked embarrassed, and Emeline's blood boiled.

"How is the underground system in Aliddser?" she blurted. Reese froze for an instant, and then gave her a sharp look. She smiled back at him defiantly.

"Is that where you're from?" Dale asked, picking up on the name.

The knight said nothing, glaring at her. She started to wish she hadn't spoken. Bless water, he was the one who knew her secret!

"Either my reputation has preceded me," he said coolly, "or someone has been asking around." She felt her face burn and opened her mouth to say that she had simply overheard gossip—that it didn't matter to *her*—but Dada spoke first.

"You can show us whatever you'd like, Sir Reese," he said respectfully, and then gave Emeline a curious glance. "Equane is a tiny village, so everything will be new to us."

Reese's face thawed. He gave Dada a wry smile and stepped out into the road, pointedly looking back at them to follow. He led him toward a large iron grate that lay flush with the road; through its bar, rushing water was only just visible, far below their feet. The sound of it was drowned out by the carriages and other noises of the city.

"The water in the houses travels through pipes into an underground level. Then it goes through a whole series of filters and comes back around and we use it again, as disgusting as that sounds," Reese said. "A man named Bastine designed it maybe a hundred years ago, and everyone insists that the filters work and the water is clean. That's all I care to know about it."

Emeline smiled as Dada and Fish crouched down to peer through the grate.

"Well, there you go, Bird," Fish said. "Doesn't sound like we ought to go down there."

"If you plan to do that, you're on your own," Reese told them.

"All right, it's someone else's turn," Dada said as the two of them stood back up.

Dale looked up at Reese then as if he were going to name their next request.

"We saw Emeline's magic," he whispered, instead. Dada stiffened. "I don't have it," he added unhappily.

"I see," Reese said, glancing first at Dada and then Emeline. She worked her dress with anxious fingers.

"Have you told anyone about it?" she asked him.

"No," he replied seriously. Emeline sighed with relief, and heard Dada do the same. "In fact, I should warn you that you're already in a position to make serious enemies on both sides of the council. Because even without revealing her magic, you will threaten the Sapients by claiming to have seen an Ithin—or two, in fact—and you will threaten the Theurgists just by being witnesses to Rellum's attempted murder. Do you understand? Everyone already knows who you are. Quaith gave you guards because he's afraid of what could happen to you."

It was sobering to hear it so plainly. Emeline studied Dada's face as the boys shuffled nervously. His brow was furrowed deep.

"Could Rellum Sapient help protect us?" Dada asked. "He traveled with us all that way."

Reese scowled and shook his head. "Rellum is not a bad

man, and he's right about many things. But remember, he wants to be king. Your testimony and, especially, her magic could destroy everything he stands for. You can't trust him."

"I don't want to destroy anything or threaten anybody," Fish said, irritated. "I just want to tell them about the Ithin and ask the king to protect Equane."

Dada nodded, glancing at Emeline. "I believe we should tell the truth about the Ithin and let the council make of it what they will," he said slowly. "But we will say nothing of my daughter."

He gave her a pointed look and she nodded quickly. But her spirits sank at the reminder.

"But you saw the Ithin too!" Aladane told Reese.

"And you captured Loddril!" Dale said. "The assassin!"

"Yes, I'm not very popular either. Not that I ever was," he replied. "But as a Lash Knight, I have a good deal of protection."

"But not us, because we're just poor villagers," Fish grumbled.

"But we're *with* a Lash Knight," Dale pointed out.

"You are." Reese folded his arms, and asked, "What's next?"

Emeline smiled. "Why don't you tell us what we should see?" she asked him.

sixteen

*T*he capital was a city of gardens, statues, and—to Emeline's joy and dismay—fountains. Vines and flowers sparkled temptingly in sprays of water everywhere. She worked hard to ignore their lure as Reese walked the villagers to an enormous thoroughfare.

A wide strip of garden ran down the center of the road, a sort of narrow park between lanes. He led them across to it when the way was clear, and Emeline saw that it had orderly pathways lined with flowers—phlox, aster, dahlia—and simple statues of kings, queens, and other important figures. There was even one of the plumbing inventor Bastine.

"This is the first place I was taken when I came to the capital. As you can see, anyone who stays here long enough gets a statue," Reese declared, waving a hand at them all.

"How long have you been here?" Dale asked, and Emeline grinned.

"Three years. Not long enough."

"Where do you live?" Aladane asked him.

"In the King's Hall, in the knights' quarters. Unfortunately, I have to share them with the other knights." Reese crossed his arms as Dale grinned up at him. He didn't seem to mind their questions; in fact, Emeline had a feeling that he liked the boys.

Dada wandered over to a stone-carved map of the city, and Emeline followed, looking over his shoulder. The capital was rectangular, with the King's Hall in the dead center. She was surprised to see many groves of trees on the map, including right by the city gates. They were certainly not there now. Was it fear of Dark Creatures that had them all cut down?

"If you see a red carriage, let me know," Reese said, looking at the traffic going by.

"Why?" Aladane asked.

"So we don't have to trudge all over the city. They're carriages for hire."

"Oh, we don't have much money," Dale told him in a confiding tone. Emeline cringed.

"I'm aware," Reese replied. He continued slowly down the path, watching the road, and they followed. Emeline found herself walking alongside him, and she glanced up, feeling strangely, suddenly shy.

He was so tall, with such big hands; his large, blunt fingers had many calluses. She tried to imagine him as a small boy, strawberry-blond and running wild on a farm. It was hard to do.

"Are you studying me?" he asked suddenly. She flinched, embarrassed, but his voice was lower, and she realized that the boys were not listening. Dada and Fish were talking to each other behind them.

She said nothing for a moment; he was watching the road. "Is there a Lash Knight academy in Aliddser?"

"You are awfully interested in my hometown," he retorted. "If you must know, it's full of alehouses, brothels, and sheep. No academies. No fish."

"Brothels?"

He turned back from the traffic with an amused expression and shook his head.

"Never mind that. I went to the Belastia up near the Dinene. The oldest and most respected academy." He said this matter-of-factly and without arrogance, which surprised her.

"Look, there's a red one coming!" Aladane shouted. Reese looked up and waved at the bright-colored carriage in the distance, stepping to the edge of the road to hail it. The rest of them waved, too, but the carriage for hire plowed along as if it had no intention of stopping.

"Hey, over here!" Dale yelled. Fish and Dada joined in the shouting, and Reese looked away, obviously uncomfortable. Emeline could see that the driver was fiddling with something in his seat, not noticing them; they were definitely going to miss it.

She put her fingers in her mouth and whistled Mama's piercing, knife-sharp whistle. Reese jumped, instinctively clapping his hand on his whip, and the driver jerked his head up, turned the wheel sharply, and pulled over to stop just in front of them. Reese gave Emeline an oddly urgent look, as if he wanted to say something; she stared back at him, waiting, but he was silent.

"That's my girl," Dada told Emeline with a grin.

The red carriage was taller and longer than most of the others Emeline had seen, and there was a step up to get in through the door. There were two girls her age already inside, who gawked at them a moment before they slid over. Reese held the door open for them to climb in, and he caught Emeline's hand to help her up the step.

To her surprise, the quick touch was electrifying. What was this? She avoided looking at him, afraid of what her pinkening face might reveal.

"The market," he told the driver, and climbed in afterward. With the two passengers already inside, the group of them only just fit; Emeline found herself squished between Dale and Fish. The carriage had two rows of cushioned seats, with small racks overhead for items to be stowed.

"So this is how you get around if you don't have your own steam-carriage?" Dada asked Reese, the girls obviously listening. One of them was studying the Equanians' clothes with a frown. Reese nodded. "Seems like it would get expensive."

"I guess you could just walk," Fish told him. The girls smirked at each other.

"Or you can simply not go anywhere," Reese said airily.

Emeline frowned at their fellow passengers; they both wore silver-and-blue motley gowns and self-satisfied expressions, and they had very straight hair. They smiled at Reese, recognizing him as a knight, but he ignored them. His head was very close to the ceiling, and Emeline grinned at the thought of what might happen if the carriage hit a bump.

"Where are we going?" Aladane asked.

"To see more things you can't buy," Reese admitted. "But it's another very public place," he added, with a quick glance at Dada. "The big market plaza, otherwise known as the crown jewel of the capital." The sarcasm rolled off his tongue so naturally that Emeline suspected it *was* simply a habit for him.

"Do they have books?" Dada asked.

"Of course," one of the girls spoke up. "They have all the new books at Halatine's."

"And you can have your hair done at the Ironers," the other one told Emeline with a kind smile. She smiled back uncertainly. The carriage stopped and the two girls rose, stepping carefully over everyone's feet and out the door.

"Good day!" they said to Reese, and he nodded.

"What do they do to your hair?" Dale asked Emeline. She shrugged.

"I don't know. It doesn't need cutting yet," she said. She caught Reese's eye and saw that he was smiling.

The carriage stopped a few minutes later at the edge of an immense square. Reese was certainly right that it was a public place: There were crowds and crowds of people, moving in throngs like Emeline had never seen. They hustled along, carrying packages, pushing carts, shopping, and calling to each other. Some were walking small dogs on leashes, and others were lingering in the gardens at the square's center. The air rang with voices.

"All the latest fashions! Right here! The softest gloves!"

"Fresh strawberries from Willen! Who's for fresh strawberries?"

"Only the finest parchment and ink!"

Dale and Aladane gaped out the window. "That's the most people I've ever seen," Dale declared.

Dada and Fish looked dismayed.

"I've got a headache just looking at that," Fish said.

Reese opened the carriage door and stepped out, handing a single payt to the driver as the rest of them spilled out behind him. Emeline stumbled into Reese, but he didn't budge; he was as solid as a wall. Flustered, she turned quickly to look out at the storefronts lining the square.

They were two-storied and built of gray-white stone, but their bottom floors seemed to have no front walls; instead, they were wide open to the shoppers who came and went, reminding her of stalls at the market in Equane. But that was where the similarities ended.

"Now remember, boys, we're just sightseeing," Dada told them. "Don't start asking for things." Dale and Aladane nodded as one, but their eyes were shining with dangerous excitement.

"I'd like to look at some of those bullet-guns," Fish said.

"There's an artillery shop on the south end," Reese told him. He started forward and they followed at his heels like children.

In no time at all, there were far too many people around them for comfort. Head spinning, Emeline grabbed on to Dada's shirt while he held both Dale and Aladane by the shoulders in front of him.

A voice cried out for everyone to "Clear the way," and then a man with leather armbands rode by slowly on a steam-bicycle. People swore at him for taking up space.

A handsome young man with long hair plowed into Emeline and apologized, then gawked unflatteringly at her country clothes; a passing woman frowned at her through a single, blue-tinted eyeglass on a chain. Emeline pulled up her hood, disconcerted.

Two little boys ran pell-mell through the crowd with a

woman wearing bells chasing after them. Then a group of young girls sporting parti-color stockings under asymmetrical skirts sauntered by, giggling.

She was fascinated and alarmed all at once.

Dada stopped abruptly at a cluttered little shop lined with books. People stood inside squinting at the shelves, some through colored spectacles. Above the entryway, a cloth banner with embroidered letters read: HALATINE'S. Underneath in smaller letters was added NO DOGS, NO FOOD.

"Look at all those books," Dada said happily, sounding like he'd forgotten all talk of magic. Emeline smiled up at him as he patted at his coat pockets. "I could read for a year. Now all I need is my pipe!"

"Why don't you stay here while I have a look at the gun shop?" Fish suggested.

Dada hesitated and looked at Reese. "Is it wise for us to split up?"

"You'll be safe as long as you stay in the market," Reese said, scanning the crowd.

"Can we go with Fish?" Aladane asked. Fish frowned at that and Emeline didn't blame him. No one wanted to keep an eye on two rowdy boys in an artillery shop.

"No, you two stay with me," Dada said. "We'll go join him in a bit." He pushed the boys ahead of him into the bookstore. "Emeline, stay with Sir Reese."

Reese raised his eyebrows at her. "Is there anything you want to see?"

She shrugged. "Can we walk a bit? I want to see everything. We could follow Mister Fish." She winced as two laughing girls pushed past her; one of them wore a pair of wire wings and both had straight hair.

Everyone here had straight hair and *no one* wore bodices.

"Walk right behind me," Reese advised, starting off. On impulse, she reached out and gripped his shirt, like she had Dada's. He didn't seem to notice. She assumed that Fish was somewhere ahead of them, but she honestly had no idea.

In the crowd, they passed a man playing a strange-looking stringed instrument and serenading passersby; Emeline wondered if he was perhaps a Keldare. A little black dog raced up to Reese, its leash trailing behind. It jumped up and whimpered and licked the knight's hands, and Reese bent down and scruffed its thick fur all over. She peered around his side cautiously; she had only known one dog back in Equane and sometimes it bit. Spotting her, this one lunged and licked her right on the cheek.

She squealed and heard Reese's nice, deep laugh. It drew smiles from a few passing people. A man came rushing forward and pulled the dog away.

Reese froze suddenly, his eyes fixed on two old men standing near a column. She understood why when she saw their blue Sapient robes.

One was gesturing impatiently to the other, two liverymen waiting nearby as if expecting instructions. People gave them a wide berth as they passed.

Reese sped ahead and Emeline followed, trying not to catch the Sapients' attention. She kept her eyes on his broad back, but when she looked up again—she couldn't help it— one of the Sapients was staring straight at her, his gaze as cold as a snake's. She stumbled, clutching Reese's shirt, and he moved faster, pulling her along.

"—from the village family...?" she heard one of the Sapients say.

"It must be. Look at her cloak."

"Keep an eye out....They're—"

The rest was lost in a jumble of voices. By the time she looked back over her shoulder, the Sapients were hidden by the crowd.

Reese pushed forward into the market's central gardens, hurrying her down a path lined with bushes of curly red flowers.

"Those Sapients knew who we were," she said, under her breath.

"Of course they did. And I'm sure they've heard that we have quite a bit to say about Dark Creatures, and maybe an attempted murder," Reese muttered.

Emeline frowned at the bushes, fingering a spiraling petal. It felt strange to be whispered about by members of the king's council. Worse than strange. Frightening.

After a moment, she asked, "What kind of flowers are these?"

"My mother used to call them lady stars. They grow well in the north."

"They must like the cool weather."

He nodded, frowning slightly.

One of the fountains splashed nearby, glinting in the sun.

"Where is your mother now?" she asked.

"She takes care of my cousins back home with the money

I send. I was too late to save my father, though. He died before I made any." His face darkened. "You see, very poor people die of diseases you contract when you don't have quite enough food. And everyone else steps around them and holds their noses."

She could hear the sharp pain hidden in his voice, and she ached for him. She started to say *I'm sorry*, but then remembered how hollow the words had seemed when Mama died, and didn't.

"How could you afford to go to the academy?" she asked softly.

"I fought my way in," Reese said, folding his arms. "I fought every rich man's son, all of them older than me, until I caught someone's attention. Then they let me in on charity and I became the academy joke...and the star pupil." He turned away and wandered toward the fountain, a simple stone bowl on a pedestal.

There was one small, white water lily bobbing near the edge. It called to her; her fingertips tingled.

"In Equane, we don't use money," she said, watching the lily. "Even though I've heard about it, I've never really thought about having any."

"Buying things gives people something to do," Reese told her.

"But there was always something to do at home, even without money," she said, surprised. He was looking at her closely now, his green eyes kind.

"There was always something to do in Aliddser," he agreed.

"Like what?" she asked, smiling.

He smirked, suddenly a mischievous little boy again. "I used to chase the sheep and make them stampede through town." She laughed. "I used to try to pluck feathers from wild birds to sell to hat makers, but mostly I got pecked to death for my trouble. I slid on the ice when the lake froze, and hunted for sweet root to eat.... And I challenged all the boys to fight."

Emeline grinned, quite able to picture it. His expression turned shy, and he glanced away.

"That's the Ironers," he said, pointing.

She looked up to see a small, crowded shop across the square, its entrance framed by floor-length red curtains tied back with cords. "The women have their hair flattened there with hot irons. It's the style."

Emeline gasped. "*That's* why everyone has straight hair!"

He grimaced and nodded. "Don't do it. I mean—do, if you like. It's your hair." He cleared his throat gruffly. "But it's ridiculous for everyone to look the same."

"I won't." But she pulled her hood up self-consciously and muttered, "I should have known it wasn't just my bodice making me stand out."

Reese broke into the same wide grin that she had seen at the practice field. "No living man would object to you wearing that."

She blushed furiously and looked away, unable to meet his gaze.

"I do like the caps the girls here wear," she murmured.

"And I like curly hair," Reese told her. "The Keldare

family that used to come through Aliddser all had red curls. They gave me food, even though they barely had any for themselves. In fact, one of them used to whistle the way you did for the carriage earlier," he added.

She laughed, her heart warming. Now she understood why he had been so impressed by the sight of Dale's armbands.

"My mama used to do that," she said. Then it occurred to her to ask him, "Why do some of the girls here wear wings?"

He snorted. "I don't know where that fashion came from, but I've heard that the Sapients don't like it."

"Because people don't really have wings?" she asked, still smiling.

"And the idea comes from folk stories—'nonsense.'"

"Well, I like it," she said.

"Emeline!" Dada called. She jumped, and turned to see him and Fish waving at her. Dale and Aladane dashed over to her and Reese.

"Fish bought a bullet-gun!" Dale exclaimed. "It was only two payts!"

"I imagine it's a beauty," Reese said, raising his eyebrows.

"The man in the shop said it's really old, but it still works!" Dale continued. "It came with five iron bullets!"

"What are you two doing over here?" Aladane asked. "We're hungry. Your dada wants us all together again, Em. He says we should go back to the Mother's Milk."

Reese grimaced. "Quaith took you to *that* place?"

Emeline couldn't resist. "The girls there seem to like you."

Reese flushed red and frowned. She laughed, and the boys looked at each other, mystified.

"Well, their coffee drink was awful," Aladane announced.

"Al spit up on Emeline," Dale said cheerfully.

The other boy was aghast. "Don't tell him that!"

"Should we eat somewhere else?" Dale asked Reese, who looked amused now.

"We have to go to Mother's Milk because we don't have money," Emeline reminded him, but her heart dropped at the thought of separating from Reese. She wanted to keep talking to him, about anything.

"I'll take you." Reese turned and led them through the garden, cutting across the square's center. Emeline decided not to mention the Sapients that had been watching her. Not yet. She hated to see Dada worry.

"Bird, you should've seen this contraption they were selling from the Outer Lands," Fish said from behind them, shaking his head. She looked back to see his new, leather-handled bullet-gun slung on his belt opposite his spring-gun. "It had a torch and some kind of propellant to shoot bursts of fire! Now that's a trick."

"No way!" Aladane exclaimed. "A *fire*-gun?"

"How did the shop get it from the Outer Lands?" Dale asked.

"Someone must've traded for it at the harbor," Dada told him.

"I'm sure they brought it in past the port. Sellers aren't fond of that harbor tax," Reese commented. Then he grimaced and added, "Don't repeat that."

"Don't repeat what?" Dale asked, missing the remark.

"If I told you, I'd be repeating it," Reese told him, and Emeline laughed.

"Oh yeah. But what did you say?" Dale insisted.

"That the king only eats fish from Equane. He considers it a delicacy."

"Yeah, right. The king's never heard of Equane," Dale said good-naturedly. Reese smiled and walked ahead.

seventeen

They followed Reese out onto a wide street, where carriages steamed past and stylish people strode by. On one side was a small lot under construction, with a long wooden wall around it to protect pedestrians from the stonework. Emeline could hear the roar of machinery and the shouts of voices over the wall, but she couldn't see the workers.

"What are they building there?" Dale asked.

"It's too soon to tell, son," Fish said, trying to peer over.

There was writing on the wooden wall, and she stopped to read it. Some of it was in chalk, some in ink, and some even looked like it was in paint.

TINDA LOVES SENINE with a heart.

LONG LIVE THE KING—followed by a morbid IT WON'T BE LONG . . . in different handwriting.

ARRANE IS A FOOL! and NEVER EAT AT HOT STONE CAFÉ.

A man in dust-splattered clothes was painting over a passage on one end.

"Look!" Aladane said, pointing at what he was covering. Emeline gasped.

The message was scrawled in large, messy red letters: BEWARE THE ITHIN!

The Equanians stopped and instinctively huddled together. Emeline shivered and tried not to think of the Ithin's terrible face in the manor, moonlight shining on its claws.

"Was there a sighting?" Dada asked Reese quietly.

"There can't have been! There aren't any woods," Fish protested.

Reese shook his head, watching the worker paint a swath of brown over THE ITHIN and then BEWARE.

"No, but I've seen that before. The Sapients haven't convinced everyone of their position, that's for sure." The warning was gone, and the painter moved a few paces to begin work on the next message; he seemed as unconcerned as Reese. "The Theurgists haven't either."

The knight continued on and they followed, Emeline glancing back at the blank face of the wall.

Soon they reached buildings that didn't look quite like shops or houses: They had small, shutterless windows, and there were few front gardens. People bustled in and out of them, carrying packages, satchels, and sheets of paper. Small groups of men dressed in long, dark-colored coats stood in doorways together, talking in serious tones; several of them wore lifted shoes that made them taller, and quite a few of them looked down their noses at the villagers. Emeline grit her teeth. Reese was walking faster now, as if eager to get through.

"If the council would ever respond to my request, these affairs could be wrapped up," a man complained to a lady with a large black hat as the two of them rushed by, carrying papers.

A woman poked her head out of a window and called, "Messenger! Come back, I forgot the signature!" A man on a bicycle loaded up with packages wheeled back toward her.

Not far behind the bicycle messenger, Emeline noticed a handsome young man in livery. He met her gaze, froze, then ducked into the doorway of a nearby building.

What did that mean?

Then it dawned on her: That liveryman resembled one of the two that she'd seen with the Sapients in the market. He was already walking along the road again in their direction. This time, he ducked his head and stopped to wipe something invisible from his shoe when she looked at him.

"He came in late yesterday too! He's just not apprentice material," a man in a striped coat announced to his companion; Emeline had almost walked into him. His tiny leashed dog attempted to dart straight for Reese, but was quickly restrained.

She looked back again. The liveryman was closer now, but he had stopped abruptly to peer through a window. She was certain he had been with the Sapients.

Had they sent him to follow her? The thought filled her stomach with ice.

"Folks are busy around here, aren't they?" Fish said.

"This is part of the business district," Reese told him.

"Sir Reese," Emeline spoke up, moving very close to him. "There's someone behind us." The knight turned carefully to look, his eyes narrowed.

"There's all kinds of people behind us," Aladane said with a look of disbelief.

"See the servant, near the garden?" Emeline asked Reese.

He nodded, unsurprised. "That one was with the Sapients."

"What Sapients?" Dada asked quickly.

"We saw two of them in the market," she explained reluctantly. She hated to scare him—but maybe he needed to be scared. Maybe they all did.

Now that all of them were looking at him, the liveryman wheeled about casually and walked in the other direction.

"What's going on?" Fish asked Reese.

"I think he was following us." Emeline bit her lip.

"Perhaps they thought we were headed to our secret meeting with the Theurgists," Reese said drily. He started walking again, but Dada stopped him.

"Should we go back to the inn?"

"I don't think we're in danger at the moment." Reese pointed to an iron gateway up ahead that marked an open courtyard; a broad building of white stone stood beyond it. "This is one of the most esteemed institutions in the capital, Mister Bird, the A.A.S. I believe you wished to see an academy?"

"What's A.A.S.?" Dada asked, reluctantly interested.

"Academy of Arts and Science, officially, but nowadays I'd call it Arts vs. Science," Reese replied. "A very public place, full of students and their professors. Despite the heated demagoguery that goes on, it is quite safe."

Dada nodded, but he put a protective arm around Emeline as they followed Reese toward the gateway and into the courtyard. She glanced up at the arch overhead and saw a banner stretched below it: PUBLIC DEMONSTRATION—AUTOMATONS, 1 O'CLOCK.

Beyond it, the courtyard was filled with many benches, most of them occupied by young people with their noses inside books. The white building had double doors propped open upon a marble veranda, and there was an enormous, ancient-looking iron clock above them. A plaque read: ROYAL ACADEMY OF ARTS & SCIENCE, EST. 981.

"Prepare yourselves for real excitement. It seems there's a demonstration in half an hour," Reese declared, eyeing the clock. Emeline grinned at his bored tone.

"What are auto-may-tons?" Dale asked him.

"No idea." Reese led the way toward the academy steps.

Aladane looked around at the people on the benches. "What's everyone reading?"

"It's school. They're studying," Emeline told him. The students were catching sight of them; a Lash Knight leading around a family of villagers was obviously an unusual sight at the academy. Some of the students frowned at the Equanians, eyeing them up and down.

A girl about Emeline's age walked out through the double doors without looking ahead, scribbling on a pamphlet. She tripped on the first step and stumbled the rest of the way; Reese made a quick move toward her, but she righted herself. One of the reading boys looked up and laughed.

"You're going to fall into a fountain one of these days!" he called out.

"It's this Mechanics lecture! The reading is so dense," the girl snapped. "And if you studied half as hard as me, you'd know what I meant!"

Reese led the way around them and up the steps, in

through the open doors. Inside, a great stone statue of a man gazing up at the sky—well, at the chamber's vaulted ceiling—greeted them. Emeline was startled by how lifelike he was: The sculptor had labored over every detail, from the folds in his robe to the veins in his skin. He held a large book in one hand, the other palm up.

An engraved plaque at his feet read: THE WONDER OF IT ALL: ENGER III, 1214. Emeline felt herself smile. This great man admiring the sky reminded her of Mama.

They followed Reese into a large chamber full of paintings and tapestries, most of them very old; students they passed tried not to gawk. Above, a circular ceiling of colored glass glowed in the sunlight, shafting reds and greens onto the marble floor.

"This lobby is a small museum called The Enger," Reese said, ignoring the students. "It's a good place to wait for the presentation to start."

"Boys, don't touch anything," Dada ordered. Even though worry was written in every line of his face, he approached the walls eagerly to examine the artwork.

Emeline moved toward a large painting of mountains glowing pink from a sunrise. The paint was so thick and soft-looking that she wanted to touch it. A plaque read: "The Spine at Dawn, *Lord Saunden, 1003. Saunden was renowned for his landscape paintings, many of which have been lost. The Spine at Dawn is a new addition to the Enger Museum, donated by descendants.*"

She couldn't believe the painting was that old—it looked so freshly done. She gazed around her again, marveling.

"Airlinna would've loved this place," Dada said softly. His face was sad and Emeline took his hand, afraid to say anything. He squeezed it.

Something caught Emeline's eye. It was a smaller piece, done in charcoal. It showed a man in crude armor, his sword drawn, facing some beast she couldn't identify. It was made almost entirely of wings—broken, jagged wings that flapped at different angles, keeping it aloft strangely tilted.

The plaque read: "Answor and the Torment of Hollolen, *Unknown, 800s. The town of Hollolen was plagued with an unnamed winged creature for decades before the young Answor finally destroyed it.*"

There was a smaller, newer-looking plaque underneath the first one, which said: *"Popular legend. No physical evidence of the monster in Hollolen exists."*

Added by the Sapients, Emeline thought, amused. She looked for another piece of art that had two plaques and found one quickly. It was an intricate tapestry that showed a dense forest in twilight. Among the branches of the trees, there were several pairs of slanted, yellow eyes, bright as the moon stitched above them. In the foreground, staring up in terror, were two children holding hands.

The first plaque said: "Beware the Gossings, *probably Minane the Wanderer, early 900s. Minane was a popular figure throughout the kingdom for his stories, artwork, and songs.*"

She read the second plaque quickly: *"Minane's tales were highly embellished versions of different legends, none of them based on fact."*

"Unknown, thought to be 700s," Dale read aloud from a plaque under a threadbare tapestry. "The 700s? I never heard of anything that old!"

"It's before the calendar starts," a surprised voice interrupted. An older woman in an elegant black-and-silver striped dress stood behind them, her expression rather severe.

"What do you mean?" Aladane asked, undaunted as ever by intimidating elders.

"Goodness, child. Don't you know how the calendar works?" she asked, shocked. "King Kindad set it at 900, marking the number of days it took to build the first border separating the kingdom from the Outer Lands. Everything dated before then is approximate."

"I never knew that," Fish said to Dada, impressed.

"Madam Professor, do you know what became of the items in that case?" Reese asked the lady. He pointed at a large glass cabinet with mirrored shelves in the opposite corner.

"Hmmph, yes. Those were the 'magical' items the Theurgists displayed," she said with a frown. "Old rings and silverwork and other such baubles. They have all been placed under the care of the Sapients to determine their authenticity."

Reese stared at her, obviously familiar with the "magical items" to which she referred. "Those objects were taken out?"

"Yes. The Sapients removed them with permission from the king himself," she told him, amused at his surprise. "And the Theurgists are livid, of course. They are forever bringing in items of dubious origin."

"That's not fair," Emeline said, looking at Reese. "Do the Theurgists get to take out things that the Sapients bring in?"

"Oh, yes," the professor said. "Often."

"That's ridiculous," Dada said angrily, but the woman had swept out the doors. "The council's bickering shouldn't have anything to do with art."

"I agree," Reese muttered as the great clock out front struck one o'clock. "Let's go see the presentation."

Back in the courtyard, the students were moving aside the benches and clearing space. Reese stepped off to one side and the others followed, curious. Several more students came out the academy doors, carrying a table between them, and an elderly man in a Sapient's cloak strode out behind them.

"Bless water, there's one right here," Fish muttered.

Dada tensed and put his arm around Emeline.

Reese frowned, looking back toward the courtyard entrance where a small assembly was filing in. "I assumed it was only a student demonstration. Let's just stay with the crowd," he murmured to Dada and Fish.

Dada put a hand on each of the boys' shoulders. "Don't draw attention to yourselves, understand?" They nodded, a little confused.

Gray-haired and bespectacled, the Sapient was directing a student carrying a box when three more Sapients appeared from inside. They were two women and one man, each wearing spectacles or holding single lenses up to their eyes. None of the lenses were colored, of course.

Their embroidered cloaks were stunning when they stood together—beautifully detailed and bright blue in the sunlight. Like Rellum, their sharp, focused eyes belied their ages. They held themselves very straight.

From the box, the students pulled a collection of metal segments: gears, joints, and wires. For a moment, Emeline thought they were parts of a complicated clock, but as the students began to fit them together she realized they were building a figurine of a person, about two feet high.

"It's a doll," she said, astonished. She looked at Reese and saw that he was watching intently. More people were filing into the courtyard now, whispering and shuffling against one another.

"A doll?" Aladane groaned. "I thought this was going to be important." Dada shushed him just as one of the Sapients cleared her throat loudly for their attention.

"Ladies and gentleman, I would like to thank you all for taking the time to attend this latest demonstration from the Royal Sapients," the woman announced. "As you all know, these demonstrations are intended to spread the latest knowledge and showcase innovations achieved through education and science."

The students had finished assembling the metal figurine and were fiddling with something on its back. It was eerily void of expression, with glass eyes, no nose, and a heavy, jointed jaw.

"I wouldn't give that doll to the worst child in the kingdom," Fish muttered.

"Today, we are pleased to demonstrate the latest advancements in automation. As some of you may already know, the figure you see before you is an automaton, a mechanical figure that can be commanded to move through the power of electricity. At this moment, instructions are being punched into a panel on its back." The Sapient tapped the nearest

student helper with her eyeglass, impatiently. Flustered, the girl quickly snapped the doll's panel shut.

The courtyard had filled up now and Emeline's view was blocked by several hats. She and Dale bobbed their heads, trying to see. Was the doll really going to move on its own?

Glancing back into the crowd, she caught sight of two old men in long robes standing near the archway. Their cloaks were like the Sapients', except they were silver velvet instead of blue, and stitched with stars instead of wheels.

Theurgists! Emeline gaped at them a moment and then ducked her head. *Both* sides of the royal council were there— and she was standing in the middle. She took a deep, steadying breath.

Not one of them knows about your magic, Emeline. Not one. Not one.

The metal man on the table still stood motionless. The student helpers were glancing at one another nervously, as if afraid that nothing would happen after all.

Then the glass eyes glowed. The metal man's hand twitched and it raised its arm stiffly.

"Bless water," Dada breathed as Emeline gasped.

The automaton's fingers opened in a sudden spasm, and then it saluted the crowd. Several people cheered—in fact, the capital folk seemed more appreciative than surprised.

The doll moved its legs next, taking two steps forward across the table.

"Wow!" Dale said. "Al, look!" He dragged Aladane up from where he sat as the crowd murmured its approval. Aladane let out a weird yelp and stared.

The automaton was walking now, marching slowly and stiffly from one end of the table to the other. Emeline was frozen with shock, and she could see that Dada and Mister Fish were too.

As the automaton walked, it turned its unsettling face to "look" at the crowd. Several people laughed, but Emeline shuddered, despite her fascination.

"You can always rely on the Sapients to bring more beauty into the world," Reese said darkly. His green eyes were bright with interest, however, as he watched the metal man turn itself carefully around.

"What in the kingdom will they think up next?" Fish said, shaking his head. "What's it for, anyhow? Children don't need walking dolls."

"I don't think it's a toy," Dada told him, staring at the living machine. "This is just...an example."

"As you can see, the automaton can follow simple commands and carry out basic tasks," the Sapient said in her gravelly voice. "As some of you may be aware, this is simply a few steps forward in a not entirely new technology. Lord Irwind was developing much more sophisticated automation, before his unfortunate departure."

The king's brother, Emeline remembered.

The automaton stopped strutting back and forth, and stood in the center of the table, its head swiveling left and right. Then it took a careful bow and the crowd applauded. Emeline clapped, too, and the boys cheered—until Dada hushed them.

"As always, we will leave you with the reminder that, in this, the year 1356, there are many new wondrous areas of study to be found at the A.A.S., as well as the Graybon and Bastine Academies," the Sapient continued. "And thankfully, these studies discredit much of the superstitions and old wives' tales that still hold sway over the minds of many an intelligent individual. Thank you, again, for attending."

There were a few disgruntled murmurs in the crowd as she and the other Sapients bowed their heads.

Emeline looked quickly for the two silver-cloaked Theurgists, but she couldn't find them. Perhaps they had marched out in disgust. The Sapients began directing the students to disassemble the metal man, and people in the front of the crowd turned to one another to chat.

But then a loud voice floated up from the direction of the archway.

"Ladies and gentlemen, after that vulgar display, perhaps you'd consider directing your attention to a more elegant discussion!"

Heads turned swiftly. The two men in silver were standing under the banner, the sun sparkling off their cloaks. One was small, thin, and white-haired, the other tall and balding.

"The smaller one is Helid Theurgist," Reese said quietly, in Emeline's ear. She gasped.

Everyone strained to see the man that Rellum believed had tried to have him killed. He had tiny dark eyes that glittered fiercely out of a wrinkled, light brown face, and his mouth was a thin line. The crowd readily gave the Theurgists their attention, even as the Sapients glared over their heads.

"Excuse me! This is *our* public demonstration!" the lead Sapient called out indignantly.

"Your chance to sway the public, you mean!" the balding Theurgist retorted.

"Someone must protect them from your *nonsense!*" she exclaimed, then cleared her throat, as if embarrassed by her outburst. The student helpers grinned at one another as they gathered up the equipment.

"So this is how the royal council behaves?" Dada asked, concerned.

"Like old folks bickering in the market!" Fish exclaimed.

"A fairly accurate description," Reese agreed.

"The Sapients can play with their machinery, but will it protect you from dark magic or Dark Creatures?" Helid called out to the crowd. "My fellow Theurgists and I have committed ourselves of late to research in the mysterious Vindane region, and we have made new discoveries!"

The crowd murmured excitedly and drew closer. Emeline remembered the Vindane region on the map of the kingdom, so painfully close to dense woods.

"Oh, please, Helid! Not Vindane again?" the Sapient with spectacles protested. There were some titters from the crowd.

Helid ignored her. "We've been studying the flora and fauna in areas where magical activity has been reported— Dark Creature sightings, curses that have manifested, and the like. As you may or may not know, we believe that magic— especially dark magic—can linger in an area until it curdles and spoils.

"I am certain that most of you have heard the story of Quilane's living dolls? The ones who violently avenged him after he was beaten by his neighbors? They were far more efficient than the mechanical one we've just seen, unfortunately for the people of Kriln. A Vindane event."

"Yeah, but that's just a story," someone spoke up. Emeline spotted a young student with green spectacles.

"No, there are records from witnesses!" another person called out.

"It's a folktale to stop people from feuding...."

"Like the royal council!" someone else hollered, and then there were shouts of laughter. They were followed by a scuffle, as if the speaker had turned and run quickly. Reese chuckled.

Helid scowled, but he quickly held up his hand. "Rest assured, I have not come here today to repeat that tale! Even if there *were* many witnesses indeed. Rather, my colleague and I would like to present to you what we discovered when we journeyed to that long-abandoned village of Kriln, and examined the area in which Quilane's dolls committed their murders." His eyes gleamed as the crowd fell silent again.

"Murders?" Fish grunted.

"It would seem that our theory of lingering magical effects is correct. No one has returned to Kriln after those terrible deaths many years ago—it has sat empty and derelict, slowly overgrown by the great woods around it. But, as we discovered, the plant life there has taken quite an interesting turn."

Helid gestured to his companion, who pulled a large satchel from his shoulder. Emeline strained to see what he took from it: a great glass orb the size of a man's head, filled with something green and black.

One of the Sapients snapped with impatience. "Helid, no one present is foolish enough to believe in some doctored specimen—"

The onlookers gasped as Helid and the other Theurgist held up the orb in full view. Inside the glass was the most contorted plant that Emeline had ever seen. Its long leaves were horned, twisted, and blackened. Bulbous growths on its stem sagged. It was bent so sharply that it seemed to have almost slithered into position.

"Bless water, what is that thing?" Dada murmured.

"Behold the schefflera plant of Kriln, poisoned by dark magic!" Helid exclaimed.

"I've never seen anything like it!"

"Maybe it's just diseased?"

"It's blighted, for sure. You don't need magic for that!"

"Is that even a schefflera?"

"This plant shall be on display shortly in the museum in the King's Hall!" Helid said. "Everyone will be able to view it on Public Days and decide for themselves!"

Half the people in the courtyard cheered with a surprising, unsettling enthusiasm. Clearly, the Sapients did not hold as much sway over the capital's residents as they wanted.

"Let this be a reminder to you all that the Theurgists are working constantly to learn more about magic and how best to defend the kingdom," Helid announced, his expression very smug. His companion quickly tucked the plant back into his satchel.

The Sapients were arguing with one another, indecipherable over the excited voices of the crowd.

"Is that plant real?" Dale asked Dada eagerly.

"I have no idea," Dada answered thinly.

Reese was frowning, watching the Sapients stomp back up the steps into the academy. "The question is, will that plant actually make it into the museum?" he said quietly. "Or will it mysteriously disappear from Helid's quarters?"

"You mean the Sapients might steal it?" Aladane exclaimed loudly.

"Be quiet!" Fish and Dada whispered, startling him.

"How come Dale never gets shushed?"

"Because he's not blurting out accusations!" Emeline snapped.

"I see what you mean," Dada muttered to Reese. "If a Theurgist could consider murder, a Sapient well might consider theft."

The knight nodded.

"And don't think for a moment that that automaton is safe either. We should go," Reese said as the crowd began to dissipate. Some people went into the academy, but most were filing out under the arch. They headed in the same direction.

"Sir Reese!" a commanding voice broke through. Emeline jumped.

Helid himself was approaching them, the balding Theurgist and a silver-liveried guard flanking him. She shrank back instinctively.

"Helid Theurgist," Reese greeted him coolly.

Helid tilted his head back to look up at him shrewdly. Then his bright gaze flickered over Dada and Fish.

"Welcome home, young knight. I've heard that you had

quite the adventure in Blyne, one involving my colleague Rel-lum Sapient," he said mildly.

"Indeed," Reese replied. There was a short silence.

"Since I know him well, I imagine he discussed certain unfounded suspicions with you. But I do hope you weren't foolish enough to believe him." Helid smiled without warmth. "In fact, it would be most *unwise* to follow him down that tunnel."

Reese's expression darkened.

"But you both have tunnels, don't you?" he asked in a stony voice. "Much like that noble beast the weasel."

Helid's eyes flashed, and they glared at each other for several moments. "I would mind my tongue if I were you, young knight," he snapped, finally.

Then he turned to look at Dada, who bowed his head warily.

"I assume this is the family that brings tidings of Ithin in their village woods." He clasped his hands together in satisfaction, his voice unbearably arrogant. "I so look forward to hearing their story! I'm delighted that it will finally convince the king of our position."

The other Theurgist whispered to him; Emeline heard something about "the museum." Helid nodded and announced, "I'm afraid we have more pressing matters to attend to. Good day!"

The two of them marched away, their guard following.

The villagers watched unhappily.

"Let's go. Now," Dada said.

Reese led them back through the gateway. The group of

them piled up against him as the last of the crowd bottle-necked there; Emeline was pressed against him, suddenly very aware of the warmth that came from his back and broad shoulders.

"Dada, how did they make the automaton move around like that?" Dale asked.

"It's a machine, Dale. Its insides must look something like a clock's," Dada explained, exhausted.

"But they didn't wind it up, Bird. And it's not steam-powered, either," Fish said, scratching his head. "As far as I'm concerned, that was a living doll, just like the ones Helid mentioned."

"But he said those dolls hurt people," Dale said. He looked at Emeline and murmured, "Do you think that kind of magic was Keldare, like yours?"

"No." Reese had turned his head to listen. "Hers is much more elegant," he said, and looked away.

eighteen

Reese hailed a red carriage to take them back to the Mother's Milk. Dada had wanted to return to the royal inn immediately, but everyone was hungry, and he had to admit they didn't have much of their own food left.

The carriage took them past a park where children were playing games Emeline didn't recognize—something with short sticks used to keep a lightweight ball aloft. The air was full of silvery jingling from the bells they wore.

"Imagine if we wore bells like that at home," Aladane said to Dale, watching the capital children with scorn. "Dale, we'd be outcasts!"

Emeline snorted as the carriage pulled up in front of the Mother's Milk; the idea of the Equane schoolhouse having standards in style made her laugh. But Aladane was somewhat popular with the girls, while Dale was oblivious, so she supposed it made sense that he was more aware of his image.

"We *ought* to tie some bells on that boy," Fish told Dada, nodding at Aladane. "It'd be a lot harder for him to stow away in wagons."

As the group of them piled out of the carriage, Emeline looked up at Reese hopefully, thinking perhaps he would eat with them. The knight stood looking in through the windows, then turned to meet Emeline's gaze.

She looked away, suddenly embarrassed—it was silly of her to want him to stay with them.

What was she thinking? What could come of it anyway?

"Thank you again for showing us around, Sir Reese," Dada told him, smiling warmly. "And for keeping us safe."

Reese nodded, running his hand through his hair. "I regret dismissing the guards that Quaith left you. Someone should be with you at dinner."

"Could we eat with you and the knights?" Dale blurted out.

Reese snorted, taken aback. "I'm afraid they aren't all as charming as I am."

"Do you eat special food?" Aladane asked.

"Yes, we eat knight food," Reese said, deadpan.

"Do you eat in the hall with the king?" Dale asked.

"No, His Majesty eats alone in his chambers."

"What about the Sapients and the Theurgists?"

"They tend to keep to themselves as well."

"And the servants?"

"Will you two stop asking questions?" Fish exclaimed. "You're giving me a headache."

"But we're not asking you," Aladane pointed out.

"Al," Dada warned.

"Do you have to eat dinner in the hall or can you eat anywhere you want?" Dale asked Reese.

"Do you have to pay money for it in the hall?" Aladane chimed in.

Reese gave Emeline an incredulous look. She smiled and shook her head, signaling that it was hopeless.

"Couldn't we eat with you? Please?" Dale pressed Reese.

"Dale, that's enough," Dada cut in quickly. "Sir Reese

has spent enough of his time with us. He has things to do."
The boys fell silent obediently, but they looked at Reese with
hopeful eyes. "We should get back in touch with Quaith. Sir
Reese is right. We need more protection."

"Quaith will be at dinner in the hall," Reese told them
slowly. "...I suppose you may as well come with me and kill
two birds with one stone."

Dale and Aladane grinned at each other triumphantly,
and Emeline bit down a smile. Reese looked at her and then
away again quickly. She felt her heartbeat quicken.

Did he want to spend more time with her, as she did with
him? Was he worried about her? Or was he just protecting a
royal witness?

"Are you sure? Will it cause any trouble?" Dada asked him.

Reese shook his head and started in the direction of the
hall's silver gates, the same ones where the other knights had
called out for entrance. She lagged behind a little as the others followed him, nervous, even when the guards opened the
gates at Reese's command. What would the fine folk on the
other side think of her and her family?

Beyond the gates, there was a pathway of polished stones,
stretching out ahead into shadow. Reese gave Emeline a concerned look, suddenly, as she made sense of the source of that
shadow.

Trees. It was a forest.

She froze, and he put a steadying hand on her arm.

"Is that...?" Dale asked.

"Woods!" Dada exclaimed. He and Fish stepped back,
horrified.

"It's all right," Reese told them. "This is the king's private grove. It is safe. I swear." His large, warm hand on Emeline's arm comforted her more than his words.

"The king has a grove? Has he gone mad?!" Fish demanded. Dale was frowning nervously. Aladane's mouth hung open.

Reese looked as if he were about to make a sharp reply, but then thought better of it. "It is completely disconnected from the world outside this wall, and it always has been," he said patiently. "It's a thousand years old. I assure you, it's absolutely safe. The king himself takes walks inside it whenever he is well enough."

"Why ever would he do that?" Fish muttered, shuddering.

Emeline took a small step forward. A safe forest? Was it possible? Reese let her arm go, watching her. The trees sighed softly in a breeze.

"Because...it's beautiful," she breathed. It had never really dawned on her before, that woods were beautiful as well as dangerous. And if one could remove the danger...?

"There should be a moat," Dada said. He stopped Dale from moving to follow her.

"If His Majesty had ever seen anything like what we saw back at that old manor, I imagine he would've told one of his knights," Reese said calmly. He stepped out onto the path and Emeline followed hesitantly, the others hanging back. Behind them, the silver doors were cranking closed, wound by a massive winch.

Then the gates were shut, and they were alone in the woods.

Fear swelled up inside her. The family padded anxiously after Reese, listening to the stirring of leaves and branches, smelling the bark and the damp earth. The trees blocked out most of the evening sky.

The image of the Ithin in the cottage flared up and she closed her eyes. *How can we do this?*

"Is this the only way in?" Aladane whimpered.

"This doesn't feel right at all," Fish muttered. Beautiful or not, it was a primal fear they were facing now.

There was no sign of the King's Hall ahead; the wood was too thick. A single lighted pole marked a division in the path, and Reese turned left, glancing back at Emeline. She followed slowly, feeling like she was in a dream, a dream that could turn into a nightmare at any moment. But she trusted Reese. She trusted Reese.

"Emeline, stay close," Dada said, low.

Reese reached another lighted fork in the path and they all hurried after him. There was a small stone fountain near the fork, carved into the shape of a boy pouring water.

"Water!" Dale whispered. He and Fish immediately plunged their hands into the basin, splashing themselves thoroughly.

A flock of birds suddenly burst into the air from the tree-tops. Aladane squawked. He and Dale broke into a run and Dada started after them, Fish following.

Emeline almost sprang off, too, but she stopped and looked at Reese, her heart hammering. Surely the hall was close now! Surely they were almost there! Why didn't he say so?

"Go left!" Reese yelled after her family, upsetting another

group of birds. His green eyes sparkled and she realized that he was trying not to laugh. Her temper flared.

"Are we entertaining you?" she demanded, repeating his remark from the practice field. But her voice was shaky.

He did laugh then, but to her relief, there was nothing mean-spirited about it: It was a little embarrassed. "I'm sorry. I suppose quite a few terrified villagers have raced through here over the years."

She nodded, the warmth from his laugh thawing her. She forgave him. They walked together quietly until they came upon a yawning doorway in a stone wall. Just inside it, Dada and Fish stood panting, the boys gaping back out at the trees.

"Emeline!" Dada called, relieved, and she rushed to join them. Reese strode in afterward and wisely said nothing as the villagers collected themselves.

They were in a high-ceilinged corridor. Several enormous, deteriorating tapestries hung from the walls, protected by panels of spotless glass. The floor was covered in smooth blue tiles, polished clean.

"Are there any more trees?" Aladane panted. "I don't think I can run anymore."

"I guess it's a good way to keep people out, anyway," Fish grumbled, peering back into the grove.

Trying not to smile, Reese led the way down the corridor. There was an armored figure standing up ahead, but Emeline quickly realized it was just an empty suit on display. It was the black armor of a Lash Knight, well-polished, but the dark plates looked thinner, much less impenetrable than Reese's suit. Like the tapestries, it was very old.

"Who did that belong to?" Aladane's voice still sounded breathless.

"Sir Rengle," Reese said.

"The first Lash Knight!" Dale exclaimed. He darted over to the armor shell.

"Not the first. Just the first to wear the black armor," Reese told him, sounding distracted. He glanced at Emeline as the others stopped to admire Sir Rengle's suit.

"Why does the helmet look like a dog's muzzle?" she asked.

"Because we're faithful to the king." He lowered his voice. "The other knights at dinner…I was serious when I said they're not as charming as I am." There was only a trace of sarcasm in the words.

She searched his face for a moment, unsure whether he meant that the knights would be unpleasant to her family, or to him, in front of them. She remembered the knight in the field who had thrown knives at him out of turn, and wanted to take his hand. But she couldn't, of course.

"It's all right," she said instead.

The corridor bent to the right and opened up into a crowded hall, the air filled with the hum of footfalls and voices. Gone was the blue-tiled floor of the outer corridor, replaced with a very old stone, worn so smooth by age that her boots slid. There were tall, dark windows on one side, paned in colored glass that would glimmer in daylight. The people bustling by included guards in leathers and upper servants in motley; snatches of conversation reached her ears.

"…And then the cook threw a pan at him! The whole kitchen was laughing…!"

"...*Sir Dinta was on board when the captain fell ill....*"

"...*Have you done the curtains yet? The ones in the library...*"

The crowd parted for a tall young woman striding along in a flowing, gold-embroidered dress, her dark hair coiled elegantly around her head, her bronze skin glowing. Was this a fine lady like the kitchen girls at the Mother's Milk had mentioned? Emeline looked sideways at Reese, but he gave no sign of even seeing her. Perhaps he was used to such beauty.

A lady's maid in a short cotehardie and wide-legged trousers followed the lady, checking a page in a small book. "And you have dinner with his father afterward, so may I suggest..."

Then they were gone, replaced by a group of boys dressed like the ones that brought the knights their weapons on the practice field. Squires? They wore the same brown tunics, and they were elbowing one another and laughing.

Dale bumped into one of them and the boy yelled, "Watch it, ragtag!"

Emeline shot him a look and he smirked back at her. *Brat.*

"Why does it take so many people to run this place?" Fish asked, bewildered.

"I'm not convinced it does," Reese replied.

"That's what I figured," the farmer muttered.

Reese led them through an archway into a large, grand room with a vaulted ceiling. It was lined with many tables and chairs, all of them trimmed in silver. In fact, everything in the room glinted with silver, even the plates and glasses carried by servers in royal blue livery. An enormous, elaborate cluster of lights dangled from the cavernous ceiling, putting the fixtures in the villagers' rooms to shame.

There were also colored-glass windows that looked out into the dusky woods. Emeline quickly averted her eyes from them.

At the tables, there were a few Lash Knights still half-dressed in their armor, but many were dressed like Reese—most of them were large, strapping men uncomfortably squeezed into their seats. There were also men and women dressed like Quaith in trim coats and motley trousers.

"That's a bird!" Aladane declared, pointing at the meat on the plates. "Look, that's a wing. Is it good?"

"When they don't burn it." Reese sauntered toward one of the side tables where empty plates and a spread of food were waiting: rolls of bread with nuts baked in; strange-looking, colorful salads; lumpy roots in a brown sauce; plenty of meat; and a yellow stew smelling of garlic. The scents were intoxicating, even if the sights were strange, and Emeline felt hungrier than she had expected.

Carrying their plates, the Equanians followed Reese past many staring eyes to a table with empty seats. He sat down with a thump and began to eat with no comment. There was some bustle as the boys moved to sit together, and then they were all seated and poking at the strange food.

"Hello!" a familiar voice said.

Emeline looked up to see Innish standing at the table. He had cleaned up since they'd seen him last, and wore an embroidered vest over black trousers, the same necklace chain still disappearing under his shirt. He was holding a silver mug.

"Hello, Innish," Dada said, and Fish nodded, chewing.

"I didn't expect to see you with us at dinner. How are you finding the capital?" Innish pulled out the empty chair next to Reese and sat down.

"It's amazing! Reese has been showing us around," Dale said. Innish gave Reese a surprised look, but the knight ignored him.

"Do you live here in the King's Hall?" Aladane asked Innish.

"Don't answer that. The questions will just keep coming," Reese warned, drinking. Emeline laughed, and his eyes smiled at her over his mug.

"I do. I live in the guards' quarters," Innish told the boys amiably. "In the old days, the knights, upper servants, and guardsmen dined separately, but since King Altin's time, we mingle freely. You, my boy—our young historian! Did you ever read anything about him?"

Dale thought for a moment.

"He went to the Outer Lands like Lord Irwind. But he came back."

"That's right, and he returned with some strange new ideas," Innish said, eyes twinkling.

"Like what?" Emeline asked.

"He proposed that academies, libraries, and museums be accessible to everyone, and he changed the royal tax system so that villages and small towns owed less than the cities," Innish explained patiently. "He also ended the royal treatment of kings' and queens' extended families, so that regular citizens no longer had to bow to lords and ladies that were cousins and so on. He generally made things less formal between the common people and royalty, you see."

"As you can imagine, these changes were highly unpopular with some people," Reese said.

"There aren't any kings in the Outer Lands, are there?" Dale asked. "Does that mean there aren't any laws? How can anything work right?"

Innish smiled suddenly, mysteriously. Emeline was struck by how different it made him look. *He's a man with more than one face*, she thought, thinking of him under the fireworks. "I couldn't tell you for sure, of course. But I've heard it said that things work better there than they do here."

Now it was Reese's turn to give him a surprised look. "I don't believe I've ever seen you smile. What's in that drink?"

Innish frowned at him. "Water."

"I'd really like to see the Outer Lands," Emeline said.

Everyone stared at her. It did sound more like something Aladane would say. But she realized she had been thinking that way for a while. "I mean, as long as I knew I could come back home."

"See, that's the thing, heart. You don't know anything for sure over there," Fish told her gently.

"Have you been?" Innish asked, raising his eyebrows.

"You couldn't pay me in gold to go there." Fish nodded for emphasis and went on eating. Innish looked amused.

"Are you going to see the council with us?" Emeline asked him.

He nodded. "I have to corroborate Sir Reese's account, especially since I saw Loddril's body as well."

A silence fell briefly over the table.

"And then we'll hear all about the fierce wild animals that roam that part of the Cinderin Valley," Reese finally said, rolling his eyes. "And how they could easily kill a man."

"Yes, the Sapients will have much to say about it," Innish replied mildly.

"Well, this is a cozy group!"

Emeline looked up to see a handsome knight standing on the other side of the table. He wore his breastplate without the rest of his armor, boasting its engraving of a pair of crossed blades. He had very dark skin and was almost as tall as Reese, but lankier, and several years older. His black hair was slicked back very carefully; it was clear that he was proud of his looks.

"Sir Gundan," Innish said in a respectful tone; Reese said nothing. Emeline remembered the name from the spectators' conversation at the practice field.

"This must be the family from Aliddser, Reese?" the knight drawled.

"No, we're from Equane," Dale said, before anyone could answer.

Sir Gundan broke into a wide grin. "My mistake!" he said mockingly. "Reese, have I gotten your noble lineage wrong all this time?"

"It wouldn't be the first thing you couldn't wrap your head around." The sudden, cold anger in Reese's tone was painful to hear. "This is not my family. They're here to see the king."

"Is that so?" Sir Gundan exclaimed, amused. "Well, if they must dine in the royal hall, I suppose it's best they keep company with someone on their level."

Emeline's temper flared, even though she knew the insult was meant for Reese. Dada and Fish were taken aback, and they looked uncertainly at each other. Dale and Aladane just looked confused.

"Excuse me, sir," Emeline snapped, "but I believe King Altin would disagree. Or don't you know your history?"

Innish choked on his water and stifled a chuckle. Sir Gundan stared at Emeline, as if he hadn't fully noticed her before.

"Who is this little miss with the unruly hair?" he asked. "Why, Reese, have you found a lady at last that's not above you?" He laughed; Emeline cringed and glanced at Reese. His face was hard as stone. "She's so quick at your defense. Good thing, too, as your defense is not your best." He gave Reese a wink and turned to go.

"Yours *is* better, but only because we're all so fond of attacking you," Reese told his back. Gundan stiffened, but continued on.

Their end of the table was quiet for a moment afterward. Then Fish spat, "What in the kingdom is killing *his* crops?"

"Crossed knives is a stupid design," Dale declared.

"He looks ridiculous walking around with just his breastplate on," Dada added.

Innish smiled again, a warmer smile than the one that had impressed Reese. "If you've read about the city of Endan in the north," he told Dale, "then you know it was established by two very wealthy households—"

"And you just met the pride and joy of one of them," Reese finished bitterly. He shoved himself back from the table and got to his feet. "It's time for me to turn you over to Quaith

for the evening. You can practice your testimony for the king tomorrow."

With that, he marched away, drawing some glances from the other diners as he went. Emeline noticed, with her heart aching, that a few knights were smirking after him.

Innish watched him go. "He'll send Quaith over. Just wait here." He stood up, nodded to them, and took his own leave.

"Capital folk," Fish said with a shake of his head.

Emeline caught sight of the slender, proper Quaith bobbing his head at Reese and looking their way in utter astonishment. Clearly, he'd never imagined they would end up dining in the King's Hall.

Then she suddenly spotted Erd, of all people, Rellum's carriage driver. He was carrying a tray of glasses somewhere, perhaps to Rellum's rooms.

His eyes met hers and he winked at her, leering, just in time for Reese to catch it. The knight scowled and stalked off.

nineteen

The following morning, Quaith arrived with the news that the king would indeed see them that day. Emeline had little appetite at the Mother's Milk. The boys chattered excitedly, but Dada was tense, and Fish kept blinking and yawning as if he hadn't gotten enough sleep. They had drilled the boys for hours to remember one essential rule: Do not speak of Emeline's magic.

It felt like no time at all before they were following Quaith back to the silver gates. He called to the guard in a much lighter voice than Reese, saying clearly, "Master Quaith returning with guests!"

The doors opened as slowly as before. Fish muttered what they were all thinking: "Here we go again."

They had to reenter the king's grove, this time without Reese to reassure them. Emeline's skin crawled with dread. Dada stepped toward her and put his arm through hers, his other one linked with Dale; Fish put a hand on first his spring-gun, then his bullet-gun, and steered Aladane forward with the other hand. They followed the knot in Quaith's hair as it bobbed ahead of them.

When they came to an arched doorway, they rushed in as a group, nearly pushing a startled Quaith aside.

"Is this the same hallway as yesterday?" Fish exclaimed, eyeing the blue floor tiles and crumbling tapestries on the walls.

"No...I think it just looks the same," Dada said, unlinking arms with his children.

"Yes, yes, all the outer corridors have a similar look," Quaith told them, quickly walking ahead. "This way, please."

Emeline glanced up nervously at the woven images as she followed. One battered tapestry was a map of the kingdom, very much like the one in the meeting hall back in Equane. She was not surprised to see that no blue star marked her village in this version.

"We are now approaching the council room," Quaith announced, looking back at them. "It is early, but once His Majesty arrives, you must be silent at all times unless signaled to speak by His Majesty or a member of the Sapients or Theurgists." This sounded like a rehearsed speech and Quaith nodded to himself after completing it.

Emeline felt like things were moving too fast for her now. There was no time to linger in the hallway and prepare herself. She wiped her sweating palms on her dress, swallowing.

The passage ended at a pair of double doors made of heavy stone. Blue-armored guards stood silently on either side, with an air of having been there since the beginning of time.

One of them nodded at Quaith and then they both moved to open the doors. The stone scraped slowly over the tile as the doors opened wide.

Emeline's first impression was of light: It was a beautiful, sparkling room, the walls covered in mirrors. They reflected the sunshine coming in through clear glass panels in the high ceiling. Silver decorations dangled here and there, chiming softly when the air stirred.

In the center of the far wall, there were two enormous, elaborately carved wooden chairs—the thrones for the king and queen. They seemed built for giants instead of ordinary people. On either side of them were boxed-in sections of small, ornate silver chairs.

Facing all of this were rows of much simpler wooden benches, but even these were trimmed with silver. The floor was covered with a soft blue carpet on which their footsteps made no sound.

"Look at this place!" Aladane hissed, his eyes enormous.

Dale nodded solemnly. Fish had removed his hat and was now just staring around him, overwhelmed. Dada couldn't help smiling, admiring everything.

All the seats were empty, benches and chairs and thrones alike. Servants were wiping down the boxed-in seats carefully, and an oversized cushion was being placed onto one of the thrones.

Then Emeline saw with relief that Reese and Innish stood waiting just to the side of the double doors. Her chest grew hot.

"Good morning, Sir Reese! Innish," Quaith said importantly. Reese was in full armor but carrying his helmet. Innish wore the same embroidered vest he'd worn at dinner, but he had trimmed his beard. They nodded to Quaith.

Emeline studied Reese's face for any sign of his anger from the night before, but his expression was blank, reserved. He didn't meet her eyes.

She bit her lip. If he was upset with them—or embarrassed—there was nothing to be done about it. They might be sent home to Equane in as little as an hour.

The thought hollowed out her stomach.

"This is where you will sit once we begin," Quaith told Emeline and the others. He indicated the first row of benches, and Fish promptly sat down, relieved to know what to do. Emeline, Dada, and the boys followed, and Quaith went to direct the people who were preparing the seats.

Emeline looked at Reese again over her shoulder, but he was talking quietly to Innish. She wished he would speak to her—she wanted him to reassure her, to tell her that her secret was safe, that her family was safe, that protection would come to Equane—that he wanted to see her again—but he didn't meet her eyes.

A soft bell sounded from somewhere nearby. Reese went to stand at attention near the thrones, leaving Innish by the door. Dale gave Emeline an excited grin, despite everything.

This was it. They were finally going to see the king. Emeline clenched her fists in her lap, her heart beating like a hummingbird's wings.

The double doors at the back of the room began to scrape across the floor again, and Emeline jerked around to look. Held open by the armored guards, the doors admitted the royal council, both Sapients and Theurgists: two lines of stately, elderly men and women, dressed in their stunning velvet robes.

Rellum and Helid were easy to spot—the Sapient wore a determined scowl, while the small Theurgist flashed his unsettling smile. They each strode forward with chin held high.

The two lines parted on cue just before they reached the benches, the Sapients swinging to the left and the Theurgists to the right.

Many of them cast critical glances at Emeline and her family, but Rellum, disconcertingly, chose not to look at them at all. Emeline felt very small under their severe gazes, sitting there exposed in the middle of that glittering room.

A moment later, a man dressed like Quaith entered, carrying an odd little machine. He sat down on the bench behind her and settled the machine in his lap: She looked over her shoulder and saw that it had little switches in rows, each one marked with a letter.

The bell rang out again, this time louder, prompting the council members and the man with the machine to rise. Emeline and her family followed suit, turning to look back at the double doors. The guards had not opened them, however, and when she looked to the front again, confused, it was to see one of the wall mirrors swing open behind the giant thrones. From it emerged two men in simple blue cloaks supporting a third man between them. He was bent over and very pale, with thinning gray hair that fell to his shoulders.

Here at last was King Olvinde. He was dressed in a black suit embroidered heavily with silver, and for a crown, he wore a delicate ring of silver that rested on the top of his head. Emeline imagined that his weak frame could not have held anything heavier. There were several gem-encrusted rings on his fingers, but they were loose. His skin hung on his narrow face and his lips were colorless.

She felt a slight and, she knew, unkind sense of disappointment at the sight of him. Despite all that she'd heard of his illness, she had still expected him to have a more intimidating presence.

The king coughed and took a shuddery breath as they helped him up the two steps at the base of the cushioned throne. The giant chair swallowed him up as he sank into it. He nodded his head at Reese, who stood closest to him, and the knight bowed in return. Then the king turned his watery gray eyes toward the Equanians who sat in his council room. He frowned and coughed into a handkerchief.

"Please be seated," he wheezed. Everyone sat down at his words, and Emeline flinched when the man with the machine suddenly gave it a loud crank. Reese grinned at her unexpectedly, and her spirits shot upward.

"I cannot even recall when last this council room held village farmers," King Olvinde said, his low voice stronger now. He surveyed Emeline and her family from his massive chair with interest.

One of his attendants in blue robes spoke up, quietly. "Your Majesty, they are witnesses—"

"Yes, yes, I have been fully informed of our business today." The king shifted uncomfortably on his cushion.

The machine was clicking steadily now, and Emeline and the boys looked back to see the man striking the lettered switches, recording the king's words.

"But first, I believe Rellum Sapient wishes to make official the inflammatory accusations he's been spreading through the hall," the king said in a dispirited tone.

The Sapient rose at once, obviously eager to tell his story. "Your Majesty, my fellow members of the royal council, I regret to have to inform you of an incident of the most serious nature," he announced. "An attempt was made upon my life several days ago, while I was traveling to visit a relative. In fact, the only reason I can stand here today is because of Sir Reese and his guard, who saved me from a hired assassin in the dead of night at an inn in Blyne."

It was early evening, Emeline thought, surprised, and she looked at Reese. His green eyes rolled up slowly toward the ceiling.

"I do recall you taking leave for a family matter. Since I've not been informed of a new prisoner, can I assume you failed to capture this assassin, Sir Reese?" the king asked, turning to the knight.

"On the contrary, Your Majesty," Reese replied politely. "My guard and I were able to secure him for the journey home, but he did not survive it. His death is part of my testimony regarding the Dark Creature sightings."

"Is that so?" King Olvinde asked, staring at him. He broke into a short fit of coughing, continuing raspily, "Well, may I ask how you and Rellum Sapient know that he was a hired assassin?"

"The man's reputation preceded him as one, Your Majesty. His name was Loddril."

"Ah. I have heard of him myself. Well, at least it appears his career is now at an end," the king said, and then turned his gaze back to Rellum. "But as I understand it, Rellum Sapient, you have strong suspicions regarding who hired him."

"Yes, Your Majesty. I believe that, given the current violent nature of our divided council, the strongest suspicions must rest upon the Theurgists," Rellum said darkly. The people he spoke of glared at him in silence. "After all, I have no enemies elsewhere." There were a few titters from the Theurgists and he cast them a furious glance, snapping, "In fact, I have every reason to believe that one Helid Theurgist is the likely culprit. It's no secret that he holds me in contempt."

At this, Helid sighed loudly and shook his head, as if he felt nothing but pity.

The king observed all this with a severe frown. For a few moments, he said nothing, but then he spoke wearily. "I am well aware that there is some dissatisfaction among the council regarding my *tentative* naming of an heir. However, a council session is not the place for speculation. Tell me, Knight, did you find anything on this assassin to suggest who hired him? Evidence?"

"No, Your Majesty," Reese said in an even tone.

"Very well." The king coughed painfully again and stirred in his throne. Emeline felt a sudden sympathy for him. It was clear that he longed to be in bed, relieved of this responsibility, done with this tedious feud.

"This is boring," she heard Aladane whisper to Dale. It was followed by a sharp elbow from Dada.

"I understand that someone must have hired this rogue to take your life, Rellum Sapient, and for that, I am truly concerned," the king said. "But I'm afraid that without this assassin's testimony, there is no evidence that points to Helid Theurgist or, indeed, to anyone present."

A tense silence rested upon the council, Rellum clutching the sleeves of his robe in frustration. King Olvinde held up his right hand and studied it for a second. It shook violently and he squeezed it into a fist.

"Rest assured that I will begin an investigation into the matter," the king said finally. "Each council member, from both factions, will submit to questioning over the course of the next few days. . . . As my health permits."

The Sapients and Theurgists looked at one another in disgust, but it was a fairer decision than Emeline had expected, and it made her hopeful that the king would be reasonable when it came to protecting Equane.

Rellum stared at the king a moment, clearly unsatisfied. But finally he said, "Thank you, Your Majesty," and sat down.

"And now to this other matter . . ." King Olvinde muttered, letting his eyes fall on the Equanians. "I understand that we are also here today to discuss a sighting of a Dark Creature—specifically, an Ithin—unusual in that it is corroborated by a Lash Knight." There was some skepticism in his voice, but curiosity too; he scrutinized Reese, and the knight held his gaze steadily. "Let us have your testimony first, shall we?"

"Yes, Your Majesty. These travelers are from the village of Equane, at the southern end of the kingdom. My guard and I intercepted them in Blyne, already on their way to report a sighting in the woods on the outskirts of their village." Reese cleared his throat and, for the first time, Emeline detected a note of nervousness. Perhaps, despite his confident air, he didn't like being the center of attention.

"And how did you discover them?" the king asked. "Were they present when you rescued Rellum Sapient?"

"Yes, Your Majesty," Reese said reluctantly, knowing the

danger this confirmation opened them up to. "They stopped at the same inn and the assassin briefly held one of the boys hostage in an attempt to escape."

There were mutterings among the council; the king peered down at the two boys. Aladane pointed at Dale, who squirmed in his seat.

"I see. We will question them about that, as well, before they leave," the king decided. The council stirred again; Dada and Fish gave each other concerned looks. Did this mean they would have to stay longer? "Please continue, Sir Reese."

The knight was frowning, but he nodded. "What these villagers saw in the woods was a shadowy creature that gave off a foul smell. But what *I* witnessed with them, Your Majesty, was altogether different. After their accidental involvement in the events in Blyne, I felt it was my duty to escort them to the capital along with Rellum Sapient, but on our journey, there was a storm so severe that we took shelter in an abandoned manor in the Cinderin Valley. The place was overgrown with trees. During the night, the young lady, Emeline Bird, wandered off. I was concerned when she was gone for some time and followed her. I found her, Your Majesty, being attacked by something in a storeroom."

The council members were very quiet now. "All I could see was the creature's head, but it did wear a hood and it was not a man," Reese told them hesitantly. "It had huge fangs and eyes, almost like an insect...and it was reaching for her with long claws."

Emeline closed her eyes, remembering.

"This was in the pitch-dark, I gather?" a Sapient asked mockingly. The others chuckled.

"Silence!" King Olvinde snapped at them.

Reese gave the Sapient who had spoken a withering look. "It is generally dark in the night," he retorted. "But my eyes were accustomed to it by then."

"Where was Rellum Sapient at this point?" the king asked, looking from the council member to the knight.

"I was asleep, Your Majesty, and neither saw nor heard any of this," Rellum declared.

"What happened next?" the king pressed Reese. Emeline noticed with surprise that his hands were clutching the wooden arms of his throne.

Reese hesitated, glancing at Emeline. She sucked in her breath, remembering exactly what had happened next: She had used her magic to drive the creature off. Magic that no one in this room could know about. She sensed the stillness of her family on the seat next to her.

"Emeline...threw some wet vines at the creature and it hissed like a snake," Reese said carefully. "Then I lashed it and pulled her away." She breathed out again, slowly, her skin tight with goose bumps. "In all honesty, Your Majesty, it was like no natural creature I've ever encountered."

The king was staring at Reese, riveted, while the Sapients groused and the Theurgists whispered with excitement. Emeline could see that nothing of the kind had ever been reported by anyone as honorable as a Lash Knight.

Honorable...Did it bother Reese to keep her secret? Surely it was part of his duty as a knight to report it, to keep faith with the king? Was he choosing her protection over that duty? Was that awful for him—was it difficult? Why would he do it?

"My guard and I got everyone outside as fast as possible," Reese continued. "But Loddril, the assassin, managed to escape in the confusion. Shortly afterward, I heard him screaming somewhere on the grounds."

The council members suddenly fell silent on both sides, almost as if afraid.

"By the time I reached him, his attacker was gone, but he was torn to shreds—clearly mauled by something with long claws." In the stillness, Reese's deep voice reverberated throughout the room. "I believe he was killed by the creature we saw in the house."

The king cursed quietly. "And you saw and heard none of this either, Rellum?" he asked with some skepticism.

"No, Your Majesty." Rellum was indignant. "I was hustled out into the night, imagining it must be an attack by thieves or another assassin!"

The king frowned at Reese. "Do you have any physical evidence of this creature?"

"Only this, Your Majesty." From a pouch at his waist, Reese produced the scrap of the Ithin's hood; Emeline had forgotten he'd kept it. He held this up, and King Olvinde gestured to one of his blue-cloaked servants, who hurried forward to accept it from the knight and bring it to the king.

"This was stuck to the end of my whip after I lashed the creature. I don't understand why, but it's burned," Reese said.

Excited gasps sprang up from the Theurgists. Several of them craned their necks to see the ragged cloth in the king's frail hands. Emeline heard one of them whisper something about "blood that burns."

King Olvinde stared down at the cloth, almost as if he were afraid of it.

Then he began to cough harshly, covering his mouth with one trembling hand; he tried to speak, but the coughing racked his thin body. His attendants quickly moved closer—one of them put a steadying hand on his shoulder, the other handed him a silver handkerchief.

"This is a—This is a new develop—" King Olvinde lost his voice again. Everyone in the room watched in alarm as he shivered and retched up something into the handkerchief.

"I need to reflect on this account," he whispered finally. The room was now quiet enough for everyone to hear it. "And I'm afraid I am unfit for...further discussion today." He winced and whispered something softly into an attendant's ear.

"His Majesty has adjourned the council session for today," the man announced quickly. "It will continue at the same time tomorrow, his health permitting. You are all dismissed."

Surprised, Emeline turned to stare at Dada and Fish—they were both frozen in place. The council had ended without any testimony from them at all. How long would they have to stay in the city?

Emeline's heart flip-flopped between fear and heat. She had more time to spend with Reese, but it was in a dangerous place, full of dangerous people.

Without another word, King Olvinde submitted to being gathered up from his throne by the blue-robed men; they led him to the mirrored door through which he'd entered. The Sapients and Theurgists, who appeared completely unsurprised, were now scraping back their chairs and rising to their feet.

Reese stood in place, waiting respectfully for them to leave first. Emeline caught his eye for a moment, but then he looked away. When would he hold her gaze again?

twenty

I'm thinking about our crops, Bird," Fish told Dada as they filed out of the council room. Reese was ahead of them with Innish. "We already lost a day yesterday, and now we've got to do this again tomorrow? How long will it go on? I hope there haven't been any pests—or bless water, any blights."

"Dilla would call on our neighbors for help. Everybody would pitch in," Dada reminded him. Fish nodded gloomily.

"Sir Reese, if I may speak to you?" Rellum Sapient's voice called. The rest of the council had left, but he and the stern female Sapient from the academy were lingering expectantly in the corridor.

Reese sighed heavily, glancing back at Emeline and the others. He said something quietly to Innish and went to meet the Sapients.

Innish waited for the villagers to reach him, then said to Dada and Fish, "Sir Reese believes you should return to your rooms promptly today. I can escort you."

His voice was calm, but the message was clear: The danger they were in was real. It was time to hide away in their rooms. Emeline looked at Dada and bit her lip; his face was grim.

"Thank you very much," he told Innish, taking Dale's hand.

She thought of the fountain, secluded in the courtyard, and her pulse quickened. Maybe she could find a quiet time to practice her magic. Maybe. She knew she shouldn't, but it was building inside her like water against a dam.

Innish hustled them back through the grove and out through the great silver doors onto the street. They walked a short distance, passing the Mother's Milk, while the guard kept an eye out for a red carriage.

The boys looked bitterly disappointed.

"Do we have to just sit in the rooms?" Aladane complained as a carriage for hire slowed to a stop for them.

"Yes," Innish told him.

"Son of a maggot," Aladane muttered, under his breath.

"Hush. I reckon you boys have had enough excitement," Fish said darkly. "I reckon we all have."

They climbed into the empty carriage and Emeline looked out the window at the gates, wondering if Reese had freed himself from the Sapients yet. What did they want with him, exactly? Were they arguing with him about his testimony?

Was he safe?

She faced forward again, fisting her hands in her lap. The driver caught her eye—he was a husky man with silver-tinted spectacles, gazing back at her intently. He nodded oddly to himself before pulling out into the crowded road, busy with carriages, bicycles, and people.

"Dog fight!" Dale exclaimed, pointing at two of them barking at each other on a corner. The owners were struggling to pull the dogs away, while some boys Emeline's age cheered them on. She was surprised to see that the boys were very plainly clad in homespun shirts and trousers. They looked more rough-and-tumble than anyone she'd seen in the capital.

It reminded her of what Reese had said in the market. About no one paying attention to the people who were poor. About the way he'd had to fight to escape it.

"Dale, Reese is from a small village like us," she said. "And he had no money before he became a knight. He did what Fish says is impossible."

Dale's face lit up, but Fish snorted.

"I'd like to know how he managed that," he said.

"Me too," Dada said.

The carriage slowed suddenly and drifted toward the side of the road. She looked for passengers to be picked up, but there were none—they had stopped on a quiet corner outside of a closed printing shop. Across the street was a small, empty park.

"Where are we?" Dada asked Innish, who shook his head, scratching his beard.

Their driver appeared at the window and stared in at them; Emeline noticed he wore a necklace with a small silver wheel pendant. "Sorry for the delay," he said tightly. "I just have to check something in the engine."

"It sounds like it's running smoothly," Innish said, surprised. The driver shrugged and disappeared from view. Innish frowned.

"I'd be curious to see the engine on this thing myself," Fish said, reaching for the door.

"No, stay inside," Innish said quickly. He opened the door and ducked out, a small fear starting to gnaw at Emeline's stomach. Was something wrong?

A second later, he reappeared at the window, his expression wary. "He's gone," he told Fish and Dada.

"Gone where?" Dada asked, startled.

"I'm not sure. But I didn't like that pendant he was wearing," Innish said, scanning the road around them. "It looked like a Sapient symbol."

"Bless water," Fish muttered.

Alarmed, Emeline reached for the door, but Dada pushed her and the boys back into their seats. "Be still," he ordered.

"Does that mean he's a Sapient?" Aladane asked, confused. Emeline heard another carriage turn onto the road behind them.

Innish's head was turned, looking down the street. "No… but he might be a supporter."

"What does that mean?" Fish demanded.

Innish didn't answer. The other carriage rumbled suddenly louder, as if it were driving very fast.

"By the kingdom…" Innish murmured. Then he yanked open the door, shouting, "Get out! *Get out!*"

Emeline sprang to her feet, but it was too late—an impact from behind sent her flying. The steam-carriage rocked forward, its back wheels up in the air. Her head struck the luggage rack. Fish's elbow jammed her in the stomach—Dale's head knocked into hers—Innish was shouting—the splintered door, hanging on one hinge, slammed against her leg.

Then the coach crashed back down—hard—throwing everyone back.

She was sprawled across the seat, breathless. Her head throbbed; it felt like the luggage rack had cracked it open, and blood stung her eye. Distantly, she heard the other carriage roar away.

"Are you all right? Em? Boys?" Dada gasped. He disentangled himself from Aladane, who groaned.

"I'm all right," Emeline murmured, her vision slowly unblurring. Everything hurt.

"What happened?" Dale whimpered.

"That thing rammed right into us," Fish breathed in disbelief.

Innish peeled the broken door back and looked in, wild-eyed. "Is everyone all right?!"

"I won't know until I get out." Fish fumbled down the mangled step.

Emeline managed to get to her feet and follow slowly, Fish helping her to the street. She was trembling.

The other carriage had crashed into them...and driven away! A Sapient supporter had tried to hurt them, maybe even kill them...!

Had he...He couldn't have been *ordered* to...?

"That was deliberate," Innish said soberly. He was staring off in the direction the other coach had taken. "The driver left us here to be struck."

She shivered, sinking down onto the pavement. Her head felt wet. Dada was examining Dale and Aladane; her brother had a bloody lip, Aladane was holding his wrist, and Dada himself had a deep scratch on his cheek and a tear in his shirt. Fish's eye was swelling up.

"You're telling me that steam-carriage hit us on purpose?" Fish demanded. Innish nodded, his hand on his gun. "We're damn lucky we aren't dead!"

"Em, your head!" Dada hurried over toward her.

She felt sick, but she tried to smile. "I'm fine. I promise."

"You're bleeding!" He was frantic, and it made her heart throb.

"We're close enough to walk to the inn," Innish told Fish.

Fish glared at him, rubbing his eye. "And what happens if someone runs us down while we're walking?" he snapped.

"We'll stay out of the open. Come, let's go quickly," Innish gestured to Dada, who pulled his children to their feet and followed.

~~~

Leather-garbed guards arrived at a merciful speed to stand at the inn's front gates. Dada had rushed everyone inside their rooms as soon as they reached the inn, shutting them up firmly. In the washroom, Emeline listened to her family talk, running warm water into the basin. The blood on her head was drying, tangling her hair.

"Bird, I think we should get out of here tomorrow morning," Fish said.

"I don't think we can," Dada said unhappily. "We're part of a royal council session. You heard the king—he wants to question us himself."

And what about Equane? Emeline thought, gingerly washing her wound. *The Ithin are real. We still need the king to send the village protection.*

"But we didn't agree to all this!" Fish exclaimed. "We already drove across the kingdom, Bird. We did our part yesterday, or Reese did it for us, and now we're done. The king knows what we saw. We need to get our wagon back and head home."

"We don't even know where the wagon is, Fish." Dada sounded so tired.

"We don't even know if the king will be well enough to see us tomorrow!" Fish threw his hands up. "We could be stuck here for weeks. You've got your family here, but I've left Dilla and the boys!"

Emeline quickly patted her hair dry and went back out to join them. Fish was pacing around the room while Dada sat slumped in a chair.

"I don't want to leave yet," Dale said quietly. He and Aladane were sitting on the beds, looking from one man to the other.

"Me neither," Aladane insisted. "But I don't think my wrist is working right."

"Let me see it," Emeline said, hurrying to their side. "Dale, go wash your lip."

"I think it's a sprain," Dada told her, glancing at Aladane.

"First they take our wagon, then they start following us and threatening us...." Fish muttered. "Now they're trying to—"

"Fish," Dada snapped, and he fell silent. Emeline knew Dada didn't want to frighten the boys. She was proud of them, though, for not wanting to run home and hide. Part of her wanted to. But the best part of her was angry. Very angry.

How dare these people attack *her family?* They could bicker among themselves all they wanted, but they had no right to hurt the ones she loved. Her people didn't deserve to be used as pawns in some mad scramble for power.

Her face felt hot as she tied a cloth around Aladane's wrist to keep it straight. She knotted it a little too tightly, imagining smothering that carriage driver in water vines.

"Ow!" Aladane complained.

"Sorry." She patted his arm and stood up with her hands on her hips.

The urge to use her magic was so strong that her fingers fidgeted against her dress. She had to slip outside as soon as she could.

~~⌇~~

It was early evening by the time she managed to get away. Everyone was hungry, but no one wanted to venture out for food. Fish was taking a nap and Dada was reading stories to the boys. She told them she needed the fresh air of the courtyard, just for a minute, and took the *History* with her.

The courtyard was even lovelier in the twilight. It was cold, but she pulled her red cloak close and sat on the tiles near the fountain. She thought of Vindane and the bizarre plant that the Theurgists had discovered, and looked up the region in the book.

The region of Vindane has long been associated with stories of magical activity and unexplained phenomenon. Many claim it is riddled with sour fragments of old magic. Keldares are said to avoid the area, as their songs and tales call it a place of shadows.

Emeline worried the corner of a page. *Old magic gone sour . . .* As if magic were like milk left out in the sun.

What even *was* dark magic, exactly? How was it different from her own power?

If only Mama were here to explain all this.

But no one was there. The courtyard was silent and empty, and Mama was gone.

Emeline stood up and leaned on the stone edge of the fountain, watching the vines drift sleepily in the water. At once, a current of magic swirled up inside her—so bright and strong, it was irresistible.

She raised a hand and summoned the dripping tendrils up into the air, making them coil and dance. It thrilled her from head to toe. Was she shimmering on the outside, the way she was inside? Maybe she glowed as she knit the vines into intricate knots and draped them along the statue girl's arms.

A night bird appeared and flitted among the dancing greenery. Then another, and another, and Emeline looped the vines over and under them, sighing at the beauty of it.

Magic was *real*. It could be wonderful or it could be dangerous, and both aspects needed to be taken into account. How could the king and the Sapients go on denying it? If they refused to acknowledge that magic was real, that Dark Creatures were real, didn't that leave Equane—and much of the kingdom—vulnerable?

And if she could prove it was real with a wave of her hand, wasn't it the right thing to do?

She was alert for the sound of footsteps, but not for the silent stride of a trained Lash Knight.

"Emeline," he said softly.

Her heart shot into her throat. Dropping her arms, she wheeled to see Reese standing near a column, watching her. His shoulders were tense, his hand on his coiled whip, but his eyes were soft. He was gazing at her in wonder.

Struck dizzy by his stare, she dropped her eyes to the ground. She waited for a sharp remark—the delight in seeing him was numbed by the shame of being caught taking this stupid risk—but he was quiet.

"You shouldn't do that here," he said finally, gently.

"I know. I couldn't help it."

"What does it feel like?" he asked, surprising her.

"It's like I'm...a part of another living thing," she said slowly. "The spark of all that life...that energy...It builds up inside of me." She gestured at the dangling tendril and it coiled itself into a spiral. "Then it rushes right out."

Reese shook his head. "I couldn't believe my eyes when those vines flew at the Ithin. I was watching one form of magic battling another."

The admiration in his voice made her lightheaded.

"Good magic versus dark magic, you mean?" She hoped he meant that.

He frowned, looking thoughtful. "I don't understand why people say 'dark magic.' Isn't magic only good or evil depending on the intention behind it?"

"Well...some say that magic can turn bad on its own," she told him. "And that it's happened in Vindane. I read that might even be how the Dark Creatures were created—old magic spoiling."

"Hmm. I suppose you better not leave your magic lying around unsupervised, then," he replied. She rolled her eyes.

His voice changed. "Is that from the crash?"

He stepped closer, leaning over her to examine the cut on her head, and she held her breath as his fingers ghosted over her dark, damp curls. It was almost too much to stand this close to him in the chill air, his warmth radiating out toward her.

When he stepped back, his jaw was clenched, his eyes furious. "If I find that black-hearted snake, I'll lash him into a thousand worms," he whispered. "Where are the others?"

❧ twenty-one ❧

Reese!" Dale shouted. Two boys leapt off the beds to greet him.

"You are a welcome sight," Dada told him, standing up as well.

Reese noted their injuries, grimaced, and glanced around the elegant room. "I suppose the fancy lodgings are meant to compensate for the attempts on your life."

"We're all right, thank the kingdom," Dada said, shaking his head. "But thank you for coming to see us."

"We should tell the king about it, right?" Dale asked Reese.

The knight sighed and folded his arms. "Innish has already given a description of the driver, and we will bring him in if we can find him. But otherwise there is no proof that the Sapients set it up," he said. "We have received a few reports of people wearing necklaces with the Sapients' or Theurgists' symbols spreading inflammatory rhetoric. But even that is unconfirmed."

"What did Rellum want to talk to you about?" Dada asked.

"He tried to convince me to alter my testimony," Reese said. "To claim not only that I was unsure of what I saw in that old manor, but also that I believed Loddril was hired by a Theurgist. For the good of the kingdom, he said. As if changing my story now wouldn't be cause for suspicion."

"What did you say?" Emeline asked.

"That it's my duty as a Lash Knight to tell the truth, as well he knows." Reese's gaze lingered on her for a moment, and she remembered that there was one truth he wasn't telling.

She chewed her lip.

"But does that put you in danger?" Dada asked, concerned.

"What if someone hires an assassin to get *you?*" Dale asked, his eyes wide.

"I'll treat him the same way I did Loddril. And if we're lucky, perhaps the Ithin will get him too," Reese said disdainfully.

"By the way, we're starving," Aladane announced, and Dale nodded. Reese blinked at this sudden change of subject.

"We are," Emeline admitted as her stomach growled.

"I'm afraid to take my family anywhere," Dada told Reese. "I figured we could stick it out until the morning."

Reese considered for a moment, looking at them. "There is a place I could take you where no one would bother you," he said. "A place it would very hard to follow you to. It may seem like a risk to be out at night...but the people there aren't the type to choose sides."

"What is this place?" Fish asked doubtfully.

"A market of sorts, but not like the one we saw yesterday. There's an old woman there who makes sandwiches for half a payt each, so good I'd trade my shield for one."

"I'll go wake up Mister Fish!" Aladane darted for the door.

"Well, if you really believe we'll be safe, then we'll go," Dada told Reese. "I wouldn't trust anyone else."

Reese looked embarrassed.

Shortly afterward, they were riding inside his simple black steam-carriage, everyone nervously looking out the windows. Emeline kept imagining she heard another vehicle speeding up behind them, ready to smash them off the road.

She tried to focus on the city. Through the great lighted windows of the passing houses, she caught glimpses of tapestries, hanging mirrors, cabinets, and bookshelves. Occasionally, she saw a person, drinking from a cup or gesturing while speaking. One woman was tying up her hair with a cord of bells.

The carriage made a sudden turn down a narrow street, one that Emeline never would have noticed. It ran along the backs of several rows of houses, and then branched off into a network of alleys. This part of the city was dim and worn. The pavement was cracked, and broken iron fences crisscrossed the spaces between houses, very small houses made of old brick. They had sloping, sagging roofs, some of them without chimneys.

The carriage slowed as strings of lights appeared ahead. Here the alleys gave way unexpectedly to a small park, completely hidden from the main roads. Even in the dark, stepping out of the carriage, Emeline could see how different this park was from others in the city.

There were no fountains or gardens, no statues or benches. The lights dangled above a cluster of stalls and a small crowd of people, all wearing much simpler clothes than she had gotten used to seeing in the capital: There were a few bells, but no wings, lifted shoes, or colored spectacles.

Several of the women had their hair tied up in wraps, which made Emeline wonder if they were hiding curls.

"It's a secret market!" Aladane exclaimed.

"Not exactly a secret. Just not widely known," Reese told him.

"A little too dark for my liking," Fish said, scanning the dimly lit crowd.

"Stay close together," Dada told the boys.

"It's all right," Reese said, and led them out into the middle of the market-goers, several nodding respectfully as if they knew him. They looked at Emeline and the others curiously.

"How did you find this place?" she asked him.

"When I first came to the capital and joined the knighthood, I didn't have money, and I didn't exactly love dining with the others for every meal," he said. "So I had to look around for inexpensive options."

He ducked under the low awning of one of the stalls and Emeline stepped up beside him. A tiny old woman leaned out to greet him with delight, her black eyes bright. She pinched him on the cheek as if he were a little boy, and Emeline laughed in surprise as Reese smiled, winced, and rubbed his face.

"How is the big boy? It's been a while! Are you hungry?" the old woman asked. She had rows of meat, cheese, and vegetables lined neatly in paper, ready to be made into sandwiches.

"That looks really good," Dale said, elbowing Emeline aside.

"I need six this evening," Reese told the old lady. She stared up at him, astonished.

"Six! The big boy has friends! Okay, six sandwiches!" she crowed. Reese frowned at her surprise, but Emeline hid a smile. "Go and sit. I'll whistle when they're done!"

"Sit where?" Aladane asked.

"In the grass," Reese said shortly. He gave Emeline an anxious look before passing through the stalls to a patch of empty grass beyond them.

She wanted to tell him that none of them would object to sitting on grass, but she didn't have to: Dada sat down immediately, stretching out his legs. It was chilly, but everyone was in their cloaks or jackets and the grass was soft. The boys stayed on their feet, but only because they were looking back curiously at the stalls.

A man at one counter handed some meat on a stick to Fish as he passed.

"Look at this!" he said, showing Dada. "That fellow gave it to me for free."

"I didn't think you could get much for free," Dada said.

He took a bite of the meat and chewed thoughtfully. "I reckon I look roughed-up enough for him to feel sorry for me."

"I hope ours is done soon," Aladane said, watching him hungrily.

Emeline jumped at a sudden shout: A tense argument had broken out nearby. Reese stood watching the two men yelling at each other, others holding them back.

A thin whistle sounded from the direction of the sandwich woman's stall.

"That's our food!" Aladane piped up.

"Stay here." Reese strode toward the stalls, casting a sharp look at the shouting men as he passed. Tall as he was, his glare was hard to miss, and they dropped their voices immediately. The argument faded into grumbles and quiet threats.

"I can't imagine many Lash Knights hang around here. Reese is an interesting young fellow," Dada said.

The knight returned a moment later with six paper-wrapped bundles. Emeline unwrapped hers eagerly. The bread was crisp on the top and soft in the middle, and the meat inside was spicy and covered with melting cheese. It was delicious. She grinned at Reese with her mouth full and he smiled. They ate enthusiastically, nodding at each other and dripping cheese onto the grass.

"What kind of peppers are in this meat?" Dada asked, trying to see it better in the dark.

"Bristle peppers from Willen, a village north of here," Reese said. "That's where she lives, the woman who makes these."

"She doesn't live in the capital?" Emeline asked.

"Willen is close enough to drive in for the day and back. I've been there a few times, just to get away from the city. It's a nice place." He swallowed and glanced at Dale, who was disemboweling the last of his sandwich, eating each piece separately. "Unlike Aliddser," he added, "where the sheep have more brains than the villagers...."

"It must be nice to live close enough to visit the capital. As long as you're not involved in any royal councils," Dada said glumly.

"And there are farms there?" Fish asked Reese, sounding doubtful.

"Farms, pastures, and a lake, if I remember correctly."

"I'd rather live *in* the capital," Aladane said.

Reese balled up the paper from his sandwich, frowning. "It gets tiresome," he said.

Emeline understood, thinking about the scathing looks and patronizing remarks they'd been subjected to. She wondered if things were more like Equane in Willen. Perhaps, if they somehow had an extra day, they could travel to see it.

She sighed, knowing what should be occupying her mind—the council tomorrow. She glanced at Dada, who was talking to Fish about the farms.

"Is it a bad thing that you haven't told the king about me? As a Lash Knight, I mean?" she asked Reese, keeping her voice low. She watched him carefully.

"It doesn't feel honorable," he admitted. He studied her as well, and she felt something in the air between them. Something confusing, distracting. She looked down at the grass, her face suddenly hot. "But you and your family are in danger as it is. I won't put you in more."

"I know," she told the grass. "But I think that the king should *know*. About me. About magic. I think . . . that I should tell him."

Reese hesitated, yanking up bits of grass from the ground. "I agree that he should know, but it's not your responsibility to tell him. You don't have to get that involved. It's too dangerous."

"But if I show the king my magic, he'll be more likely to

believe in the Ithin, won't he?" she asked. He nodded reluctantly. "And then he'll be *much* more likely to send help to Equane. That's what I'm worried about most of all. Equane."

"But Equane has a moat."

"Yes...but we never knew for *sure* that Dark Creatures truly were on the other side of it. Now we do. And how do we know that it's only the Ithin?" Emeline asked him. "Do we know for sure that *no* Dark Creature will cross the moat? What about something with wings?"

Dada glanced over at her and she lowered her voice again, picking at the grass. "It's all peaceful families in Equane. I'm worried," she said in a forced casual tone.

"I know." Reese rested his hand a second on something at his belt—a small item wrapped in cloth. Then he dropped his arm absently. "It's brave of you to want to help at your own risk," he said, the admiration in his voice making her smile. "But you'd have to demonstrate your magic to everyone in the council, with the more witnesses the better. Do you understand what that means?"

Emeline squirmed at the thought, glancing over at the boys, who were throwing their sandwich wrappers. "What will happen?"

"Well, first, they will all lose their heads. Then the Sapients will accuse you of trickery and insist that you be taken into custody, to be examined. Next, the Theurgists will insist that *they* be allowed to examine you instead. Both sides will do their best to use you for their own ends."

"But what about the king? What will *he* do?" Emeline asked, embarrassed to hear her voice shaking.

Reese sighed. "I believe—I hope—that he would keep you and your family secured away from the council, and perhaps have you examined by someone neutral. But I'm not entirely convinced that he's strong enough these days...or that there *is* anyone neutral in the hall."

Her family was watching the two of them now. Dale started to say something to Emeline, but Dada shushed him.

She pictured Equane, with its lovely canals and cottages, the villagers walking to the market or coming in from the fields. Her stomach twisted into knots at the thought of anything happening to them.

But was it fair to put her family in the fire to protect them?

If she didn't, though...if she didn't, they might all face danger in their own homes anyway when they returned. There was no easy option.

"What do you mean when you say 'examined'?" she asked Reese. "Just that I'll have to demonstrate it over and over again? Explain how it feels?"

"I don't really know," he admitted.

"What if I tell them I won't show them anything unless they promise to keep my family safe?"

"I think that if they're afraid of you, then it might work," he said seriously. "You'd have the upper hand. But I doubt they would be."

Reese cleared his throat. "It's getting late. I should bring you back to your rooms." He stood up and nodded at Dada, who was watching him; the rest of them got up too, brushing themselves off.

"What were you two talking about?" Dale asked.

"The council," Emeline said truthfully.

"Miserable, hateful group of people..." Fish muttered. "They all ought to be locked up."

"It wasn't always this way. For one thing, the Sapients didn't attack the idea of magic so much," Reese said wistfully. "They used to just focus on science and technology, which is more than worthy of pursuit. The Theurgists' mistrust of all of that will actually hold us back, as a society. But ignoring the uses and dangers of magic will too."

He looked up at the sky, where stars cut through the deep blackness. "I keep thinking that we need both philosophies." He crushed up the last of the grass in his hands. "I don't understand why one side has to be completely right and the other one completely wrong. But I'm not someone anyone of importance would listen to," he added, sounding dispirited.

Emeline felt the truth of his words.

Perhaps she or Reese could bring something to the council room—like a recently watered plant. Then she wouldn't have to decide now. She could make up her mind during the council herself whether to show her magic or not.

It was her decision. Something felt very right about that.

≈≫ twenty-two ≪≈

A group of boys suddenly appeared among the dwindling market-goers. They were joking loudly and shoving one another roughly, dressed in holey trousers and dirty-looking shirts. As if their arrival were a signal, the stall keepers began to pack up.

"Let's go," Reese said, leading the villagers back toward the carriage. Emeline watched as the new arrivals overturned a stall, and laughed when the keeper yelled at them.

"Some of those boys need a good whipping," Fish said, frowning at their antics.

Reese stiffened.

"They'd like it if you tried. They're just poor, and angry about it."

Fish went quiet at that, and Emeline glanced up at Reese's face. He looked very tired, suddenly.

He took a roundabout way to avoid the crowd. A little girl screamed nearby, and Emeline looked up to see a woman hushing her.

"Your brother's just trying to scare you!" the woman said. "You know there are no Dark Creatures here. There're no woods in the city!"

Except for the King's Grove. A cold breeze blew and she hugged herself. She and Reese were ahead of the others now.

"Reese," she said softly. "Would you bring a plant to the council room? Just in case I decide to do it?"

He met her gaze, his eyes bright with concern. He nodded.

Then he said, "Here," and pulled the little package from his belt that she'd noticed earlier. He handed it to her, looking away. "It's getting colder. This might help keep you warm." He sounded gruff, uncomfortable.

Astonished, she unwrapped the parcel and found a round woven cap folded up inside. It was a deep red that perfectly matched her cloak. Wish a rush of joy, she remembered how she'd told him that she liked these caps.

"Thank you!" she breathed, looking up.

But Reese had walked off already, striding down the road as if no one were following him. Her happiness faded into confusion. Was he embarrassed? Did he already regret giving it to her? She squeezed the soft cap tightly.

Then the boys caught up to her, and she hid the gift in her cloak pocket.

Before long, they were riding through cleaner, busier streets, lit by lantern-topped poles and the lights of carriages and bicycles. They were back to their rooms soon enough, where the two guards greeted them silently at their doors; Dada and Fish sighed heavily with relief.

Emeline tried to catch Reese's eye as they thanked him several times and said good night, but he just smiled at the boys and drove away.

That night, in a restless sleep, she dreamed about Mama. She saw her the way Fish had described her, arriving in Equane as a girl, her bright blue eyes peering out from under her shock of black hair. She had more worldliness in a single glance than anyone in the village, but she liked it there—she *loved* it—and she made her decision.

Then, all at once, she swirled up into the sky like a column of colorful air. She danced among the clouds, faded into the stars. And she gazed down on Emeline lovingly . . . admiringly.

Yes, I have the magic too, Emeline thought in her dream. *And I can make my own decisions.*

~ ~

"How come we have to eat here again?" Aladane asked at the Mother's Milk in the morning. Quaith had sent a liveryman and fresh guards to take them to the café and then back to the council room. Emeline sat in her blue dress with the stars and the red cap from Reese, her heart hammering and her palms slick. She drank the bitter coffee because it warmed her up, but it made her even more jittery.

Of course, Dale had asked her where she'd gotten the cap, but Dada had surprised her by changing the subject: *Someone gave it to her. Look at that bicycle, Dale, it seats three.*

Was telling the king really the right thing to do? She could not even ask her father, because she knew he would stop her, for her own safety. But it felt wrong keeping it from him. She chewed on her lip and drank more coffee.

"We have to eat here because it's free, remember?" Dale told Aladane.

An aproned girl arrived at the table at that moment and caught his words. She hooted and Emeline looked up in surprise.

"Nothing's free here, honey," she declared, drying her

hands on her apron. Dada and Fish gave each other worried looks.

"We're supposed to have the royal lodger breakfast," Dada said politely, repeating Quaith's words. The girl's eyes widened and she looked them up and down incredulously.

"You're a pack of villagers! Or else I'm a goose!" she exclaimed. Emeline's face grew hot, but another server appeared then, the one who had witnessed Aladane's coffee accident.

"You *are* a goose, Setta," she hissed, pointing at the guards who were watching them. "They're *important* lodgers. Go take the back table." The other girl turned red and then scurried away.

"I'll be right back," the regular girl told them, and swept off toward the kitchen.

"A pack of villagers! What are we, wolves?" Fish grumbled.

"Well, *she's* a goose," Dale said, grinning. Aladane laughed at that and Emeline had to admire her brother for not being bothered by the girl's words. How had Reese gotten used to this?

That afternoon, the liveryman returned and they were rushed to the King's Hall. Outside the brilliant council room, a gardener stood holding a potted plant.

Emeline stared at it, her heart in her throat. It was a lady star, the red spiral-flower that Reese had identified at the market. She knew it was no coincidence that it was here. He had chosen it for her to use, if she decided to.

Then they were ushered inside, right next to Reese and Innish in their place near the doors. The servants were once again straightening seats and preparing the room for the council. Innish stared across the room, fingering the mysterious chain around his neck, lost in his thoughts.

Her hands shook, but her eyes met Reese's and he smiled. There were shadows under his eyes, as if he hadn't slept well. She colored up, remembering that she was wearing his cap.

"I feel like my true self when I'm around you," he told Emeline suddenly, in a quiet, fierce voice. When he looked at her again, his eyes were on fire with a sweet, intense warmth she had never known before.

She took his large hand and held it tight, her heartbeat spiraling wonderfully out of control. It was so nice just to hold his hand, to feel the strong, warm fingers. She knew that others might be watching, but she didn't care. She didn't care if the king and the council saw them. Then Reese squeezed her hand and let it go.

She walked unsteadily to the seat that held her family, afraid to look at them. Dada glanced at her for an instant, then looked away. The boys were thankfully distracted, fascinated by the man with the recording machine, who sat behind them once again.

"Can you keep up if someone talks really fast?" Dale asked him. The man was very surprised that anyone was addressing him.

"Oh, yes," he said, blinking. "I've been trained to. I'm very fast."

"Did you have to learn at an academy?" Aladane asked.

"Oh no, my father taught me," he said, amused. "He was the council transcriber before me."

"Maybe that's what we can do when we move here, Dale. I mean, unless you can't be a village boy."

Emeline cringed at his words, but the transcriber smiled kindly. He was younger than Dada, but old enough to have children of his own.

"You can be from anywhere for this job, son. You just have to learn fast and work hard," he said, just as the bell announcing the arrival of the Sapients and Theurgists rang out.

The mirrored door opened to admit King Olvinde and his attendants. He seemed impatient, as if he were eager to get started, or perhaps eager to finish. He wore a blue suit this time, and his expression was sharp, his hands steady, even if he still had to be helped into his throne.

"Good morning," he announced hoarsely. The transcriber cranked his machine and began to punch the keys. "Thank you for reassembling. I apologize for my hasty dismissal yesterday. I've taken a cure-all from the esteemed Doctor Nallor, however, and feel vastly improved." As he spoke, he shot an amused look at his council, which erupted into bickering.

If the king was exercising his sense of humor, he was clearly in better spirits than yesterday, at least.

"Today I believe we will hear from the villagers, who did not travel this far in order to sit silently in my council room," he declared, his gray eyes pinning Emeline in place. "I shall attempt to move things along more quickly. Which of you saw something in your village woods? Please rise."

Dale gave Emeline an anxious look, and she was reminded all over again of the village meeting. It was strange how far they had come since then. She stood up, pulling her brother to his feet next to her.

"Please state your names."

"Emeline and Dale Bird," she said, a little shakily. Olvinde nodded and then began to cough, gesturing for to continue. "My brother, Dale, was playing by our moa the village. It's there to separate us from the woods, and one crosses it. But he ran across a plank bridge, and I ran aft him." It felt easier than before to tell this part of the stor "Then we heard something rustling in the woods, and we sav a shape moving. It *did* look like it had a hood, just like the one Reese and I saw later—"

Emeline was interrupted by outright laughter from both sides of the council. Startled, she saw that the king's eyebrows had shot up to his hairline.

" 'Reese and I'?" Helid echoed, incredulous. "Is she so familiar with this knight?"

Emeline felt herself reddening from her head to her feet. She had spoken without thinking, leaving off the "Sir." She and her family had casually dropped his title altogether, without realizing it.

What does it matter if I say "Sir Reese" or not?

Reese cleared his throat and Emeline forced herself to look at him, afraid she had embarrassed him. He was scowling, but to her relief, it was at Helid.

"We're not used to titles, Your Majesty. We don't have them in Equane," Dale spoke up. She stared at him, impressed. There was a snort or two from the council.

"Please, go on," King Olvinde said, amused now. "What did you see?"

"It was kind of like a man in a hooded cloak, but it moved… weirdly, more like a snake," Dale told him while Emeline kept

her eyes on the floor, wishing she could just sit down again. Or perhaps even crawl underneath the benches. "And then Emeline grabbed a water lily from the canal and threw it," he said proudly. "And the thing hissed! Then we ran away."

Silence followed from the council, and the king's intense gaze moved from Dale back to Emeline. His eyes seemed to bore right into her head, but she forced herself to meet them.

When he finally spoke, the king's voice was filled with unexpected respect. "Young lady, am I to understand..." he asked slowly, "that *twice* you have fought these things with water?"

The words made no sense for a moment—she'd been expecting a rebuke. But then her heart leapt like a fish. *He believes us! He must!*

In no time at all, the council room was ringing with voices. "Your Majesty!" a Sapient shouted. "Surely you don't believe this!"

"It must have been some wild animal!" another added.

"The knight saw the other one with his own eyes!" a Theurgist argued.

"No one has any proof!"

Dismayed, Emeline and Dale watched the council's men and women wave their arms and shake their fists.

"Both times, water deterred it! What does that tell you?"

"It was in the dark! They don't know *what* they saw!"

The king tilted his head to one side, listening wearily to the outburst before a coughing fit overtook him. Gradually, the council members noticed and fell silent.

Finally, he regarded Emeline and Dale once more. "You

appear somewhat battered this morning," he declared hoarsely. "Or do I imagine it?"

Emeline put a self-conscious hand up to her injured head and glanced at Dale, whose lip was swollen.

"We were in a carriage accident," she told the king, anger rushing in suddenly at the memory. She cast a defiant look at the council. "We were in a carriage for hire with Innish and the driver wore a Sapient symbol. He parked the carriage in an odd place—"

"And then he left us!" Dale chimed in.

"Just in time for another carriage to crash into us," Emeline finished sharply. "It was deliberate, Your Majesty. The carriage that struck us didn't try to stop."

Several Sapients glared back at her, but most appeared unconcerned, even amused. The Theurgists whispered excitedly to one another, which she found almost as loathsome as the Sapients' nonchalance.

"I see." King Olvinde's voice was icy as he regarded his council members. "And where is this driver?" he demanded.

"Your Majesty," Reese spoke up, "my guard and I have put out a notice with his description."

The king succumbed to another attack, filling the room with his wracking cough. Then he clenched his fist and rasped, "Let us hear from the guard."

All heads turned to Innish, who stood like a statue in the back of the room. He strode forward and stopped on a level with Emeline and Dale, bowing low.

"Did this carriage accident take place the way the young lady described it?" the king asked him, barely audible.

"Yes, Your Majesty, exactly," Innish said, keeping his eyes on the king's feet. He spoke in a deeper voice than usual, which was strange.

"Did you see the creature in the abandoned house as well?"

"No, Your Majesty. But I did see what it did to Loddril, the assassin. He was torn to shreds, just as Sir Reese said. A normal animal could not have done it."

This was followed by sounds of disgust from the Sapients and exultation from the Theurgists.

King Olvinde studied him for a moment. "You strike me as rather familiar. How long have you served in the King's Hall?

"For many years, Your Majesty."

The king rubbed his eyes, nodding a dismissal. The guard spun and took up his place by the doors again. King Olvinde cast his weary gaze on Dada and Fish.

"And these men?" he asked. "Have they testimony as well?"

Dada and Fish frowned at each other and then stood reluctantly. Dada put an arm around Emeline and Dale.

"Yes, Your Majesty," he said. "My name is Wender Bird and this is Airn Fish. We went to investigate the spot where my children saw the Ithin in Equane, and can testify that something gave off a terrible smell."

"Not just terrible, *unnatural*, Your Majesty," Fish added. "So we came to report it."

"And based on the two incidents, we'd like to ask that some forces be sent to protect our village. Guards or knights—whatever Your Majesty sees fit," Dada said, and bowed his head. "There is something in our woods."

The king studied him a moment as everyone waited in silence. He glanced at Aladane, the last one left on the bench.

"Aladane's just a stowaway," Dale told him. Emeline winced at his familiar tone and Aladane glowered, but Fish suddenly laughed. It was oddly loud in the quiet chamber.

King Olvinde cleared his throat, and then gestured impatiently for the villagers to sit down. They sat quickly, Emeline eyeing Reese. He was watching the king sharply as one of the blue-robed attendants produced an enameled vial and passed it to the ailing man. Emeline suspected this was medicine—*real* medicine.

The king took a long drink, then regarded everyone with weary eyes. "And so we've come to the difficult task of deciding what actions to take. Do I send investigators to this manor in the Cinderin Valley, or perhaps to this southern village? Let us discuss this in a civilized fashion."

The king's voice grew stronger as he addressed one of the Theurgists, a large, white-bearded man. "Grimdi, what say you, who recently returned from a similar journey?"

"Well, Your Majesty, there is no reason to assume the Ithin at the manor would still be there, but we could send a group to Equane."

"But the evidence from the manor is much stronger!" a balding man said, the Theurgist who had been at the academy with Helid.

"We could examine the surrounding woodland in the Cinderin Valley," Helid suggested.

"And what good did it do on that journey His Majesty just mentioned?" a Sapient asked. "You found nothing to report in Basten, Grimdi, except for hysterical rumors."

"It was never determined what the lights were that those families saw in the trees," Grimdi said stiffly.

"Exactly!" Rellum exclaimed. "That is my point!"

"I meant that there was no rational explanation!" the bearded Theurgist insisted. "It must've been the Anthrane!"

"No explanation except for bioluminescence!" a Sapient called out. "You conveniently ignored it!"

"You fool! You'd call the very ghost of your mother bioluminescence!" another Theurgist snapped.

"Well, it *would* be!" the Sapient retorted, and a few others laughed.

The king cleared his throat loudly. In a few moments, the room was quiet again.

"Your Majesty, I would just like to remind everyone," Helid said pompously, "that the head schoolteacher in Bellash saw those lights as well, and he is a well-respected man in the town."

"That's still hearsay," Rellum spoke up. "Even Sir Reese's testimony is hearsay. I saw none of it!"

Reese cast a dark look at the Sapient whose life he had saved.

The king frowned too. "Sir Reese, although young, has been a faithful Lash Knight for three years. His account is not to be taken lightly."

"And he has cloth from the Ithin's hood!" a Theurgist shouted. There were angry mutters from the Sapients at this.

"That could be from *anything!*"

Emeline sighed tightly and looked at Dada, who was watching the council in dismay.

"Yes, yes," the king said, sounding exhausted. "There is no denying that in all this time, there has been no indisputable evidence that the Dark Creatures exist. Or magic, for that matter. Yet the stories and sightings are so persistent they cannot be ignored." He grimaced. "I will admit that I was facetious before, however, as Doctor Nallor's tonics certainly do nothing. As is the case with all 'magical' cures I have seen."

"Your Majesty, you put your life in danger when you saw that man," Rellum declared.

"My dear Rellum Sapient, my life is constantly in danger," King Olvinde told him drily. "In point of fact, it is a very large part of being king." The Sapient flushed red.

At that moment, King Olvinde broke into another fit of coughing. He waved his attendants away angrily, as if determined to get through this council session.

"But as we are in the midst...of investigating the crime against Rellum Sapient," he wheezed, "I am of a mind to hold off on sending anyone anywhere...." He shuddered, leaning back in his great chair, and whispered, "At least...for the present."

The Theurgists were crestfallen, the Sapients smug. Emeline's hopes plummeted. With one short argument, they had already wiped out all possibility of protection for Equane. How long could her little village be left undefended at the shoulder of the forest?

That languid shadow lurking between the trees...the hiss!

She watched the ailing king as he struggled to breathe, and a sudden, terrible thought reached her: If he died, and Rellum became king, there would be no help for Equane ever. Ever. No matter what the Ithin did.

King Olvinde rode the line between the factions, holding both Sapients and Theurgists at bay. Without him, that medium would be lost. What would become of the kingdom then?

"Sir Reese!" Emeline blurted, startling everyone. She only just remembered to include his title.

Dada put a hand on her arm in alarm, but she did not heed it. Not now. Reese gave her an expectant look, calm and steady, knowing exactly what she was going to say.

"I want to show them." She kept her eyes intently on him.

Reese nodded and turned to address the king, who was frowning indignantly. "Your Majesty, there is something you should see."

Then he raised a hand to Innish at the back of the room, just as Emeline heard Dada mutter, "Em, no!"

twenty-three

Innish rapped on the doors to the council room and they slowly opened. Emeline stood up slowly, shaking off Dada's hand. She was afraid to look at him, afraid to look at Dale or any of the others.

"What is this interruption?" the king asked, coughing again. The council members were looking from Reese to Emeline to one another suspiciously.

"Emeline!" Dada demanded softly. He was sitting on the edge of his seat, his dark eyes wide. "What are you doing?"

"It's all right, Dada," she told him, and her own steady voice surprised her. "It's the right thing to do."

Her father turned pale and started to rise, but Fish caught his arm. He looked alarmed too, but he shook his head at Dada, watching Emeline.

Innish reentered the chamber, carrying the potted plant from the corridor; it was freshly watered, dripping. He brought it carefully up to Reese, but Emeline could tell from his expression that he had no idea what this pretty, curling flower was for.

There was a short silence, and she looked at Reese, not sure how to begin. He nodded and announced, "Your Majesty and members of the council know of the Keldares' stories—tales of magic as unlikely to some as the Dark Creatures. Emeline Bird's mother was a Keldare."

Emeline swelled with pride at his words. Several of the Sapients were scowling now, whispering angrily to one another, and the Theurgists watched in suspense.

Reese smiled at her encouragingly, even though his eyes were worried. She stepped forward and took the plant from him.

"What is this nonsense?" someone demanded from among the Sapients.

Ignoring it, Emeline held her hand out over the lady star. The shimmer of magic spread hotly up her arms until it filled her, her palms almost aglow. The flower sprang up into the air, following her fingers like a dancing red snake.

The council room exploded into a fury.

Theurgists and Sapients leapt from their chairs, shouting at the top of their lungs. The king's attendants cried out and recoiled in fear.

"By the kingdom!" Innish bellowed.

King Olvinde sat perfectly still, his face drained of any color it had left.

Bolstered by the potent magic inside her, Emeline held her ground, spinning the flower in elegant spirals.

"What trickery is this?!" a Sapient screamed.

"Stop her! Stop it right now!"

"Don't you touch her!" a Theurgist brayed.

"This is proof! This is *absolute proof!*"

"Nonsense! Chicanery! Call the guards!"

There was a sudden crash of chairs falling and Emeline

snapped out of her spell. Reese was standing between her and the Sapients, some of whom had rushed down from their seats. She realized that Dada and Fish had jumped up and stood on either side of her, ready to beat back the Theurgists too.

She had done it.

"Stop, girl," the king rasped at her. He was rigid in his throne, his skeletal hands clenching its arms. Quickly, she let the flower fall, drooping over the side of the pot.

"It's real, Your Majesty!" The words rushed out of her, in nearly the same way her magic did. "Magic is real and so are the Ithin!"

"Lies!" the Sapients shrieked.

"This is why Equane needs help!" Emeline shouted at the king. "Your Majesty, please! Please help us!"

"The plant must be examined!" Rellum roared. Helid's expression was beatific.

The king grabbed hold of one of his attendants and spoke urgently into his ear. Collecting himself, the attendant pulled a small bell from his robe and produced the chime that had sounded earlier. It startled the council members enough to create a pause.

"His Majesty demands silence!"

"This changes *everything!*"

"Your Majesty, this is everything we've tried to tell you!" a Theurgist called out.

The king beat his fist on his lap and the attendant shouted, "Silence! By order of the king!"

Emeline's head was pounding, but Dada was holding her hand tight and Reese was a fierce wall in front of her. There were one or two more shouts, mostly incoherent. Then followed a strained silence.

King Olvinde's eyes bored into Emeline once more, his thin chest heaving. "Sir Reese," he said, after a moment, "bring me that plant."

Obediently, Reese took the pot from Emeline and passed it to the closest of the king's attendants.

"It's an ordinary lady star, Your Majesty, from one of the royal gardens," Reese said.

The king held the pot in his lap and studied the drooping flower. The council members murmured as he poked in the dirt and ran his shaky hands along the bottom of the pot.

"Young lady, explain to me *how* you manipulated this plant," he commanded Emeline.

"It's plants and water together," she told him in a rush. "I can make them move. I discovered it in Equane, with the water lilies in our canals."

"Your Majesty, she also used it to defend herself from the Ithin in the manor," Reese said, and Emeline felt a small weight lift from her. Now there was nothing he hadn't told the king, on her account.

"So you've witnessed this phenomena before?" the king asked him. He nodded.

Emeline clenched her fists and added, "I had to show you, Your Majesty, to make you understand that our village is in danger! If the council just keeps arguing and attacking itself, then nothing will be done to protect our people! Don't you understand?"

This was followed by outbreaks of bitter rumbling from the council. It was clear that the silence would not last long.

She looked at her family; they were pale and breathless, Dada most of all. She longed suddenly for them all to be far away from that airless room.

King Olvinde cast a wary look at his divided council. Then he nodded slowly to himself.

"I hereby decree that we should waste no time in investigating either this girl's ability or the areas in which the Ithin were seen," he declared.

The council members had no time to react.

The double doors flew open and crashed against the walls. "Your Majesty!" a voice roared.

Emeline's heart jumped into her throat. It was a blue-armored guard with his bullet-gun drawn.

"We're under attack!" he shouted, half-panicked, half-confused.

The king dropped the plant to the floor and the pot shattered.

"Attack?" he echoed. "By who?" Another guard raced into view and nearly crashed into the first one, heaving. His face was terrified.

"It's the *Ithin!*" he cried out, his voice trembling. "The Ithin are in the grove!"

Suddenly, the council room seemed to spin. Voices broke out all around Emeline—the king's, the Sapients' and Theurgists'—someone shouting—

Numbly, she felt Reese's arm around her, pushing her back toward the seats. "Stay calm," he said, his deep voice cutting through the bedlam.

"There is *no such thing!*" a Sapient bellowed.

"I saw one with my own eyes!" a guard yelled.

"How did they get in my grove?" the king demanded, horrified.

More guards and servants appeared in the doorway, shouting and running. The pandemonium was sudden and intense.

"Take the king to the tower!" Reese commanded the royal attendants. Then he started for the double doors. The Theurgists leapt to their feet as the king's attendants helped him up—a few of them started for the mirrored door themselves, as it was the closest exit. The Sapients watched them, frightened, but stubbornly rooted to the spot.

"This is another trick!" one of them bellowed. "Just like this village girl!"

A loud scream burst from somewhere outside the hall, chilling Emeline to the bone. Everyone stared at one another in horror.

Helid Theurgist shot up from his seat a second later, as if he'd been stabbed from below. His wrinkled face was slick with terror.

"They've come back!" he shrieked. His fellow council members stared at him in astonishment, not comprehending. Then his face burned red, and he gathered his robe up quickly, struggling to leave. The king looked back in confusion before he and his attendants disappeared through the mirrored door.

Then someone else shouted from across the room: *"It was you! You let them out!"*

Everyone turned toward the voice. It came from the doors, through which Reese and Innish had not yet left. To Emeline's amazement, Innish stood taut and furious, his finger pointed at Helid. His face was nearly unrecognizable. Reese was gaping at him.

Then the guard flew toward the council. He threw himself in front of the mirrored door as it closed behind the king, blocking anyone else's escape. Helid recoiled from him, suddenly looking very old and weak.

"Bless water," Dada whispered, holding Dale and Emeline tight. Innish seemed delirious.

"You let them out!" he roared, sounding like a madman. "And now they've come home!" Grabbing Helid by his sleeve, Innish called out to Reese, across the council room. "We must flood the grove, Reese! The water will destroy them!" His voice was so altered now that he seemed to be a different man.

Helid trembled as Sapients and Theurgists alike rushed away in different directions.

"Flood the grove," Fish repeated. "That might work! It's walled in!"

Reese was staring back at Innish as if a wild realization had struck him. Innish turned and swung himself and Helid through the mirrored door; Reese looked at Emeline and the others, and she could see his thoughts whirling, fast as a whip crack.

"Follow Innish!" he shouted at her. "Into the tower!"

Dada rushed them toward the empty thrones obediently. "Into the tower," he said feverishly, pushing everyone past the chairs and toward the mirrored door.

Emeline looked back at Reese, her heart pounding. He had bolted out of the double doors.

"We're going into the king's tower?" Aladane hissed in disbelief.

"Come on!" Fish exclaimed, and shoved him.

In a second, they were through the mirror and it had closed soundly behind them. Emeline blinked rapidly in the gloom.

Gone was all the glass and silver. They were standing in a dark, low-ceilinged hallway made of ancient stone bricks. She remembered that the tower was older than the rest of the King's Hall, dating back to the beginnings of the capital. There was a faint smell of mildew.

Innish and Helid had vanished already, and the king and his attendants were long gone. The hallway curved to the left ahead of them, passing a narrow window before it disappeared into darkness.

"A 'king's grove'!" Fish burst out in disgust. "The royals should've known this would happen! It's a wood, just like any other wood!" He tore off his hat and slapped it against the stone wall.

"What was Innish saying?" Emeline asked, panting.

"I don't know, but let's get farther in," Dada said. They started for the curve up ahead and Dale paused at the nearest window slit.

"Maybe we can see what's going on!" he said.

"Em, you showed them your magic!" Aladane exclaimed, incredulous.

"I had to," she said, glancing at Dada's ashen face. "To protect Equane."

She squeezed against Dale to see out the window, squinting in the bright sunset. It looked down on a rooftop, some portion of the hall. Beyond it, they could see only the buildings of the capital, stretching out like a very real tapestry.

"The grove is on the other side," Dale realized. They turned and hurried around the corner, the boys bumping into each other in the musty darkness. They climbed several stone steps, catching sight of another window slit ahead.

Suddenly screams broke through the air, and everyone froze. Emeline flew to the window, her heart in her throat.

Where was Reese? Was he all right? She could see the trees of the grove now, just in view on the left. *The next window,* she thought, and bolted ahead, not waiting for the others.

Dada called after her as she raced around the corner, stumbling over the steps. She found the next window, trembling. Now she could see the grove directly below; the treetops were dense and green, and deceptively still. She spotted several guards standing atop the great stone wall that sealed in the grove; they were holding massive hoses, pouring water out over the trees.

The others joined her just as she heard a noise ahead, around the next corner. They all stopped and listened. It sounded like something scraping against stone.

"There's someone here," Dada said, alarmed.

"Maybe it's Innish, still acting like a lunatic," Fish said grimly.

"Get behind us." Dada stepped in front of Emeline and the boys, and Fish followed him, both of them tense. They led the way cautiously toward the corner, listening as the scraping became louder. It was accompanied by heavy breathing.

They rounded the corner and came upon Innish himself, attacking the tower wall with a long, heavy spear. The villagers halted, startled. He gave them one quick glance and then continued, slamming the point of the spear into a crack between the stone bricks. The weapon looked like a decorative piece that he'd taken from a wall somewhere. Helid was no longer with him.

"I told you," Fish muttered.

"Innish, what are you doing?" Dada demanded.

"There is a secret way down into the grove." Innish heaved, stabbing fiercely into the crack. "Only Olvinde and I know it." His face was not that of the man they'd traveled with; gone was the serious, guarded expression. Now he looked feverish, his eyes enormous.

"Olvinde...!" Dale repeated, staring. Emeline had caught it too—Innish had called the king by his name alone.

With one more blow, a stone in the wall pivoted and fell crashing to the floor. Innish grabbed hold of the stones on either side and pulled them out, widening the hole to expose a cavity inside the thick wall. It was wide enough for a man to fit inside.

Emeline inched forward past Dada and Fish, peering inside the cavity. Then she gasped: there was a smooth silver pole running vertically through the hollowed wall.

"I am the king's brother, Irwind," Innish said shortly. He tore more stones from the wall, making the hole wide enough to step through. "Those fool Theurgists let my Ithin out. We are *all* responsible for...so much destruction..."

He reached inside the hollowed wall and grabbed hold of the pole with both hands. Then he slid down into the darkness, out of sight.

"Innish!" Dada cried out. They all crowded around the hole and stared down into the shadows. He was gone.

"Innish is the king's brother?" Aladane exclaimed.

"How can he be?" Dale asked, looking back at Dada and Fish. "Wouldn't the king know?"

"Maybe he doesn't recognize him," Emeline murmured. Irwind had run away to the Outer Lands years ago—or so the story went.

"*His* Ithin'?" Fish said, bewildered. "He's just gone mad, Bird. He's babbling!"

"Look at this pole, Fish," Dada said quietly. "How did he know about this?"

"Maybe he's been snooping around! I don't know!"

"How could he have his own Ithin?" Dale exclaimed. "Does that mean he can control them?"

Dada rubbed his face, staring down after Innish. "Irwind was a scientist...an inventor," he muttered. "Maybe..."

Emeline listened, thinking rapidly, gazing down into the secret entrance to the grove. If the guards were flooding it, then all the trees and plants would be wet.

Wet vines wrapping themselves around an Ithin's head...

One form of magic battling another...

Reese was down there fighting monsters, and she could help. She could help! If she followed Innish—whether he was who he claimed or not—she could be there in an instant.

Without another thought, she grabbed on to the pole and threw her legs around it.

"Emeline!" Dada roared. He grabbed her by the sleeve, but she yanked free. Then she loosened her grip and she slid, surprisingly fast.

The silver was perfectly smooth and she dropped like a stone into nothingness. The others shouted down after her, their voices echoing. It was more like falling than sliding; her skirts flew up around her and her hands burned against the pole.

In a moment, she had landed, her feet striking dirt. Dizzy, she glanced upward and saw only darkness. She couldn't hear the others calling anymore.

Before her was a large hole full of sunlight and she crawled through it, wincing at the burns on her hands. The stones of one of the grove paths lay in the dirt before her, and she followed them, hearing the water hoses in the distance, and smelling the fresh, frightening scent of the woods.

The age-old dread crept into her bones and she shivered. The tree branches blocked out the sky, and there was a mist in the air she knew must be from the hoses. Water dripped from the branches overhead and she stepped in a puddle, soaking her foot. Everything was quiet. There were no birds chirping, and she saw no one.

Where were the knights? Had they already destroyed the Ithin? Or been destroyed by them?

She heard a distant cry and gasped, her heart hammering. Every instinct told her to run away, to find a door and get back inside, but she was here to help Reese. She steeled herself and hurried toward the sound, walking off the path. Her boots sank into cold mud and she opened her arms to shake out her damp cloak.

A movement on either side made her freeze. She saw only dripping branches...but some of them were twisted toward her.

She dropped her arms, afraid to breathe, and the branches moved back, springing drops of water into the air. Her breath came out in a rush as she realized what had happened. She hadn't even been trying! The energy was boiling inside her, right below the surface.

Slowly, she reached out an arm toward the trees, and a single branch stretched toward her. It cracked and groaned as it came.

There might be monsters in the world, but she had magic too.

She rushed forward again, faster, deeper and deeper into the woods. She went with her hands outstretched, and the branches followed, splintering and crunching as she passed. The power danced through her, crackling like lightning, thrilling and frightening at once. She felt like she was moving in a dream.

Then she saw a shape in the gloom ahead, lying in the mud—a figure in black armor. She froze, staring at the fallen knight in absolute horror.

But relief came quickly. *It's not him!* The figure was too thin.

She stepped closer, breathing again. The knight's helmet was askew, but not enough to see his face. His breastplate was battered, crushed inward. She realized the design was of two crossed blades.

Gundan. Pride of the city of Endan. Dead.

The breastplate had been beaten in right over his heart. *They eat the hearts of men.* An Ithin had tried to tear out his heart!

She reeled away from the dead knight. Would Reese's armor not protect him?

She could hear herself panting now, and she closed her eyes and leaned against a tree trunk, trying to calm down.

There was a distant clang of metal on metal. Her eyes snapped open. A deep voice roared, and she ran toward the sound, plunging through mud and undergrowth, slogging through wetter and wetter grass. She could hear the hoses rushing, not far away now.

Then she heard Reese yell, heard the crack of his whip. She plunged through a cluster of soaking bushes and saw him. He was fighting a creature wrapped in a tattered, hooded cloak. The thing was nearly his height, but it was hunched over, its hooked forearms protruding from the cloak.

An Ithin.

It lunged and snapped its jaws, slicing at Reese's shield with a horrible, metallic sound. It struck again and again, in strangely jerky movements. Reese kept putting ground between them, struggling to crack his whip.

"Reese!" Emeline screamed.

He whirled his whip around the Ithin's neck suddenly and yanked it to its knees, but then he jerked his head up to see Emeline. The Ithin grasped the whip in its claws and pulled. Reese stumbled forward.

She threw out her arms at the nearest tree and its branches swept down. The wood smacked into the Ithin's head as she swiped across the air, and she could almost feel the physical blow in her arm. The creature tumbled backward, Reese falling with it; he let go of his whip quickly and leaped to his feet.

There was a white-hot anger inside her. Tree branches

beat the Ithin bodily, rolling it across the ground until the wet grass rose up and twisted over it. The thing hissed violently, clawing at the plants, and Reese snatched up his end of the whip. He jerked it tight as the Ithin rolled in the opposite direction—tearing its head clean from its body.

Emeline gasped as the Ithin's head flew through the air—it landed with its fangs still gnashing. The headless body kicked and writhed on the ground.

Out of nowhere, white sparks shot out of the head. Emeline stumbled back. Reese swore. The Ithin's hood came off as the head jolted and writhed on the ground, and the round, insect-like face lay exposed, its giant eyes blank and dark. The fangs fell apart and were still.

Then the tree branches slowly withdrew, the bark crackling as they settled. Reese stared at Emeline a moment and then he ran toward her, yanking off his helmet.

"What are you doing here?" he demanded.

He caught her up in his arms, and she kissed him without thinking, all her relief pouring out at once. He grabbed the back of her head and kissed her back, almost roughly; it set her whole body on fire. The world disappeared in a rush of dizzying warmth.

But then he pulled away and glanced around them quickly, shoving his helmet back on.

"Innish says he's Irwind, the king's brother," she told him in a rush. "He showed me a shortcut into the grove."

"Irwind?" Reese exclaimed. "Innish is Lord Irwind? What madness is that? Are you sure?"

Emeline nodded, breathless. The Ithin's head sparked

again, and she turned away, shuddering. Water was puddling around their feet.

"Reese, he called the Ithin 'his,'" she added uncertainly. Reese grimaced and stared down at the monster lying in the mud.

"I always knew Innish had a secret...but I can't believe it," he said quietly. "He's been my best guard for a whole year."

twenty-four

A sudden rustling broke out behind Emeline. She turned to see something spring from a tree—a mass of claws and a ratty cloak. She shrieked, but Reese swung his black shield in front of her and knocked the Ithin into the groundwater. He lashed his whip around its neck and broke it, just as another one slithered into view behind him.

Emeline swept out her arm and the nearest tree slammed its branches into the creature. The Ithin fell, and she whirled up several vines, flinging them around it. Hissing and snapping its fangs, it jerked its way toward her, crawling in the water. Then Reese slammed the edge of his shield down on its neck, slicing the head right off. Water and sparks flew.

Emeline wheeled to face the next one, but for the moment, everything was still.

"You should be in the tower," Reese said sharply.

"I came to help you," she insisted, and his eyes widened.

"To help me?" His voice was both angry and admiring.

"Look, the grove is really flooding now," she pressed, as the muddy water visibly rose. Her feet felt numb inside her boots. "That's why I knew I could help. Everything is wet."

"Emeline," he said, his voice catching in his throat. "I don't want you to help. I want you safe in the tower."

"I'm staying here!" she told him, clenching her fists. "*I'm* the one with magic, remember?"

He started to argue, but then he grabbed her arm, looking down at their feet. The water was inching up toward her knees.

"We should both go back," he said quickly. "The water will stop the rest of them." He scooped her up off her feet, her cloak dripping back into the dark water. Then he started off through the trees, brandishing his shield before them. All of her senses were strained, anticipating, dreading the next Ithin to appear.

Suddenly, an Ithin loomed out of the shadows. She screamed; Reese froze. She expected it to lunge at them—but it didn't move. It stood there like a statue, its claws protruding crookedly from its cloak. Neither she nor Reese breathed.

In the dim light, she couldn't quite make out its face. Did it not see them? It was drenched and streaming water. Was it dead, then? Did they die standing on their feet?

Reese took a cautious step forward as Emeline's heart pounded. The Ithin was still. He took another step and then another, both of them staring at the inanimate creature.

Then Reese started to run again. Emeline twisted to look back over his shoulder, bewildered. Dead or alive, the Ithin did not follow. Turning back around, she realized she had no idea which direction the King's Hall was, but he was splashing through the wood with assurance. They came to an opening in the trees and she saw that they were at the fork in the path with the fountain.

Without warning, a hissing Ithin sprang out before them.

This one was alive for sure. It jerked forward and backward, as if confused and angry—steam burst from its head and it spasmed, struggling in the water.

Reese set her down quickly to fight, but she waved at the undergrowth and it swelled up, tripping the creature. It crashed into the groundwater, sparking and smoking. Reese stared down at it in disbelief.

"Are they machines?" he demanded.

Emeline shook her head, not comprehending. Her mind spun for a moment as Dada's last words came back to her: *Irwind was a scientist, an inventor. . . .*

Reese took her hand and they plunged onward, sloshing through the water. Soon they were passing windows with colored glass, some with faces pressed up against them. Emeline recognized the dining hall.

The thought suddenly reminded her of her family. She had counted on them being safe in the tower, but now a terrible realization struck her:

Dada was much more likely to have followed her.

Is he in the grove?

Emeline stared back behind them as Reese pulled her along, making for the archway that led to the first corridor. Its doors were closed tight against the rising groundwater.

Without warning, Innish stepped out onto the path, drenched to the bone, his limbs and beard dripping. He stood nearly as still as the inanimate Ithin, and in his eyes was a mixture of awe and fire that she had never seen. He wasn't looking at them; his gaze was directed behind them.

Fear flooded her.

"There she is," Innish said in a hushed tone. "The original."

Reese and Emeline spun quickly. Her heart stopped at the sight of the weird thing that struggled through the water behind them.

It was an Ithin, but it was smaller and rattier than any she had seen. Its cloak and hood were totally unlike the others': They looked more like an outer layer of flesh or hide than cloth. Its claws were clicking together and its head was weaving side to side. Its huge eyes were not blank, but bright and roving, taking in all three of the people in front of it.

Just as Emeline realized that its movements were fluid, not jerky and stiff, she was struck with a horrible stench. *Rotting flesh!* The smell that Dada and the others had described! She couldn't breathe and Reese gagged.

It was like some ancient tomb had opened up—a tomb for something unnatural...but old as the land and sky.

Dark magic.

There was a magical spring deep inside of Emeline, but *this* thing was magic in and of itself. The difference struck her with a certainty that took her breath away.

Reese crouched as the creature writhed in front of them, not stiff and clumsy, but liquid like a shadow. She fought the instinct to run as it snapped its jaws at them and hissed. Even its hiss was different from the others': It was much louder, and it sounded like many terrible voices whispering at once.

"Innish, what in the kingdom have you done?" Reese roared.

Before Innish could answer, the Ithin lunged forward.

Reese's whip cracked just as fast, stopping the creature midway. It hissed again and clicked its claws.

Frantic, Emeline summoned the grass beneath the water. It shot upward, wrapping around the Ithin's legs; the monster let out a gurgling cry and fought against the wet, clinging grass.

"That's right, trap her!" Innish shouted.

Reese slashed his whip around the Ithin too. The grass and whip tangled around the creature, and it cried out again, an eerie, strangled scream. Emeline shivered, her blood running cold.

All at once, the Ithin threw itself forward and crashed into them, knocking them down into the water. Emeline caught a muddy mouthful before she struggled to her feet.

Still snarled in the grass, the Ithin was on Reese's chest, wrestling with him. Its claws found the skin between his helmet and his neck, and blood sprayed, shockingly red. Innish shouted from somewhere nearby. Desperately, Emeline flung up whatever plants she could command from the water.

No! Don't kill him!

Then a shovel swung through the air, knocking the Ithin off the knight—it was Dada, looking wild with terror. Reese staggered up and clapped his hand on his wounded throat.

The hall doors were open; Dada had come flying out of them, brandishing the first thing he found. Fish rushed out behind him with his bullet-gun, just as two more of Irwind's Ithin emerged from the trees. He fired at the first one, and Emeline's ears rang with the sound. The Ithin's left eye flashed and exploded; it dropped stiffly to the ground as Fish aimed at the second.

"Get inside!" he roared. "Come on!"

But the real Ithin turned toward Dada, hissing and shrieking, its horrible stench thick in the air.

"No!" Emeline shouted. Panic smothered her as he stepped back, gripping the shovel, the monster advancing. She heard Fish fire again and curse; heard Reese roaring something she couldn't make out.

I won't let you hurt Dada!

With all her might, she strained her arms at the nearest tree and heaved—not at its branches, but at the base of its massive trunk. Energy snapped through her, searing the air, tearing at the soaked, twisted roots beneath the ground.

Not Dada! Never!

Her hair rose from her scalp, heat swallowing her up.

The great tree groaned and rocked forward, tilting wildly toward the Ithin. Irwind and Dada cried out at the sight, just as Reese slashed his whip across the Ithin's back. The creature gave an ear-splitting screech.

Emeline pulsed with the enormous effort... with the incredible force of the *magic*. She felt as if she hovered above the ground. Wonderful and awful, it was too much; her muscles were screaming. It was impossible. She couldn't do it—could she?

With an explosion of shattering bark, the tree fell. It smashed down upon the Ithin with an impact that shook the entire grove, sending a wave of groundwater into the air.

She collapsed into the filthy water herself, streaks of light across her vision. There were shouts and two more gunshots. Then Reese and Dada were grabbing hold of her arms, pulling her to her feet. Bless water, they were both still alive.

She stumbled as they ran for the doorway, pushing past the giant network of tree roots exposed to the air. She glanced back at the trunk across the path and saw nothing of the Ithin underneath. It was gone.

Then she was dimly aware of being suddenly inside, of Reese slamming the doors shut. He shoved a thick bar down across the handles to lock them.

The group of them stood there for a long moment, in shock. The corridor was flooded from all the water that had come in; Emeline stared down at the tiles blankly.

Then Dale and Aladane flung their arms around her, snapping her awake. Fish was holding up Dada, while all around them people were splashing through the hallway in panic.

"Emeline, you went into the grove!" Aladane said, absolutely appalled. "Why did you do that?"

"Because of the water. Because she could use her magic to fight them," Dale said. His face was pinched, but his voice was thick with pride. "Did you see that tree fall?" Aladane's mouth hung open.

"I was so afraid...." Dada put his face in his hands.

Fish hugged his shoulders. "She's all right, Bird. She's all right," he said. Emeline threw her arms around her father, too, and he squeezed her tight.

"Don't you ever do that again," Dada whispered fiercely.

She shook her head, tears stinging her eyes. First she had revealed her magic to the king, and then she had flung herself into a battle. It was a wonder that her father's heart had not stopped. But she had won. *They* had won.

"Innish!" Reese's voice boomed suddenly. They all turned

to see him grab the older man by the collar with one hand, the other still clamped on his neck. Emeline gasped at the blood seeping through his fingers. "Perhaps you'd like to explain yourself now!"

Innish went limp for a moment, closing his eyes. Then he straightened himself and said, in the strange new voice he'd used in the tower, "I will. But I must find Olvinde first and make sure he's safe."

Reese stared at him for a few seconds. Then he let go, shaking his head. "If you're Lord Irwind, prove it. Prove it." His tone was uncertain now.

"Here is my proof, Reese!" As they all watched, Innish pulled out the chain that hung under his shirt. On it was a large silver ring, engraved with a symbol of stars and wheels interlocking.

Emeline looked at Reese as he studied it. His green eyes went wide. For a moment, he said nothing, but then he swore under his breath. Abruptly, he knelt low to the floor.

"By all the fish in the canal," Fish said, watching him kneel.

"This is the ring of my birthright," the king's brother told them. "But there's no need to bow to me, Reese. I owe you an apology for lying to you." He sighed heavily and looked down the hallway with a troubled expression. "Though that's nothing compared to the other wrongs I've committed, and must atone for now."

"You built these monsters, didn't you?" Reese demanded, standing slowly. "They're automatons!"

Fish gasped. Emeline looked at Dada, who was frowning

and watching Irwind. He had already begun to suspect it in the tower, she knew. She almost didn't believe it herself, but the sparks and the steam...and the Ithin standing absolutely motionless....Everything clicked in her mind now.

It had broken down. They were machines, malfunctioning in the water.

"But not that last one," Reese said, and looked at Emeline, his fierce face drawn. It was the first time she had truly seen him look afraid.

"Reese, you're bleeding," she protested, coming to his side.

He glanced down at her, barely comprehending, but then he pulled off his helmet, wincing. The Ithin's claws had slashed him deeply. He knelt wearily and wrapped one arm around her waist as she examined his wound. She pulled off her drenched red cap, for lack of a bandage, and pressed it against the blood flow. Even in the midst of her concern, his arm felt wonderful around her. It felt like it belonged there.

"No, not that one." Irwind put his hands up to the sides of his head and closed his eyes again. "Let us find my brother and I will explain. Come with me to the tower. The grove is flooded and the danger is over." He turned and strode down the corridor, trailing through the water.

twenty-five

"Do you remember, Olvinde, when I journeyed to Vindane all those years ago?" Lord Irwind asked, studying his brother. "To see the mineral springs? I became lost for several days in the woods there."

"You never would take an escort!" the king retorted.

Emeline and her family watched from a soft divan in a glittering blue-and-silver sitting room inside the tower. It was less ostentatious than the council room, but more comfortable. The king and his brother were seated in padded armchairs, their hands clasped together between them. Emeline couldn't imagine what the king was feeling, now that he knew his missing brother had been hiding in plain sight for an entire year.

Reese was missing the story after all, to his clear frustration, having been ordered to report to the infirmary at once by the king.

No more of the creatures were stirring in the grove. It remained locked and flooded, but most of the hall's residents were still in a panic. The surviving knights were trying to restore order.

No one but the people in that room yet knew that all but one of the Ithin were automatons. Emeline marveled at the irony of a handful of villagers knowing such a secret before anyone else.

"Truthfully, I never had an interest in the springs," Irwind continued. "I went to the Vindane region because I was concerned by the persistent folklore surrounding it. You know where I stood in the royal argument. I was thoroughly convinced that the Theurgists were deluded in every sense, and I wanted to see for myself what innocuous wildlife populated the area." He laughed grimly. "So I went, with every intention of debunking those myths. And instead...I found her."

"Her?"

"An Ithin, brother," Irwind told him, his eyes glittering. "A real-life monster, flesh and blood."

King Olvinde's sunken face turned even paler. "Beyond all doubt?" he whispered.

"Beyond all doubt. A Dark Creature itself, from the old legends. She was tangled in a hunter's trap and dying. She was so fearsome, her smell so horrible!"

Irwind smiled despite what he was describing, and the effect was strange—almost sinister. It reminded Emeline of the weird look on his face underneath the fireworks.

"Imagine my horror and shock. After all that time, to discover that the stories were true!"

"But you told no one?" King Olvinde demanded.

"And admit my mistake? No...never," Irwind said, reddening. "A common fault in this city."

Emeline couldn't believe her ears. She looked at Dada and Fish, who shared disgusted glances. She could only imagine Reese's reaction.

"But I was desperate to study her. The issue was getting the subject of study back into my labs under the hall, undetected," he said. "I paid my driver into silence, of course, and only managed to strap the creature to our carriage because she was so deteriorated."

"You should have brought the cursed thing straight to the council!" the king exclaimed.

"Yeah!" Aladane muttered.

Irwind hesitated, dropping his eyes to the floor. "...Forgive me, brother," he said finally. "That *is* what I should have done." He put his hands up to the sides of his head and closed his eyes again, as he had done in the corridor beyond the grove.

The king made a furious, exasperated sound.

"But instead, I brought the Ithin to my lab through one of the subterranean tunnels and began to study her. Her strength was incredible, even in that injured state! Her movements so serpentine... How she frightened me, even locked up in a cell... One thing became very clear, Olvinde: The kingdom needed protection from these creatures." Irwind gazed at the king and for a single instant, Emeline could see Innish again—the staunch protector they had traveled with across the kingdom.

"Perhaps because of my skills at automation, the idea struck me that I could build a mechanical Ithin—one of equal strength and fearsomeness, but one that I could control. And if I could build one, why not many? What better defense against Dark Creatures than our own army of them?"

"I confess I had no idea how advanced your automation had become," the king murmured, staring at him in awe.

Irwind brushed that off with a wave of his arm.

"But surely you see the logic?" he insisted. "I began at once, but it was a long and difficult process. I could never duplicate the exact odor the Ithin projected, so I left out that detail, but I designed a simple attack-and-defense program. I built an army of twenty, as deadly as the real one languishing in her cage, and just as aggressive. I gave them automatic reflexes. I even devised a way to make them seek out woods, as a shelter from rain." His eyes lit up with pride for a moment. "I had them pacing in the cells, testing their movements and strength against one another."

Emeline grimaced at the image of a pack of Ithin roving about in cells and tunnels underneath the King's Hall.

"My plan was to present them to you, Olvinde, and give you the controls—once I had finished them. But all along I *knew*—I ignored the fact that those prying council members were attempting to discover my secret." He shook his head in fury. "I never imagined any of them could be so wicked as to use it to their advantage."

"Helid Theurgist!" Dada said, suddenly comprehending. "He let them out!"

"Yes." Irwind's voice dropped to a bitter murmur. "Before I could finish their controls, someone released them through the tunnels in secret. My monstrous army was set loose upon the kingdom."

Emeline gasped.

"And now I know that it was Helid, the same vile man who hired Loddril," he declared.

"Why would he do that?" Dale blurted out.

"To ensure that everyone believed in the Ithin and the

Theurgists would regain power," Irwind told him. "You see, at the time, the reports of Dark Creature sightings had become rather few. And with my Ithin roaming the kingdom, the chances of such sightings were much higher."

"But didn't he know the machines could kill people?" Fish demanded.

"Oh, yes. He could not have seen them in action without knowing that," Irwind said darkly. "It was a sacrifice I suppose he was willing to make, in exchange for the favor of the king."

Emeline felt a sickening twist in her stomach.

"But there were two things that miserable old man did not know. One, that a real Ithin was among the machines, and two, that the others were programmed to return to the hall, once they began to need repairs. The latter is why they ended up in the grove." He paused and shook his head. "I confess, I don't know why the real Ithin returned with them, unless to her, they had become family."

Silence filled the room.

"That man should be put to death!" Fish growled suddenly.

"He will be," King Olvinde rasped.

Irwind nodded and then closed his eyes again. "But you see, I didn't know what he had done. I believed the Ithin had escaped through some fault of mine, and I...I could not face it." He looked at the king, and his face crumpled in shame. "The programming was unfinished! There was no way to find them all, to bring them back! But they were designed to be attracted to the woods, and I knew that would minimize the damage. People were already afraid of the woods."

"The knights could have hunted them down," the king

said, and his voice was flat, expressionless. "You should have told me."

"But I didn't," Irwind whispered. "Instead I ran away to the Outer Lands...where my foolish eyes were further opened. Very few people I met there thought the existence of magic at odds with science and invention. There are sophisticated people outside this kingdom, brother, people whose technology is beyond our imagining." He looked at Emeline then, and she flinched, uncomfortable with his attention. "I finally understood that our divided council was waging a pointless war. Both sides are right, of course," he said quietly.

"And while I was out there, berating myself, I learned that the Theurgists had begun to use the more frequent Ithin sightings to influence you, Olvinde. And at that, I became suspicious. So I returned to the capital in secret and secured myself employment as a guard. When Reese suspected foul play among the Theurgists, I knew I had allied myself with the right man."

The image of Gundan lying on the ground returned to Emeline abruptly. Young, handsome, dead. Arrogant, yes, but that was not a crime. Because Irwind's Ithin were modeled after the legends, they must have been designed to aim straight for the heart. And they had crushed his.

How many others had died at the hands of his machines? Today, or anywhere in the kingdom? Adding to the number of existing Ithin, had the machines caused more deaths than they ever would?

It struck her that, in the wrong hands, science could be even deadlier than dark magic. Perhaps the problem with all power was that the wrong hands reached out for it.

In the silence that filled the room, Dada picked up the tattered journal that Irwind had left on the table between them and the two royals. It was his diary of how he had designed the Ithin, as well as his other discoveries, ideas, and projects over the years. Emeline knew that it must be wondrous, but she wanted to toss it into the fire.

"Yes," the king said suddenly, startling everyone. He had been quiet for so long, listening and thinking, his trembling hands knotted together in his lap. "You were right in that, brother, that one matter—that both sides are right." Although he addressed Irwind, he seemed to speak to the air, looking at no one. "In fact, I have had enough of this foolish feud, once and for all, and I shall end it."

His eyes turned to Emeline, and she held still under his piercing gaze. "You who so bravely demonstrated that magic is not only real, but also elegant, and not limited to these terrifying creatures...you deserve, first and foremost, the promise that I will send royal guards to protect your village."

Dada and Fish beamed at her and each other. Her heart soared.

"And second, you have won the right to be the first in the kingdom to hear my decision." The king cleared his throat. "It is to become royal law that the council be once more combined into one. There will be no more Sapients and Theurgists. It will not be easily done," he added grimly.

"Reese always believed in both. Science *and* magic," Emeline heard herself say. Then she winced, and added quickly, "*Sir* Reese."

"Yes, he is a good knight," the king replied. There was no

mockery in his voice at her familiar address. "I understand why you have formed an attachment."

Her face grew hot. Most of them had seen Reese with his arm around her in the corridor. Dale and Aladane were grinning at her—Aladane even winked—but Dada's expression was serious. With a sudden pang, she wondered what he was thinking. Was he afraid that she would refuse to go home to Equane?

"And what about Emeline and her breathtaking magic?" Irwind asked. She looked up again and saw with alarm that he was studying her, fascinated.

"It's her mother's magic, Your Majesty," Dada said guardedly. "As you said, it doesn't have anything to do with the Dark Creatures."

"Yes," the king said thoughtfully, watching Emeline. "Magic even the Theurgists know little about."

"It's *stupid* that I don't have it," Dale muttered, and Aladane nodded in sympathy.

"I would like to see you demonstrate it again," Irwind told her eagerly. "With your permission, of course," he added to Dada.

Dada's face darkened, and Emeline couldn't blame him: She had immediate misgivings herself about his interest.

"I believe we would all benefit from learning more about your gift," the king told her, and she nodded reluctantly.

"But please, Your Majesty, my daughter must be *safe*," Dada said quickly. "I'm sure you understand—she must be kept safe from the council members. From being used or hurt."

"Indeed. I give you my word that she will be." With sudden violence, Olvinde snatched up a handkerchief and retched into it, his whole body shuddering. Irwind turned to him in concern; the last of his brother's color was fading fast in his weary face.

"And then there is the matter of my heir," the king whispered to himself. He stared at Irwind as if he could not quite fathom who his brother had become. "Things have changed now."

Emeline had forgotten that the king's brother, now that he'd returned, certainly had the best claim to the throne. Dada and Fish gave each other unhappy looks: This new heir was a man who had designed and built murderous automatons, after all.

"I must retire. Someone should collect this family." The king's voice was barely audible.

"I'll call for Quaith," Irwind said quickly, standing up. He stepped over to the wall and pulled a round knob that was hidden behind a tapestry; a faint ringing reached their ears.

"Take the young lady to see her knight," the king breathed.

The king was a complicated man, she realized. As fierce and proud as he had seemed in the council room, he had spoken well of Reese, without concern to his birth. And despite the serious matters that lay before him, he had taken a moment to acknowledge her feelings.

twenty-six

When Quaith arrived, looking much shaken and disheveled by the events of the day, Irwind told him to take Emeline to the infirmary and return the others to their guarded rooms, per the king's command.

"She'll be perfectly safe in the infirmary," Quaith was telling Dada, sounding exhausted. "I'll bring her home whenever she's ready."

The word "home" hung in the air in an odd way. She gave Dada a fierce hug and then turned to follow the servant that Quaith had summoned, out into the corridor. After many turns, they pushed through a pair of white doors and into a large room filled with a sober hush. It was partitioned by several white curtains, and men and women in blue cloaks walked through, speaking in low voices.

"Not done?" Reese's deep voice broke the silence. Emeline gasped. "What else are you going to do, paint it over?"

There was a thump and another voice, soft but stern, answering. Emeline broke into a grin and ran forward, just as one of the curtains was yanked back by a large hand.

Reese stood there in his trousers and bare feet, a large bandage taped to his neck. There was an impatient frown on his face. His bare chest was badly scarred—the life of a Lash

Knight was not an easy one—and Emeline stared. An elderly doctor, looking very tiny next to him, marched away with a shake of his head.

"Lash Knights," he grumbled.

Reese caught sight of Emeline and his eyes lit up. Her stomach flipped.

"Are you all right? What happened?" he asked a bit gruffly.

"I'm fine. We've been sitting with the king and Innish. I mean, Lord Irwind," she corrected herself, ever more aware of the fact that he was half dressed.

"Sitting with the king! Well! Things have changed a bit, haven't they?" he said, regarding her seriously.

"I don't understand all that. I don't understand any of that." She scowled, not realizing she was copying a look he wore often. "Why it matters who we are and where we're from and who we sit with." She felt a world of weariness rush out of her as she stood there, huddled in her damp cloak. She wanted to go home to Equane—except she didn't; she absolutely didn't.

"It *doesn't* matter. Not to anyone worth knowing." Reese folded his arms, watching her.

"All that matters is that the king promised to send guards to Equane," she told him.

"Good. What did Irwind have to say about his charming toys?"

Emeline lowered her voice and told him the story quickly, stopping whenever a doctor or attendant passed.

"Son of a maggot," he swore, glaring at the floor. "So

first that lesion Helid let loose a pack of deadly automatons on the kingdom, and then he tried to assassinate the king's heir."

"And now Irwind might be the heir," she told him, unable to keep the concern out of her voice.

"I suspected as much." He sounded grim. "I hope the king is wise enough not to allow that."

"Irwind wants to study my magic," she whispered.

"I imagine he'll end up frustrated. It's not something he can copy, is it? It's a part of you. I can be there when he summons you, if you'd like," he offered, studying her face. She nodded eagerly. "Good. Let's leave this place."

He took her hand and led her back toward the white doors. The smell of medicine, sweat, and the woods rolled off him, making her a little dizzy. They stopped by a row of hooks in the wall, where he collected his shirt and his boots.

"Where's your armor?" she asked, watching as he carefully pulled on his shirt.

"They sent it up to my quarters." He looked at her for a moment. "Do you know why I have a ring symbol on my breastplate?"

She shook her head. He took her arm and gently pushed up her sleeve. It sent tingles up her to shoulder, but it also revealed her gold armband, which was, naturally, in the shape of a ring.

"The Keldares?" she exclaimed.

"Lash Knights are required to bear a symbol when we graduate from the academy. Most wealthy families have heraldry already, but I had none, of course. So I thought of the people who had been kind to me." He smiled, and went out through the white doors. Emeline followed down a hall, enormously flattered, and happy to walk alongside him, wherever they were going.

He turned around a corner, and Emeline found herself greeted by fresh night air. They were in a secluded nook with a small balcony, which overlooked the practice field and the city beyond. The capital was brilliantly lit, glittering away into the distance.

A cold gust of wind blew her hair back, and Reese wrapped an arm around her and held her close. She felt herself melt into his warmth. A sigh escaped her, and he leaned down and kissed her.

In all of her sleepy life in Equane, she had never imagined this kind of happiness. She could never have dreamed up this gruff, kind young knight, who wore armor that honored her mother's own people.

"I love the way you look at me," Reese murmured. "Your eyes don't judge me...except when I deserve it," he added, grinning. "When I've forgotten my manners." Emeline laughed at that. "But not because of my 'lowly status.'" He kissed her hair, and then added, with a chuckle, "Although you didn't know that I was lowborn for quite a while, did you?"

"It was the kitchen girls at the Mother's Milk who gave it away," she said. "But all it did was help me understand you better."

His expression turned suddenly serious. "Remember Erd, Rellum's driver? I overheard in the infirmary that Helid

already confessed to hiring Loddril, and he named Erd as his informant. He's the one who revealed Rellum's travel route."

"Erd did that?" Emeline exclaimed. She remembered that Rellum had dismissed suspicion of him during the storm.

"He did, the little weasel. He's been locked up with Helid. But I owe him a favor, or perhaps even two," Reese said, grinning unexpectedly. She gave him a confused look. "Well, if he hadn't been an informer, I would never have met you that evening in Blyne." She smiled, realizing it was true. "And when he leered at you at dinner, I realized just how strongly I felt."

"What do you mean?"

"I was boiling with jealousy," he admitted. "And anger. I could tell you didn't like his stares, that eel." Emeline leaned against him and laughed, remembering how mad he'd looked in the dining hall. He kissed her again, and suddenly her heart panged at the thought of the journey home.

"I don't want to leave," she murmured.

"I don't want you to leave," he said, his voice fierce.

"But my father? And Dale?"

Reese was quiet for a long moment. "Let's take it one day at a time," he said, and kissed her on the forehead.

"Yes." She felt comforted by that kind of reasoning. There was nothing else they could do tonight but sleep away the terrors and revelations of the day. "What is your room like in the knights' quarters?" she asked curiously.

"Do you want to see it?" Reese asked.

"Oh." Emeline blushed embarrassingly. "I was just

wondering...I mean, I'm supposed to ask Quaith to take me home. I mean, to the inn...."

Reese started laughing and she cursed herself for babbling.

"It's late. I'll call Quaith."

She nodded, ducking her head against his shoulder. Bless water, he smelled good.

twenty-seven

*I*n the morning, the sky was thick with gray clouds, but still bright; the air smelled like rain was on its way. Emeline looked out the inn window and shook her head. Rain would certainly have been helpful the night before.

The villagers had been woken by a liveryman at the door with a letter from the King's Hall, requesting her presence before the king and Lord Irwind the following day. Fish's face clouded at the continued delay, but he said nothing, looking at Dada. Dale and Aladane gave each other small smiles.

The liveryman left without any mention of breakfast, which sank everyone's spirits.

"Maybe the guards can take us to the Mother's Milk," Dale suggested.

"Maybe so," Dada said hesitantly, watching Fish. He had started pacing slowly in the room. Emeline watched him too, her shoulders drooping. It was unfair to ask him to stay.

"So now they expect us to wait around while they sort themselves out," the farmer muttered. He didn't sound angry as much as determined. The others watched him quietly. "Irwind might not manage to see her for days and days."

He stopped pacing and faced Dada, looking tired and hungry. "Bird, I don't blame you if you want to stay awhile. I know that what Emeline can do has changed some things…and you have to figure out how much," he said. "But I would like to go home. And I think I should bring the stowaway back to his family."

"What?" Aladane exploded.

Emeline stared at Dada, not having considered the idea of splitting up. She saw that her father had, however; he seemed more contemplative than surprised.

"I just don't know how you'll get back home, if I do take off," Fish said, frowning.

Emeline looked at the boys and saw that they were stunned, their eyes darting back and forth between the grown-ups. She suddenly felt stomach-twistingly guilty—her magic, and her feelings for Reese, were causing this. She was responsible for splitting up the group. Wasn't she?

"I know your families are missing you," Dada said slowly. "And you're right, this is just about my family now. We did our duty together and reported our story to the king." He paused and looked at Emeline. Her heart beat loudly in her ears. "Let me find out first how I can secure a wagon and horses to get ourselves back home. If Irwind insists on talking to my daughter, then he ought to be able to help us with that, at least."

Dale heaved a sigh of relief, and then flashed a guilty look at Aladane. The other boy kicked at the tile floor and said nothing.

Fish nodded and shook Dada's hand. "I will take care of your crops, Bird. As long as you don't stay too long," he said with a grin. Dada shook his hand with both of his.

"Thank you very much. And thank you for helping us out

there in the grove. If you hadn't been there at that moment..."
His voice broke and Fish patted him on the back.

"Say nothing of it, my friend."

Everyone stood there for a few moments, trying not to relive the night before. Then Dale shifted his feet and asked, "Can we go eat now?"

Dada turned to address the guards just as they heard the sound of a carriage approaching. It was Quaith's small carriage with its open top—a welcome sight.

"Hello!" he called breathlessly, quick-stepping toward them. "My apologies for not attending to you earlier. As you can imagine, things are in a turmoil."

He glanced at Emeline with absolute awe for several seconds. It was quite a change from his usual condescension, and she looked away, flustered.

"Mister Quaith, what's going on?" Dada asked. "Has there been an announcement about Lord Irwind? Or the Ithin?"

"Not yet. People have heard about the attack, of course, and that it was dealt with. But His Majesty will issue a statement this afternoon."

"Where's Reese?" Dale asked, not bothering with his title.

"Sir Reese has been helping drain the King's Grove this morning, but I imagine he will be free soon. He inquired after you as well," Quaith said in a tone that suggested it wasn't quite appropriate.

"Can we go eat with him again?" Aladane asked.

"Actually, Mister Quaith, we have a better question for you," Fish spoke up. "It looks like our company will have to split ways, since the king wants to see Emeline tomorrow."

"Oh?" Quaith asked.

"Yes, my friend here needs to get back home to Equane, but if he takes the wagon, then the rest of us won't have a way to get home," Dada explained. "Is there some way that His Majesty can help us with that?"

"Ah." Quaith started blinking rapidly, as if it helped him think. "I'm afraid I don't know the answer to that. Why don't we go straight to the hall and I will try to find out?"

~ ~

They found Reese arguing disinterestedly with a red-haired man in the dining hall, someone Emeline recognized as one of the other Lash Knights. There were other knights milling around and filling their plates. A few of them ogled the villagers, especially Emeline. Gone were the sneers and the amusement, however; it was clear that news had spread.

Reese's face lit up as they approached and Emeline's heart did a little spin. He cut off the red-haired knight with the disparaging remark, "As much as I'm enjoying this, Asai, we'll have to discuss your tournament wins later." Then he stood up and shook Dada's hand, glancing shyly at Emeline. The other knight's eyes widened at the group of them and then he slipped away.

"Sir Reese, I'm afraid the Equanians were neglected this morning as far as breakfast is concerned, and since they also have a question for His Majesty, I've brought them here," Quaith told him.

"Go get some food before it disappears," Reese told Dale and Aladane. They darted off for the side table, and he asked Dada, "What's the question?"

Emeline lingered for a moment, but the smells from the knights' lunch were too delicious. She left Dada and Fish to explain and followed the boys. This time, there were thick slabs of bread to load up with spiced meat, cheese, and vegetables. There was even a pitcher of coffee, which Emeline helped herself to, having developed a taste for it.

They returned to Reese's table with their plates full. Fish clapped his hands together as Emeline sat down and said, "Perfect! Al and I can head out right after we eat." Aladane's face fell immediately and he sat down with a thump.

"What happened?" Dale asked.

"Mister Fish will take the wagon back. Reese thinks Lord Irwind will grant us a carriage ride home when it's our time to leave, and Reese will escort us," Dada explained. Emeline smiled at Reese, realizing he had just given them more time together. He winked.

"Can't we leave in the morning?" Aladane asked Fish. "Isn't it better to start early?"

Fish looked at Aladane, considering. "Well...maybe," he said, frowning. "I don't know, son, I'm so hungry I can't think." With that, he went off to the food and Dada followed, smiling.

"Al, you might have some crazy adventures on the way home," Dale said sympathetically.

"Yeah..." he grumbled, and took a huge bite of food.

"You should get Mister Fish to teach you how to shoot," Emeline suggested. He perked up a little at that and nodded, chewing.

"He got the Ithin through the eye, just like that thief," he said.

"What are you doing today?" Dale asked Reese with his mouth full.

"I see you have the table manners of a Lash Knight already," Reese told him. "I have some more work to do, but then I thought I would make a visit to Willen, that village nearby. Would you like to come?" He looked at Emeline and she smiled.

"Yes," she said eagerly as Dale nodded, keeping his mouth closed.

"Oh, good. If you're just going to see a village, then I don't mind if I have to miss it," Aladane declared.

~ ~

It was a couple of hours later that the group of them headed out to Willen. They rode in a steam-carriage driven by a young servant whose eyes flew from Emeline to Reese in sheer astonishment, noticing the way they smiled at each other. She could imagine the gossip back in the King's Hall.

They headed north along a mostly empty road. Past the outskirts of the city, there were few houses or cottages, and the land was dotted with clusters of trees. The clouds broke and rain came down, rattling pleasantly on the carriage roof.

"What will the king's announcement say?" Fish asked Reese after they'd been riding for a while. He had been persuaded to wait until the morning to leave, and now he seemed eager to see what a village so near the capital was like. Aladane was hanging his head out the window.

"I've heard some speculation that he may leave out the part about Irwind's original model," Reese said drily.

"You mean, he might tell everyone that *all* the Ithin were automatons?" Emeline exclaimed.

"In order to avoid widespread panic, yes," he told her. "But the story about your magic is circling the hall, and he certainly still plans to combine the council."

"That's the important thing," Dada said, catching hold of Aladane's sleeve. "If you fall out and bang your head, Al, you do still have to go home."

"I see some cottages coming up," the boy announced, ducking back in. "And a big lake!"

The carriage slowed to a stop a few minutes later and Emeline looked out to see a larger village than she'd expected. The cottages weren't round and red like in Equane, but many were built with a white clay that was pretty in the watery sunlight. There was a large ring of them around a glittering lake, with farmland beyond. Emeline climbed out with the others and admired the scene.

"This is a sight for sore eyes," Fish declared, and Dada nodded, smiling.

Aladane shrugged at Dale. "It's kind of like home."

"Yeah, but so close to the capital!" Dale said, amazed. Emeline agreed. It was hard to believe that their short journey had taken them here.

Reese led the way down a dirt path, following the curve of the lake. Some children ran past the group of them, stopping to stare at Reese for a second. The knight was conspicuous with his whip coiled at his hip, but also for his size. The Equanians didn't get much more than a glance, for once. The children were dressed like Dale and Aladane, simply, although one little girl wore a bell tied around her neck with a ribbon.

"Look at the birds on the water," Dale said, pointing at the lake.

"Are there no ducks in Equane?" Reese asked, surprised. Dale shook his head, watching the birds glide serenely across. "They're delicious. So are these." He gestured at a handful of chickens and geese being herded along by a woman in a dress printed with flowers. She gaped at Reese as they passed.

"What do they grow here?" Dada asked, looking out toward the fields.

"Everything, I suppose," Reese said. "I know they raise a lot of animals and sell meat to the capital."

"Must be good fishing in the lake," Fish commented.

"I wouldn't know," Reese said with a grimace. Emeline grinned.

"Let's find the market and see what they got," Fish told Dada.

"It's in the village center up ahead," Reese said, and Fish snorted.

"We know how to find a village market, son," he told him, and sauntered off ahead. The boys followed Dada and Fish, and Emeline moved to join them, but Reese pulled her back gently.

"Let's catch up to them later," he said, putting an arm around her. "Since they know everything anyway."

Emeline leaned into him and they walked in a different direction, cutting across a small courtyard in front of a cluster of cottages. She didn't worry about Dada wondering where she was—not here, with Reese. She listened dreamily to the voices floating from windows and the animals clucking and lowing.

"I have to confess I had an ulterior motive for bringing your family here," Reese told her.

"What's that?"

"I wanted to see if you liked it—all of you. Because…I had the idea that maybe your father might consider moving here." He sounded uncharacteristically nervous now, fidgeting with the handle of his whip. "If I offered to help, of course. I know it wouldn't be an easy undertaking."

Emeline's heart was close to bursting. She had no idea what Dada would think about such a huge change in their lives. But he had been so delighted by the books in the market, the art in the museum, and the academies. Perhaps he *would* like to be closer to the capital, especially in a place like Willen.

"I don't know," she told Reese slowly. "I want it more than anything, though."

It started to drizzle, and Reese pulled her under an overhanging cottage roof. There was a lovely flower bed at their feet, and Emeline admired the dahlias and blue roses, bobbing in the rain.

"I could train Dale, if he's serious about going to a knight's academy," Reese said thoughtfully. "And if I add that to the offer, he might just badger your father into saying yes."

Emeline had to laugh. "That's a strong possibility!" She couldn't even imagine how Aladane would react—he would absolutely stow away again on that trip.

"Let's bring it up later," he said, encouraged. "Anything is possible."

For answer, Emeline held out her hand over the wet flowers at their feet. That delicious energy rushed out more readily now, more readily than ever. She drew the leafy stems straight up into the air, then curled the flowers around the two of them in a sweet embrace.

Acknowledgments

Thank you to my extraordinary family, who keeps me alive, and who never seemed to doubt that I could do this, despite the considerable odds. Special thanks to my Wonder Woman mother, who helps me find the magic on the darkest of days. And thank you to my good friends for their excitement and support, and to my long-lived but dearly departed cat, who was on my lap for so much of the writing in my life. I'm also eternally grateful to Holiday House and my editor Mora Couch, for all the hard work that went into the shaping of this book, as well as her positivity and enthusiasm for the story. And finally, thank you to Sara Kipin, for the gorgeous illustrations.